THE FUTURE
MR. DOLAN

THE FUTURE MR. DOLAN

CHARLES GORHAM

CUTTING EDGE

ISBN-13: 978-1-962896-17-7

Published by
Cutting Edge Books
PO Box 8212
Calabasas, CA 91372
www.cuttingedgebooks.com

For HAROLD LAVINE

PART I

CHAPTER ONE

I COULD FEEL New York as soon as the train left Newark. Outside, through the dusty window, the Jersey Meadows were rolling by, a million acres of salt marsh with dirty grass as tall as your chin, black with soot from the trains going by, thick cattails that looked like hot dogs sticking up along the edges of streams that wandered through the marshes. It is a mean approach to the City.

When we entered the tunnel and the lights came on I got up and carried my bag to the door. I leaned against the iron brake wheel and swayed with the train, watching the lights, red, green and amber, and the long shiny ribbons of the rails, turning into switch points, then running straight, right into the heart of the City, deep underground. We coasted slowly into Penn Station and I opened the door before we stopped, and hopped to the platform, running a little. I was the first one off the train.

Cabs were rolling down the incline, loading and unloading fast. I took the first one in line, although it was filthy and falling apart, with shredded cloth showing through the imitation leather seat and an old piece of clothesline lashed to the door to hold it shut. At least it was a New York cab and not one of those southern hacks that look like private cars.

"Eighty-sixth and York," I told the driver. "Go through Central Park, huh?"

"Okay, soldier."

He turned his head, showing glasses and a lot of nose. I read his name on the Hack Bureau card in the rack over the glass curtain: HYMAN NOTENSTEIN. He didn't look like the photograph that was pasted to his license.

"Civilian, Hymie," I said. "Since this morning."

"Okay, soldier," he said.

We climbed the ramp out of Penn Station and turned uptown. I sat back and enjoyed the ride. There is no town like New York and this was one of its good days. It was the first week in September, 1946, and not too hot. I wound down the window and took a deep breath of the air from the Park—trees and grass and everything you smell in the country, with something else in it too, the smell of the City. The drive through the Park wound around, eating up nickels on the taxi meter but I didn't care, because I was home. I could see Fifth Avenue on my right, with the rich side streets running east, and beyond that I knew there were Park and Third and First, and beyond that York and the East River—my neighborhood. When we stopped at the corner of Eighty-sixth and York I handed Hymie a dollar and a half for the dollar I read on the meter.

Big-shot Dolan.

I felt wonderful because I was out and because I had four hundred dollars pinned to the pocket of my uniform shirt and because I was nineteen years old with a whole future in front of me. The sun felt good and I stood on the corner in front of the bank, just smelling the old neighborhood, taking a good long smell to make up for the year I had been away in those southern states, looking at nothing but red clay backroads and coca-cola signs, smelling nothing but niggers and whores and the tarpaper smell of army camps.

East Yorkville might not smell sweet to an outsider: a peasant from some small town. To me it smelled wonderful. It is a mixture, that smell, of stale beer from the saloons, of clothes drying on the courtyard lines, of motor exhaust and manure from the street, of the River, which is right around the corner, of half-burnt fuel oil from the furnaces of the big apartment houses toward Gracie Square, and mixed with it all is the heavy sour smell of the old, old houses and the people in them. You can always smell something cooking. Usually cabbage.

After a little I walked up the block and went into Greene's saloon on the corner. The bar is on the left. A plywood partition, painted mahogany, runs down the center and on the right are a dozen tables with red-checked cloths. Each table has its own bottles of Heinz Ketchup and A1 Sauce. Greene tries to make the place look like a well-known steak house. All the way back, near the men's room, is a new juke box with a bright colored front, the kind with levers instead of buttons. The walls are covered with photographs of fighters, wrestlers and politicians. Behind the bar, over the cash register, is a long picture of fifty guys, posing with a fish about twenty feet long, all of them drunk, including the fish: ANNUAL OUTING, HIAWATHA DEM. CL. AUG. 1940. *Biggest Fish, O. Mahoney.* Greene's is the big Tammany hangout, the best saloon in the neighborhood.

I stood in the doorway with my feet apart and my barracks bag on the floor between them, looking at Murph and the Wop, who sat on stools, staring at their beer. Greene leaned on his forearms across the bar, reading the *Daily News*. None of them noticed me.

"For Christ's sake," I finally said. "Where is the body? When is the funeral?"

They turned around, a little suspicious, like sleeping dogs that have been disturbed. It was early afternoon. Then Murph climbed down from his stool and walked over to shake hands.

"For Christ's sake!" he said. "For Christ's sake! Mattie. Mattie Dolan."

"In person," I said. "How are you, Murph?"

"Fine. Fine."

I walked up to the bar.

"Hello, Guinea," I said to the Wop. "Hello, Greene."

They both said hello. I sat down and ordered beer for the four of us.

"Thanks," said the Wop, as if he didn't mean it.

"Thanks, Mattie," said Murph.

We all drank.

Murph is big, six feet two, with a red, dumb-ox Irish face, a grin, and hair which is thick and blue-black, except for a white patch in front where he was clubbed by a reform school guard. He is a year older than I. The Wop is about my age, dark, with a thin Italian face, and you never know what is going on behind those mean Italian eyes. When he knows something, and you don't know it, he laughs at you back in his throat: *"Heh-heh-heh!"* *"Heh-heh-heh!"* It is a laugh he learned from a radio program, "The Shadow," and the way he does it makes you feel uncomfortable, as though you'd stepped on a snake or a dead bird.

"When did you get out?" asked Murph.

"This morning," I told him.

"You must have been born lucky," he said. "How long were you in? A year?"

"Fifteen months," I said.

"Yeah," he said. "Johnny-Come-Lately."

"Lay off that," I said.

I was tired of having suckers from combat call me boy scout and Johnny-Come-Lately simply because I was lucky enough to avoid getting shot at.

"Lay off it," I told him.

"Sure," he said. "I was only kidding. But how did you get out so fast?"

"I was an orderly room clerk. I typed the lists of guys to go to the Separation Center."

"Heh-heh-heh," laughed the Wop. "And after D comes Dolan."

"That's right."

Murph slapped me on the back.

"You were always smart, Mattie," he said. "Spring for a beer, huh?"

I tapped the bar with my empty glass and called to Greene: "Three more."

Then I turned back to Murph and the Wop.

"What are you guys doing?" I asked. "Anything new? Making any money?"

They both laughed.

"I am in the Fifty-two Twenty Club," said the Wop. "Very exclusive. There's only about a million members."

"How about you?" I asked Murph.

"I got a pension," he said. "From the Marines."

Murph was a chump. He hung around the neighborhood for a year after they let him out of reform school, then joined the Marines: a volunteer. Being too dumb to duck and too big to hide, he was badly hit at Tarawa.

"Look," he said. "I'll show you."

He pulled up his pants leg and shoved down his sock. From the knee to the ankle the leg looked as if the flesh had been chewed by a rat. A long scar ran from the heel to the knee, turning in like the scar on an old tree that's been patched up by the Park Department.

"Big piece," he said. "Big piece."

He dug into his pants pocket and took out a chunky piece of metal, ribbed and corroded on one side, jagged and sharp on the other.

"That's the big piece," he said. "There were lots of little ones."

I held the fragment of shell in my hand, then gave it back to Murph.

"Jesus," I said. "Does it hurt?"

Showing his leg made Murph feel big. The leg and the fact he had been in jail were his only claims to fame. He shook his head and rolled down his pants.

"Nah-h," he said. "It don't hurt. But it's good for a sixty per cent disability, so should I complain?"

"Yeah," said the Wop. "He's going to get a tin cup and sit on the sidewalk with his pants pulled up, like a beggar with a wooden leg."

"That's right," said Murph. He staggered a few steps toward the bar, pretending to be a cripple with a cane.

"So what's the matter with you guys?" I asked. "Are you sick? What's the matter with working?"

"Heh-heh-heh," laughed the Wop. "Working."

"For what?" asked Murph.

"For money, you dopes, what do you think?" I said. "Money. Moolah."

"Thirty a week?" said the Wop.

"Thirty a week," said I. "Am I a chump?"

"Thirty-five?" said the Wop.

"Whaddya mean, thirty-five?" I said. "I've got a good job waiting for me. My old job, at Langley, making airplanes. It's good for sixty, seventy per. What's wrong with that?"

"Heh-heh-heh," laughed the Wop. "He's got a good job." He swung around on his barstool and tapped me on the chest. "Listen, junior," he said. "It's Nineteen Forty-six."

"Yeah," said Murph. "Going on Forty-seven."

"The war is over," said the Wop. He turned away and looked at the mirror, smoothing down his black hair. Murph slapped me on the back so hard he nearly knocked me off the barstool.

"You look heavier, Mattie," he said. "Bigger."

"Yes," I said. "One ninety."

"Are you going to play any football? We might get up a team. You can be captain."

"Sandlot ball?" I asked. "Do you think I'm a sucker?"

"Ten bucks a game," said Murph.

"Can they spare it?"

He laughed. "Buy another beer, huh, Mattie?" he said.

I took the money out of my pocket.

"Why don't one of you chiselers spring?" I asked. "Would it break you to buy a beer?"

"Because we're broke, that's why," said the Wop. "Wait till you try to live on the twenty a week Mister Whiskers puts out. You'll be chiseling beer yourself."

"Yeah," said Murph. "Or what I get from the Marines, for my leg."

He reached down and started to pull up his pants leg again but I stopped him.

"You showed it to me already, Murph."

I bought another round of beers; Greene flattened the collars neatly with a yellowed ivory beer knife.

"I've got a good job," I said. "Sixty, seventy dollars a week. I got it coming to me."

"Yeahyeahyeah," said the Wop, reaching for his beer. "You and your sixty-seventy a week."

I didn't like the way he said it.

"Cry about yourself, will you, Wop?" I said. "Let me cry about me."

We drank the beer and Murph started to eat pretzels from a cut-glass bowl on the bar, popping them into his mouth fast, the way you eat peanuts. Greene picked up the bowl and moved it down the bar.

"Don't you eat home?" he asked Murph.

"Aw, I get hungry," said Murph. He turned and stared out the window.

"Look," he said. "Look at the push-push."

A group of girls in bobby socks were standing on the sidewalk, peering into the bar. They were fourteen and fifteen, high school kids, wearing cotton jackets with shoulder patches and navy rating badges sewed to them. Most of them wore heavy makeup, whore makeup, and they carried schoolbooks hugged to their breasts. One girl stood apart from the crowd and I noticed her right away. She had red lips, wet and shiny without any makeup, and big, deep eyes, wide apart.

"Who's the one in back?" I asked. "The one without any lipstick."

The Wop looked out and made a Bronx cheer.

"Stiff," he said. "A Newman Club kid. Strictly nothing doing."

"For you, maybe," I said, "nothing doing. For me I would make a bet it's the business."

Murph laughed his dumb Irish laugh.

"That's jailbait, Mattie. Jailbait. That can get you twenty years."

"That'll be the day," I said to Murph. "Who are those kids?"

None of them looked familiar to me.

"Kids from the neighborhood," Murph said. "Just kids from the neighborhood."

"They look like prosties," I said. "Except for the scared-looking one in the back. She looks like a nun who wants to break her vows."

"Lay off that, Dolan," said Greene. "Lay off the Catholic Church."

"Yeah, Mattie," said Murph. "Don't say a thing like that."

He crossed himself.

"Yah-h, Protestant putz," said the Wop.

I had to laugh. The neighborhood is Catholic, mostly Irish Catholic. I am Irish, but not Catholic, because my old man comes from Antrim, in the North. But I always got along all right with Catholic boys like Murph.

"I'm sorry," I said. "I didn't mean anything."

I looked through the window at the girls. Three or four of them stood in front with their noses pressed against the glass, staring at us as if they expected to see a free show. I went to the door and they scattered and ran. The scared-looking one without any rouge was on the corner, standing by herself. A thin, hard, foreign-looking woman crossed the street and grabbed her arm.

I heard her say: *"Get home, get home,"* and then she slapped her on the cheek so the skin turned red. I went back into the bar.

"They hang around all the time," said Murph. "Greene don't let them in the bar, so they hang around the window, watching the fellows. They used to hang out in Times Square, looking for soldiers to buy them beer."

"But now there aren't any soldiers," I said.

"Except thirty-year men like you. Peacetime soldiers," said Murph.

"Listen," I said. "I'm out."

I touched the yellow discharge emblem sewed to the breast of my shirt. Both of them laughed.

"Our hero," said the Wop.

"Don't talk, Wop," I said. "How long were you in the Navy? Six months?"

"Ten," he said. But he shut up.

I bought another beer, then said, "I guess I better go home and see if my old lady's alive. Will you jerks be here later?"

"They're always here," said Greene. "They live here." He wiped the bar with a damp towel and moved the pretzels away from Murph again.

"So long, Mattie," said Murph. "I'm glad to see you back in the neighborhood, no kidding. We'll have some good times, huh? The way we used to."

"Sure," I said.

We shook hands.

"So long, Murph. So long, Wop."

"So long, sucker," said the Wop. "Heh-heh-heh!"

I went out into the street and walked up York Avenue to my block: Eighty-seventh. The house is old, with a high stone stoop and an areaway protected by a cast-iron railing with red lead showing through the black paint. There were four cans of ashes and one of garbage standing on the sidewalk without any covers.

It was mid-afternoon and the sun was high and hotter than it had been earlier in the day. I went into the house. The hallway stank the way it always did, of stale coffee and dog dirt from the hound they kept on the fourth floor and were too lazy to take to the street. I went upstairs, two at a time, and found the door to the apartment unlocked. I walked in.

"Hello," I said. Then I slammed the door. There was no answer.

"Hello," I said. "Is anybody home?"

I walked down the hall, into the apartment. It was dark, as usual, a back flat with the windows on the courtyard instead of the street. The old lady sat in the kitchen with her back to the door and she didn't turn around.

"Hello, Ma," I said. I said it again. I said it three times. Finally I walked over and put my hand on her shoulder.

"For Christ's sake, Ma," I said. "It's me. Mattie. What's the matter, you slopped or something?"

She looked up and said: "Hello, Mattie," as offhand as if I'd been to the corner for a pack of cigarettes instead of away in the Army for a year.

"Jesus," I said. "You might at least let on to be glad to see me, even if I'm not a hero like Rusty."

She stood up and put her arms around me. I got the reek of her cheap perfume, through the smell of her beer and mine.

"Sure I'm glad to see you, Mattie. Sure I am," she said, trying to kiss me on the cheek.

"For Christ's sake, Ma," I said. "Let me get my breath, will you?"

She let go and sat down. I walked into the front room.

The old place looked just the same, dark and dirty and full of the stink of sour beds and old beer. The front-room carpet was worn out so the burlap backing showed through in patches and felt slick under your feet. Through the windows you looked at a wall and clotheslines holding the washing for half a dozen families. There were two bedrooms, one for the old man and old lady, the other for my brother Rusty and me. There was a scarred round oak table in the front room. We ate there and usually the old lady forgot to put the sugar and salt away, so they sat there in the front room, sometimes with the bread plate beside them. The kitchen was where the family hung out, because it was light and fairly large, with a table and four wooden chairs. The kitchen window looked down on the court at an angle, so that you got a glimpse of York Avenue. We had lived in the place for fifteen years and the only good thing about it was the price, which was twenty-four dollars a month. There were times, during the depression in the Thirties, when the old man had trouble getting up the twenty-four, when he was on relief and WPA.

I walked back to the kitchen.

"So what's doing, Ma? What's new?"

"Same old thing, Mattie," she said. "Same old thing. Your father's not doing so good with the cab."

"Did he ever?" I asked.

"Aw, Mattie. ... "

She used to be a natural blonde, but now she has her hair bleached at a German beauty parlor on Eighty-sixth Street, bleached and waved in a cheap permanent, so that it's brittle as excelsior. She would go hungry to have her hair done. Hungry, but not thirsty. With her hair fixed in those little curls and eyes blurred by a dozen whiskies, she can sit on a barroom stool and admire herself in the barroom mirror, half-believing she looks the way she looked when Rusty was born, when she was sixteen and well-known as the prettiest girl in the block, the block she was born in, down the avenue. When she was drunk she thought she was happy, sometimes, and she would talk, talk, talk. I didn't want to hear it so I went into the bathroom and took two ten-dollar bills from the roll pinned to my shirt, then returned to the kitchen with the money in my hand, hoping she would believe it was all the money I owned.

"Here, Ma," I said, handing her one of the tens, "I'll go halvies with you."

She took the money, folded it, and tucked it into her bosom.

"Would it break your jaw to say thanks?" I asked.

"Aw, Mattie, don't be like that." She looked up and patted her hair. "Thanks."

"You're welcome."

I sat down and riffled the pages of the *Daily Mirror;* the *Mirror* was her paper.

"Didn't you get your mustering-out pay that they give you? Three hundred dollars?"

I shook my head.

"Rusty got it," she said.

"That comes later," I explained. "They mail it to you. And I only get two hundred. I wasn't overseas."

"Oh," she said.

She got up and took the ten dollars out, looked at it to be sure it was real, then put it in her pocketbook. She pulled her dress down over her hips; the dress was a little tight.

"I got to go to the store, Mattie," she said. "You going to be home for dinner?"

"Sure," I said.

She started out. I knew the name of the store she was going to: Moylan's Bar and Grill on Third Avenue. And I knew about how long the ten dollars would last, at five drinks an hour.

"Watch out the old man doesn't hang one on your chin when you come home," I said, calling after her.

But she was gone, halfway down the stairs.

I lit a cigarette and looked around, then dropped the burnt match and stepped on it, grinding it into the front-room rug. When I took a good look at the place I felt sick to my stomach; disgusted. I sat down in the old man's chair, with the ends of the arms as slick as glass from the grease and sweat that were always on his hands, and looked through the window at the wall, a brick wall painted white, with the red of the brick striking through where the old paint had flaked off. The blinds in the windows across the court were pulled down as if someone was dead and in one window, outside the blind, hung a service flag with one gold star and three blue ones, curling at the edges as if it had been there, hanging in the window, for a long time and had been forgotten.

I found the old man's *Daily News* that he brought home at night after putting up the hack. I tried to read but it just annoyed me. The paper might have been a year old for all the news I found in it. I folded it up and shoved it under the chair, then got up and went into the bedroom where Rusty and I slept. The bedroom looked cleaner than the rest of the apartment and there were fresh-looking sheets on the double bed.

I thought I would try on my civvies, but as soon as I slipped into a coat I knew it was no use. It was tight across the chest and shoulders and the sleeves were too short. I had filled out in the Army, grown a little and filled out. I tried on a civilian coat of Rusty's, but it was small, as bad as my own.

Rusty's summer Eisenhower was hanging in the closet, his officer's uniform, with the wings and all the other junk: two rows of ribbons covered with stars and clusters. I tried it on and looked at myself in the mirror. It was snug around the waist, but you want it that way. I thought for a gag that I would wear it out and see if I could pick up a girl on the strength of Rusty's ribbons. I rolled up the jacket and tucked it under my arm, because I didn't want anyone in the neighborhood to see me wearing it. I got into a taxi on York Avenue and buttoned up the jacket, sitting in the cab.

"Where to, soldier?" the driver asked.

"West Side," I told him.

I went into a bar on Eighth Avenue, one of those sucker traps for soldiers, and had two whiskies all by myself, just looking at the mirror and the bottles in front of it, and at the reflection of myself in Rusty's suit. I couldn't work up any enthusiasm for anything. In Greene's, with Murph and the Wop, I had wanted to go home. When I got there and found the old lady half slopped, bleary with beer, I wanted to get her out of the house so that I could have the place to myself. As soon as she left I felt restless and couldn't get away fast enough. Now, sitting in this strange place on the West Side, that might just as well have been in Atlanta or in Montgomery, Alabama, for all it meant to me, I couldn't even get interested in drinking.

After a while two girls came in and sat at the end of the bar near the street, so that the light came through the window behind them and made them look like cardboard cutouts, like an ad for coca-cola. One was a blonde with brass-colored hair who looked like a copy of a good-looking girl. The other was small and nigger-dark: a Wop, maybe, or a Jew. Sometimes it's hard to tell.

They ordered whiskey and talked to one another. I kept my eyes on the blonde and, sure enough, when she looked up, she gave me a big hello. I called the bartender.

"Give the ladies a drink on me," I said. "Whatever they're having."

"Sure, soldier, sure," he said.

He set them up for the girls and I saw him jerk his head in my direction, and say something I couldn't hear. The blonde sat up straight on her stool, looking over the bartender's head.

"Come on over, Lieutenant," she called. "Don't be so stuck-up."

I moved to their end of the bar and bought four or five rounds, sitting between them and concentrating on the blonde. After a while the dark one got up and said: "Excuse *me!*" When she was gone I said to the blonde: "How's about you and me?"

"Sure," she said, showing her teeth. "But let's get everything straight."

"So?"

"Twenty bucks," she said.

"What?"

"Twenty dollars," she said. "What do you think this is, the Salvation Army?"

"What do *you* think this is, bank night?" I asked her. "In the South I paid three. Four, maybe, at the most."

"That's the price," she said. "Twenty."

I looked at her, noticing her bad teeth and her dead-pale skin, rough under the makeup. I thought of the nunlike high school kid who had been looking through Greene's window, and decided this would be a waste of time.

"I'd rather have a nice cold bath," I said.

She just looked at me and said, "That's probably more your style anyway. I don't like officers."

"Why, you tramp!" I said.

She threw her highball in my face and blinded me for a second. The bartender came up carrying a club, the kid's baseball bat they used to mash up the ice in the beer trough.

"Let's not have no trouble, soldier," he said, tapping the edge of the bar with his bat.

I went out. The blonde laughed as I closed the door, and thumbed her nose at me through the window.

I tried other places on Eighth Avenue but they were dead, two or three lonely civilians drinking by themselves, playing the juke box from piles of change lying on the bar beside their glasses. It was depressing and getting dark, so I caught a cab and rode home. I took off the officer's jacket in the cab and folded it up. When I came into the house I threw it in a corner, then walked into the front room.

Rusty and the old man sat across from one another at the round table. Rusty was reading a thick book; the old man had the *Daily News* spread out in front of him. The old man was wearing his cap, black on the sides where his greasy hands had touched it, union buttons pinned to the band. Rusty wore an officer's suntan shirt, opened at the neck, without a tie. His hair was redder than I remembered it and he looked older. But he hadn't gained weight the way I had.

I kicked the doorframe and both of them jumped when they heard the noise. Rusty stood up and shook hands.

"Hello, Mat," he said. "Glad to see you home."

"Hello, Rusty," I said.

The old man squinted at me from under the peak of his cap.

"So you're back," he said.

"Yep."

"You had a nice short war," he said. Then he returned to the *Daily News,* frowning over the pictures.

"Aw, lay off him, Pop," said Rusty. He went to the kitchen and punched open three cans of beer. We drank a can apiece. It tasted good after the whiskey, cold and bity. I sat down at the table between him and Pop.

"What are you doing, Rusty?" I asked, closing the book so he lost his place. "Improving your mind?"

"Oh," he said. "I go to school. College. I'm going to law school next year."

"On what?" I asked. My marks had always been better than his; I wondered why he was going to school, instead of learning to drive a truck.

"GI Bill of Rights," he said. "Courtesy of Uncle Sam."

"Sucker," I said.

He laughed.

"What are you going to do?"

I teetered back in my chair and balanced my feet on the edge of the table. The old man shoved them off, so my heels hurt when they hit the floor.

"I don't know," I said. "Give me a chance. I thought I'd go back to my job at Langley, making planes. It's good for seventy, eighty a week. Give me a chance to look around, and see what I can promote."

"If the job's still there," said Rusty.

"Sure it's still there," I said. "The law says so. I'm a veteran, right?"

"Veteran!" said the old man, snorting into the newspaper. "Where did you fight? The Battle of Fort Benning? What makes you think you're a veteran?"

I had an answer for that one.

"The Government says so," I told him. "The United States Government."

"That's right, Pop," said Rusty. "Even a punk who was in a month is a veteran on paper."

I stood up, with my hands on my hips; I was bigger and tougher than either of them.

"What do you mean, punk?" I said. "Lay off me, will you? Is it my fault I didn't get shot at? Is it my fault I'm nineteen and didn't get born soon enough to get killed?"

I sat down again; neither of them answered.

"I thought I might go see Fred," I said. "After I'm settled at Langley. Fred might do something about getting me a start somewhere."

"Fred!" said the old man. "That black-market bum!"

He sat up straight in his chair with his shoulders back but it didn't make him look a bit more impressive.

"That bum," he said.

"Since when is a guy who makes two thousand dollars a week a bum?" I asked.

"He's a bum," the old man insisted. "A dirty black-market bum."

You couldn't reason with the old man. During the war, when Fred was selling red ration tickets, he gave me a handful to take home to the old lady. The old man threw them in the toilet; I fished them out and dried them off and enjoyed a dozen steaks from them.

"Fred *is* a bastard," said Rusty.

"So what?" I said. "The world is run by bastards. You think people get ahead by being nice to one another? The world is run by guys who would just as soon cut your throat as look at you. Maybe rather."

"It shouldn't be," said Rusty.

"Lots of things shouldn't be," I said. "They just are, that's all."

"That's no attitude," said Rusty, picking up his thick book.

"A-nnnh, don't mind him," the old man said. "He's a wise, fresh punk." He turned to me, tapping my chest. "Listen," he said, "you hang out with Fred and you'll turn out to be a bum just like him."

"Can you guarantee it?" I asked. "I'd like to be sure of it."

"Wise punk," he said. "Rusty! Get some more beer."

Rusty put down his book and went into the kitchen; I noticed that the old man didn't try to order me around. He had been looking at me, sizing up the weight and reach I had added since he'd seen me last. I sat, grinning at him. I had to laugh at what he had said, because if you compared my uncle Fred with my old man no one would have to write you a letter to tell you which one was the bum.

We sat, drinking beer, talking about the neighborhood, who was back and who was married, who had been killed and who was in jail. The old lady came through the door at nine-thirty, tanked to the ears, humming a dumb tune to herself as she came down the hall. She stood in the doorway, swaying, wearing a foolish grin on her face as though she was proud as hell of it.

"Good old Mattie," she said. "Darling, dear old Mattie. Gave his mother ten dollars. Good old son Mattie."

"Shut up, will you?" I said.

The old man rushed her into the bedroom. He closed the door and after a while we could hear him slapping her around. Then Rusty went to the door and said, "Oh, Pop, for Christ's sake, leave her alone. She can't help it."

The old man came out, red-faced and sweating a little.

"Whaddya mean, she can't help it?" he wanted to know from Rusty. "She comes home stinkin', no dinner, the place a mess, me out in the hack all day, workin' like a nigger. Whaddya mean, she can't help it?"

"She just can't help it, that's all," said Rusty.

The old man got mad at me.

"Whaddya give her money? you little bastard," he yelled. "You knew she'd get boiled."

"Aw, for Christ's sakes," I said. "She's my mother, isn't she? I got a right to give her dough if I want to."

He moved toward me, meaning to hit me, and both of my fists came up.

"Listen, Pop," I told him. "You lay a hand on me and so help me Christ I'll knock you into next week, old man or no old man."

Rusty got between us.

"Oh, for God's sake," he said. "Knock it off, will you? Let's go out and get something to eat."

"Okay," the old man agreed, as if he was doing someone a favor. He looked at me, wondering whether I really would have hit him, then pulled down his cap, toughie style, and put on his coat over the heavy suspenders he always wore.

"Come on," he said. "Let's go."—right away leader, as if eating had been his idea.

We ate dinner at the Chink's on Eighty-sixth Street, run by a Chinaman who used to be chef to the President of the United States, so the food should have satisfied my old man. But he didn't notice the taste of anything. He just stuffed himself, shoveling food. I paid. I thought it would make him feel better, but all he said was: "You seem to have plenty of it to throw around."

He was surly, really mean, worse than he was before I was drafted, sour, as though his insides had curdled, never laughing at anything, except somebody else in trouble. I figured the old lady was worse and that he wasn't doing too well with his cab, so I thought

I would overlook it. On the sidewalk in front of the Chink's, I said, "I'm going to have a beer. You want one, Pop? Rusty?"

"I'm going to have a beer," the old man said, "but not with you. I'm going to Mallin's."

He would sit in Mallin's with his old Irish pals, telling lies until four o'clock, drinking, maybe, five or six beers. He wasn't a drinking man at all, but he liked to get out of the house.

"Suit yourself," I said.

We watched him walk away, trying to get a military swagger into his middle-aged walk.

Rusty laughed: "Don't mind him."

"How about you?" I said. "Do you want a beer? I've got money."

"One," he said. "I've got to study."

We went into Greene's. There was a crowd at the bar, people I knew, and you heard them as we walked down the bar to an open space at the end:

"Hi, Mattie!"

"Hello, Dolan!"

"Hi, Mattie!"

"Hello, soldier."

"Hello, Dolan, what's new?"

"Hello, sucker."

I put a ten-dollar bill on the bar.

"Hello, soaks," I said to the crowd. To the bartender I said, "Drinks for all. If that's not enough there's more where that came from."

He set them up. I turned to Rusty.

"Are you really going to be a lawyer?" I asked.

"Sure," he said. "Why not?"

"What's the P.C.T.?" I asked. "What's the percentage?"

He shrugged his shoulders.

"I don't know. Something to do."

"It takes too long," I said.

"Yeah," he said. "I guess so."

He finished his beer and put the glass on the bar.

"I have to go. So long, Mattie."

"So long, sucker," I said.

He went home to study. I stood at the bar in Greene's, buying beer until four in the morning, then walked home alone, feeling sick from all the beer on top of the Chinese food. I stood on the curbstone in front of the house, hanging on to a lamppost, and after a while I was sick in the gutter. A big, young-looking cop came by, swinging his stick so it touched the sidewalk, making a ringing, woody noise.

"Take it easy, soldier," he said, laughing a mean cop laugh.

I tried to tell him to go to hell but I was so sick I couldn't talk. I stood there in the gutter, sick, hanging on to the lamppost, until the dawn began to show pink in the sky above the buildings on the edge of the East River. There was no place to go but home and when I thought of the apartment I got sick again. Stretched across the street, from the fourth-storey tenement windows, was a big faded banner made out of cheap flag bunting:

THE BOYS FROM THE NEIGHBORHOOD

There was a picture of a soldier, a sailor and a marine with their arms around one another the way you see them in cigarette ads. Underneath the picture it said:

SERVING THEIR COUNTRY FROM
EAST EIGHTY-SEVENTH STREET
YORK AVENUE TO FIRST AVENUE.

"GOD BLESS OUR BOYS"

I lip-farted at the damned banner, then turned and went into the house... no place to go but home, sick again on the smelly stairs. All in all, it was a hell of a homecoming.

CHAPTER TWO

The next day I went out to the Langley Aircraft plant and talked to a small, mean-looking boss who wore a blue suit that made him look neat. He stared at me along his nose, as if I wore a street-cleaner's outfit instead of an army uniform. The office was in the corner of a factory unit, two walls of concrete with wire-glass windows, two of movable metal partitions painted olive green. You could see the I-beams overhead, and the fake oriental office rug looked out of place on the concrete floor. The building vibrated under your feet, from the heavy motors out on the floor, driving the big power lathes.

"What makes you think you have any right to a job here, Dolan?" the guy in the blue suit asked.

"The law says so, doesn't it? I was here when I was drafted and the law says you have to take me back at the same money."

He laughed and picked up a long ruler with a brass edge that shone in the light.

"Not quite, Dolan," he said. "Not quite."

He very carefully put down the ruler, then got up and opened the drawer of a file case standing behind his desk. He took out some cards, clipped together.

"You came here in Forty-three," he said, referring to the cards. "How old were you then?"

"Eighteen," I said.

It was a lie; I went there when I was sixteen, a punk kid with no experience except three years of high school.

"I see," he nodded. "And you left here in June of Forty-five to go into the Army."

"I was drafted," I said. "So I got a right to my job back."

He put down the cards and picked up the ruler, stroking the sharp metal edge with the fingers of his left hand. He seemed to admire the ruler.

"For one thing, Dolan," he said, "the job you had no longer exists."

He pointed out the window with the ruler. The Langley plant covers fourteen blocks, big, glass-walled factory buildings with a high electrified fence surrounding the whole business, and gates with sentry boxes and uniformed guards, just like an army or navy establishment. I saw that a lot of the buildings had been shut down and I could hear it, too. During the war, when the plant was rolling twenty-four hours a day, you heard the hum of the motors for miles, all over Sunnyside, big dynamos purring like tigers, big motors that whined when they were stopped or started. You didn't hear them now.

"We've curtailed operations, you see," the personnel man explained. "Besides," he said, "the job you had belonged to a man who was drafted too. You replaced him."

"So?"

"And the man he replaced was drafted too."

"So?"

He smiled; his smile was beginning to annoy me.

"So even if a job existed, which it doesn't, *you* wouldn't be entitled to it. And neither would the man whose place you took."

I argued, but what was the use? After a few minutes' talk he put down his ruler and stuck out his hand.

"If you really want to work, Dolan," he said, "I can send you to a man who is hiring veterans."

"Doing what?" I asked.

"Office work," he said. "It's a chance to learn the business."

"Running errands?"

He smiled again, fiddling with his ruler.

"Something like that."

"For how much?"

"Well," he said, "you can't expect to make what we paid you here you know. The war is over, Dolan."

"How much?" I asked.

"I believe he starts his people at thirty. With a raise to thirty-five in six months if you make good."

He took a scratch pad marked INTEROFFICE MEMO and with a ball-point pen wrote a name and address on it in a neat handwriting. Under the name and address he wrote: *Introducing Matthew Dolan,* reading my full name from the record card. He tore off the sheet and handed it to me. It looked like a doctor's prescription, with his name scribbled at the bottom. I held it in my hand and looked at it, then folded the thick, expensive paper and creased it with my thumbnail until the fold was sharp as a knife. Then I tore the paper in half and dropped the pieces onto the rug.

"Stick that job up your bucket, mister. Or take it yourself. What do you think I am? A sucker?"

I heard him laughing as I walked out. The guard unlocked the big wire gate, swung it open, and let me out.

"No luck, huh, soldier? Tough," he said.

I looked at him, with his uniform and gun that belonged to the private police outfit he worked for.

"Save it, will you, clown?" I said. "Cry about yourself."

There is a saloon a block and a half from the plant, one of the places I played a lot when I worked there, during the war ... a run-down place in an old frame building with the paint peeling off the clapboards, looking like the kind of bar you'd find in a mean, tough mill town. The fixtures and furniture are cheap, but the turnover, during the war, must have been five or six thousand a week. Saloons make money at all times, but during the war there was a fortune in the business.

"Rye," I said to the man behind the bar.

"Okay, soldier," he said, spinning the shot glass on the bar. He was one of those cheerful bartenders, with a chummy, confidential manner.

"Don't call me soldier," I said.

"Okayokay!"

The place was empty, in the middle of the morning. At lunchtime it would be crowded with Langley employees, drinking beer and eating the sixty-cent-plate lunch:

!Special!

Pot Roast w. *Red Cabbage*

60c

!Special!

The sign hung over the bar mirror; it had been just as special at the time when I worked at the plant; it was special the way the hamburger steak and home fries are special in a Greek coffeepot.

I sat, looking at the whiskey, not wanting it. I come from a beer-drinking neighborhood, but last year, in the South, I learned to order whiskey, because whiskey is what southern girls expect you to buy for them.

Through the window of the saloon I saw a few of the Langley buildings ... long, low, temporary factories, prefabricated in sections. At the gate a private cop walked a thirty-foot beat, swinging his club. He looked lonesome. I guessed that they would be tearing the place down soon.

"Looking for a job, chum?" the friendly barkeep asked.

"Yeah, I guess so."

"Nothing doing over there," he said. "They're laying off already. Business is getting dead here."

"Yeah."

"But it was a good place during the war. Big dough. Everybody spending."

"You're not kidding," I said.

So far as I was concerned, back in Forty-three and Forty-four and Forty-five, when I worked for Langley, the war could have just gone on forever. I earned a dollar twenty an hour and some weeks we worked sixty hours. Figure it out: 60 × $1.20 $72.00.

I was sixteen then, and seventeen, making the money and spending it, having a good time. There were women in the plant, plenty of women, with husbands in the service or working in war plants out of town ... women who always had taken a beating because the husband had the job, and his few dollars made him king. All of a sudden, during the war, the women had money, plenty of money: sixty, seventy, eighty a week. Naturally, they were independent. They did what they pleased for a change and if the husband didn't like it he knew what to do.

For me, it was made to order.

A Polack named Emma worked one of the machines and she kidded a lot, sidling past me, brushing her breasts across my back, pretending it was an accident. I was afraid to speak to her, but one day she whispered: "I'll see you when the lunch whistle blows, kid. Around the back." Her lips were close to my face and I smelled the pick-up she must have stopped for on the way to work that morning. She was high enough to be reckless. I met her at lunchtime.

She wore a clean, faded workshirt, overall pants, silk stockings, high-heeled shoes and nothing else. Her skin was white, dead white, and she had a loose Polack mouth, painted on. She wore mascara, even to work, and the blood-red polish on her nails was chipped. She always had a laugh and a wisecrack ready. She enjoyed life, and life to her meant eating and drinking and making love.

She took me to a shed behind our building, slits of light showing through the cracks between the warped boards, dust from the dirt floor playing in the light. Afterward, we sat in the sun, eating lunch out of tin boxes, resting our backs against the warm brick wall.

"You got a lot to learn," she said. "And I'm just the tramp to teach it to you."

Money didn't matter then. The girls went with you because they liked you. They weren't working any other angle. Emma, for instance, made as much as I did, and she had a husband in the service who sent her a hundred a month allotment. If we went out, drinking or dancing, she paid her way, always half. Money didn't mean a thing. It was just something they gave you to spend.

Emma lived in a Sunnyside apartment and one night we were in the bed when the door opened and in walked the husband. He was a sergeant in an infantry outfit getting ready to ship overseas, ugly, tired, and half-drunk. He looked tough and had the hands of an iron worker. I thought he was going to hit me, but he just stood there on the bedroom rug after he snapped on the light, with his hands on his hips and his haversack dangling from one shoulder. His uniform was rumpled and dirty from sleeping all night in the day coach.

"Jesus Christ, Emma," he said. "Is this the best you can do for yourself? A kid like this?"

Then he slapped her hard, across the face, and she laughed.

"Get your clothes on, punk," he said to me. "Get out of here before I get mad."

Three days later she showed up with an eye that was colored blood red and purple under the flesh-colored paste she'd put on it. She wore the mascara just the same.

"Oh, he clouted me around," she said. "Can you blame the poor bastard?"

After that he went overseas and I spent two, three nights a week with Emma. We ate steaks from the black-market Greek and drank beer right out of the can, made love if we felt like it, just slept it off if we didn't. Paydays we would draw our checks and head for the bar I sat at now. They would be five or six deep in the place, all drinking, all spending. And nobody worked himself to death.

A soft touch until I was drafted, two days after I was eighteen, in June, 1945. At that I was lucky that the war ended before they sent me overseas, because if I had gone I might be dead and buried on one of those little Pacific islands.

But I wasn't dead and I wasn't buried. I was here in Sunnyside sitting in a bar, looking at a whiskey I didn't want to drink and thinking about the good old days when I was sixteen and seventeen, the good old days when the money rolled in, during the war, before I was drafted. I got so mad, sitting there, that I kicked the bar with enough anger to hurt my foot through the GI shoe. I took half a dollar from my pocket and dropped it on the bar so that it bounced, then started out, leaving the rye.

"Hey!" the barkeep called after me. "You got change. A dime."

"Keep it," I said. "Feed it to the chickens."

There was a cab going through the street so I flagged him down. I had ridden the subway to Sunnyside when I was sure I was going back to a job at seventy dollars a week. Now, just another discharged soldier, with no job and no money except for the few hundred dollars I brought out of the Army, I rode in a cab as if I owned the world. I looked out the window at the rows of houses, block after block of them, all alike, built on an ash-heap and a garbage dump, breathing the soot from the Pennsylvania Yards, and I wondered why anyone, taking his choice, chose to live in Sunnyside or Long Island City. When we crossed the bridge and turned uptown I had an idea.

"Don't go to Yorkville," I said. "Go over to the West Side. Central Park West."

"Okay, soldier," answered the driver.

CHAPTER THREE

Fred answered the door himself. He wore a maroon silk robe with a script *F* embroidered on the pocket, and under the robe he wore a white shirt with a heavy silk twelve-dollar tie. He had just shaved and looked neat, the way he always did. He reminded me of Edward Arnold, except that Fred was smoother— a big man, more than two hundred pounds, with a chuckle that started down at his heels, and neat, always neat and well dressed. He had twenty-five suits, made to order, and fourteen pairs of shoes, hand-sewn. You caught the smell of his dollar cigar the minute he opened the door.

"Kid!" he said. "Come in, come in. Come on in."

"Hello, Fred."

We shook hands and I followed him down the hall to the living room. Fred had five rooms in a house on Central Park West. He paid a decorator ten thousand dollars to furnish the place and it looked it: modern furniture that was close to the floor, cork walls, a built-in bar, lots of lamps at two hundred each, springy rugs an inch thick, four big sofas you sank into, with a glass-brick ashtray always right at your hand. It was on the eighteenth floor, and from the living-room windows you got a view of the Park that looked like a map—all of Central Park, from Fifty-ninth to a Hundred and Tenth Street, laid out for you neat and green, with the winding roads and the bridle paths and the straight cross-drives showing up sharp. The cars were like toys, creeping along. It looked like a model for the City of the Future, as if the trees were faked out of moss and the grass lawns faked out of thick green felt. Beyond the Park was the East Side, with the flat-faced houses on Park Avenue, and beyond that, over the rooftops of East Yorkville and a million washlines, you caught a glimpse of the East River, flashing like silver in the sun.

"Sit down, kid. Sit down," said Fred.

I took off my army cap and sat in one of the sofas. Fred stood in the middle of the room, the expensive cigar in his mouth, looking at me and rubbing the palms of his hands together. He seemed nervous, a little embarrassed.

"What's the matter?" I asked. "Aren't you glad to see me? I can go."

I started to get up.

"Sit down, sit down."

He came over and ruffled my hair.

"Don't be so touchy. Sure I'm glad to see you. How about a drink?"

I nodded. "I just left one standing on the bar," I said. "Bought and paid for. But I'll have one with you."

He poured bourbon into two heavy crystal glasses, then added plenty of ice. I watched the soda bubbles run up my glass; he took his with plain water.

"Get the drink cold," he said. "That's the secret of a good drink."

I took a sip. It was bonded bourbon, rich and fruity, almost like brandy, the kind that costs a dollar a drink. Fred tasted his, nodded, then took a mouthful.

"So you're out," he said.

"I'm out. In more ways than one."

"What's wrong, kid? Is it dough?"

He sat beside me on the sofa. I could smell his cigar and the stuff he used after shaving. He smelled rich. He smelled like money. Being with Fred made me feel confident, made me look at things differently from the way I did with the old man, or my brother Rusty, or Murph and the Wop—any of the slobs from the neighborhood. I told him what had happened at Langley.

"So there goes my seventy per," I finished.

"Yeah," he said. "That stuff is out. The peasants go back to being peasants and the chumps go back to being chumps."

"I only wanted the job for a while," I told him. "Just until I looked around. Found some real opportunity." I didn't want Fred to think I was willing to work in a factory for the rest of my life.

"What do you think you'll do?" he asked.

I got up and put my glass on the table, then walked to the windows and looked at the Park, at the whole city stretched out down there.

"I don't know," I said, after a while. "But I'm not going to go to work for any thirty-five dollars a week. I know that much."

He stood beside me with a hand on my shoulder, pointing down with the other hand.

"Look at that town down there," he said. "Seven million people and most of them jerks, suckers just begging to be taken."

I nodded.

"Don't be a sucker, kid. Don't ever be a sucker."

"No."

"And if you aren't a sucker," he said, "you have to be one of the people who take the suckers. Some do the eating and some get eaten."

I nodded.

"Yeah," I said. "I saw that. In the Army."

We walked back to the sofa together and sat down.

"So what are you going to do?" he asked.

"I don't know. I thought you might have some ideas."

"For a job?"

"Not a job," I said. "Just something to do."

He looked at the blue-grey smoke from his cigar, rising and curling like a thin silk scarf, then shook his head.

"No, kid," he said. He got rid of the ash on his cigar with a delicate touch against the side of the glass tray. "I could get you something to do. Something that would pay off two, three hundred a week."

"Honest?"

"Sure," he said. "But you don't want it."

"Are you crazy?" I asked.

He put his hand on my knee.

"I like you, Mattie. I don't want to see you in jail. Or in some alley with a belly full of bullets."

"Are you in jail?" I asked.

He smiled.

"I have been."

"But not for long."

"No," he agreed. "Not for long."

During the war, when he was selling meat and gas ration tickets, the Federal people picked him up and held him downtown for a couple of days. I think I made myself solid with him then, because I was the only member of the family who went to see him.

"Look," he said, tapping my knee with the tip of his finger. "During the war you could get away with murder. What I was doing was practically legal, it was so simple. It was just like prohibition. They had a law then that said people couldn't drink. Did they stop drinking?"

"No."

"They didn't stop eating meat, either, just because Whiskers told them to. So it was simple, during the war. But things are different now."

"So?"

"So stay on the legit. If I had it to do again I'd hardly break any law at all. I'd run up a stake and then go into some legitimate business. That's what you want to do, kid. Be a businessman. You'll make money all right. You're a smart kid."

I got up and walked to the windows again, leaning against the steel frame, looking down at the City.

"It isn't only money," I said. "You can make money and still be a slob. I see them: guys from East End Avenue, from the big houses on Eighty-sixth, guys making twenty, twenty-five thousand a year, but for what they do to earn it they might just as well be in jail. They're scared, scared guys. You can see it in their faces."

Fred nodded. Talking to him, in this room, with the smooth, expensive bourbon working, I thought I saw exactly what I wanted.

"I don't want to be like them," I said. "And I don't want to be like my old man. I want to be independent."

He looked at me for a long time, as though he saw me for the first time. Then he nodded, slowly, and took the cigar out of his mouth.

"I think I know what you mean," he said. "I think I know exactly what you mean."

"Yes," I said. "I thought you would. I can talk to you, man to man. Rusty and the old man, they just think I'm a fresh punk, too smart for my own good. The guys in the neighborhood—what are they? Slobs. Dumb, ignorant slobs."

"What do you want to do?" he asked.

I stared at the shiny, neat bar.

"For a starter," I said, "I'd like to open a spot. A saloon. After that, who knows?"

"Why a saloon?" Fred asked.

"Where else do you find the same percentage? Saloons always make money. Good times, bad times, they always make money. Guys will starve in order to drink. Starve or rob or beg. Dames too. Look at the old lady."

"How is she?" he asked. My old lady was Fred's sister.

"Worse," I said.

"Too bad," he said. "It's your old man. I tried to get him a job once, during prohibition, driving a rum truck. He wouldn't take it."

"He's a chump," I said. "A no-good chump."

"Yeah," said Fred. "How is Rusty?"

I laughed.

"He's going to law school."

"How about that?" Fred laughed, a deep belly laugh. "A shyster."

He picked up the glasses and carried them to the bar. While he was pouring another drink he spoke to me, not turning around: "Why don't you do that? Go back to school?"

"Me?"

He held the drinks, one in each hand.

"Sure," he said. "You're smarter than Rusty."

"I know that," I said. "Rusty's dumb. But what would I learn in school?"

"Did you learn anything in the Army?"

I nodded.

"I learned how to break your arm or your leg before you know what's happened. Or your neck. They call it unarmed combat."

"Anything else?"

"I played some football at Fort Benning. Not much, but I learned some tricks."

He got excited.

"Look, Mattie," he said. "Why don't you go back to school? Play some ball. You should be a cinch against those kids, with what you know. Maybe get a scholarship to some college. Get a rep'. Then, when you open your place you'll be somebody, not just a punk kid from the neighborhood."

I looked at him across the top of my glass. I knew that part of what he had in mind was to keep me out of the rackets, at least out of some petty spot where I'd get caught or get hurt; the other part might have been on the level and it might have been just to get me off his mind, so I wouldn't be a bother.

"I don't know," I said. "What am I going to use for money when the time comes to open my place? When I'm twenty-one? Buttons? How can I waste my time in school?"

"Don't be a chump, kid," he said. "Let me worry about the money."

"What do you mean?"

"I mean what I said. Let me worry about the dough."

"You mean you'd put it up?"

"Why not?"

I could see that he meant it, the part about the money.

"Go back to school," he said. "Get a reputation. Then, when you're twenty-one, you can open your place."

"That's two years," I said.

"Is that long? You've got a whole lifetime in front of you. A whole future."

He got up and went into the bathroom, and came out with a package of sen-sens.

"Here," he said, "chew a couple of these."

"Thanks."

"And remember," he said. "One rap and there goes your license. So keep your nose clean."

"Sure," I said.

I stood up and put on my hat. We shook hands and I walked toward the door.

"Hey!" Fred called.

I turned around.

"How are you fixed for money?"

"All right, I guess."

I had a little under three hundred and fifty dollars; not a lot at these prices.

"Wait a minute."

Fred went into the bedroom and came out with a new bill folded in his hand.

"Here." He shoved the money into my hand. "Cigarette dough."

"Thanks."

I put the bill in my pants pocket; in the hallway, waiting for the elevator, I looked at it. It was a hundred-dollar bill.

CHAPTER FOUR

Five-thirty, standing on the corner, I watched Rose Eberle get off the crosstown bus, stepping from the bus to the curb with a bright flash of pretty leg. I stood up straight, pushing myself away from the wall I was leaning against.

"Hello, Rosie," I said. "Can't you say hello to an old pal?"

She was my age: nineteen. I used to take her to the high school dances, love her up a little in the movies or in the Park on the warm summer nights. She was a good Catholic kid: a teaser, but all right. She was dressed up, in clothes that were better than the ones she wore when we went to school together. She stopped and turned when I called.

"Why, Mattie Dolan!" she said. "When did you get back to the neighborhood?"

"Yesterday," I said. "Just in time to take you out. How about tonight? We'll go to a show and then go dancing. Anything you feel like."

She hesitated.

"Gee, Mattie," she said. "I can't."

"Why not?" I said. "I've got money."

"Gee, Mattie," she said, "I'm engaged to a fella," and she took off her white net glove to show me a ring worth, maybe, forty dollars.

"No kidding?"

"Honest," she said. "To a fella from uptown that works in my place. From the Heights. I'm moving out of the neighborhood as soon as we're married next month."

"How did this joker find an apartment?"

"Gee, Mattie, you know what he did? He gave the super two hundred dollars like a bribe."

"Some Four-F bum, I suppose?" I said.

"He is not!" That made her mad. "He was in the Army, an aviator. Like your brother Rusty. He got out of it a long time ago, a year and a half. On points."

"Okay," I said. "So I'm sorry. So what about tonight?"

"Gee, Mattie, I can't."

"Okay," I said. "Forget it." She wasn't just what I wanted anyway; to do more than feel her up you would have to be inspected by the priest and married, so that you'd never get out of it. "What are you doing with yourself?" I asked.

"I'm working," she said. "I got a good job, fifty week."

"Yea-h-h-h?" I said. "Doing what?"

"Secretary."

"For fifty a week?"

"Sure," she said. "Private secretary. To a fella."

"Jeez," I said. "The best I've been offered is thirty a week."

"Well, gee, Mattie, don't blame it on me."

"Who's blaming you?" I said. "Where's Sally? Sally Reilly?"

"Oh, Sally, she's engaged. To a fella."

"No kidding?" I said. "Not to a gorilla? Where's Fran?"

"Gee, Fran, she's married. She got a kid already a long time ago. Six months."

"How about Loretta? Betty?"

They were all girls I went to school with, kids I had taken to parties and dances, kids about my own age.

"Loretta's married. She lives in Detroit."

"Betty?"

"Betty's gone."

"Gone where?" I said. "To heaven?"

"You know. Gone. She got into trouble with some soldier, a marine, and she left the neighborhood."

"You mean she's a tramp? A regular whore?"

"Mattie Dolan!" she said, "don't use that kind of language to me in my presence. Yes."

"All right," I said. "I'm sorry."

"Accepted," she said.

She looked at the ribbons on my uniform: Good Conduct, American Theater, Victory.

"What's that?" she said, touching the Good Conduct ribbon.

"Distinguished Service Cross," I said. "Five bucks extra a month."

"Gee," she said. "I didn't know you had that."

"Sure."

"You still in the Army, Mattie?"

I looked at her.

"What do you think? I'm discharged, dopie."

"How come you still got the suit?"

"I got some tailor making me a suit," I explained. "The same guy that makes clothes for my Uncle Fred. Hundred and a half a copy. It takes a few days, fittings and all, but it's worth it for what you get."

She agreed.

"Well, Mattie," she said, "I'm glad to see you back, no kidding."

"Sure," I said. "Yeah, sure."

"Will you come to my wedding, Mattie, next month?"

"Sure," I said. "St. Mike's?"

"Yeah," she said. "Father Fliegel."

I watched her walk away from me, trim and neat in her nice little dress, with good-looking legs on high-heeled shoes. Jesus, I thought, what the hell: a million-dollar body and a two-cent head. After that, standing on the corner and watching the people getting off the bus, coming home from work, I wondered what I was going to do for a girl friend, now that I was back.

CHAPTER FIVE

The next day I went to Tuppers on Madison Avenue and bought a suit for eighty-five dollars, sharkskin, banker's grey. I didn't like the cheap clothes Murph and the boys from the neighborhood wore; this suit was an investment in front. Inspecting myself in the three-way mirror, I decided that in this suit I looked like a smart professional athlete—football player or fighter—the kind of guy who invests his money and later becomes a businessman.

"Shall I send it, sir?" the clerk asked.

"I'll pick it up," I told him. "When will it be ready?"

"A week from today, sir," he said.

"A week from today," I said.

Back in the sun on the crowded street I kept seeing my reflection in the shop-front windows, still in that lousy uniform. I wondered why I hadn't asked the clerk to send my suit to the house; then I knew it was because I was ashamed of living in Yorkville, the old neighborhood.

People who don't know the City think it is the same from the Battery to the Bronx, except for Broadway and Park Avenue, Wall Street and the shopping centers.

It isn't that way at all.

The City is made up of neighborhoods and if you come from one section you never feel exactly right in another. For instance: I'm from East Yorkville. An outsider might not notice the difference between Yorkville and, say, East Harlem, but there is something about it, something you feel. Some sections you see are different, right away. Take Washington Heights—what they call Kike's Peak or the Kosher Alps. You notice the difference between that and Yorkville, because what you see on the Heights are Jewish delicatessens and Appetizing Stores and what you see in Yorkville are saloons. Fordham is another thing, up in the Bronx, half Irish and half Jewish. The West Side is something else. They are all different, but in a way they are all the same. Kids get born in a neighborhood, grow up in it, go to school at the P.S., marry a girl from down the block, and then, as often as not, they set up housekeeping in the neighborhood. It's just like a small town except that the City is always there like a jungle, pressing in on the neighborhood: seven million people.

I turned around on Madison Avenue and walked back to Tuppers—four blocks. The clerk stood near the door, leaning against a glass showcase filled with seven-dollar ties, stripes, regimental stripes.

"Is anything wrong, sir?" he said, taking his elbow off the case.

"I decided to have the suit sent."

He wrote on a card while I gave him the address.

"A week from today, Mr. Dolan," he said.

"Okay," I said. "A week from today."

All the people hurrying along, salesmen with cases trying to look important, office boys with big manila envelopes, women window-shopping antiques, genuine big-shots going back to give out some orders after enjoying a two-hour lunch, all these people who seemed to be busy made me nervous and aware of the fact that I had nothing, nothing to do. I thought of Fred and of what he had said about going back to school.

I was the one who had been good in school, out of all the kids in the neighborhood crowd, but when I quit in Forty-three I never meant to go back.

School, I thought, walking up Madison, a fine rich street ... school, where they tried to turn you into a sucker willing to work for thirty a week … school, where the teachers knew less than the students about anything that really matters.

Our public school on York is more than a hundred years old; it smells like the public toilet in the subway at Times Square. It is a big brown sandstone building that looks like the jail in a poor southern county, except that a jail would have to be cleaner because of the prison laws. The toilets are outside. In winter you freeze when you go and in hot weather the flies are so thick you have to fight them off. The classrooms have small windows, not big ones like they have in new schools, so that during the winter months, when it gets dark in the afternoon, they have to turn on the lights. We used to sit two in a seat because there were fifty, fifty-five kids in a classroom built for thirty-five.

And the teachers—toughies from all over town, mean old maids with religious medals and dried-up faces, or moonfaced dames married to cops, red-skinned and bloated from beer, the kind you see watching for Tammany Hall at the neighborhood polls on Election Day.

A good-looking teacher had a hard time because of the boys in the eighth grade, lots of them fourteen and fifteen, left back. When Murph and the Wop and I were in the eighth we had a teacher who was brand new, twenty-one or twenty-two years old, with a body that gave you ideas, made you squirm when you watched her walk. Every big boy in the class changed his seat to the back of the room so that he could slump down and try to look up her skirts when she sat at the desk. She knew about that after a while and kept her knees together and her dress pulled down. But she couldn't do anything about the fact that just looking at her was exciting, and when she stood at the blackboard and stretched to write, you heard the boys in the back row whistling and making cracks.

Murph was fifteen and she drove him crazy. He promised the rest of us he would love her up even if it got him kicked out of school. One day he waited after class, pretending he wanted to talk about his lessons. When he and the teacher were alone he shut the classroom door.

"Come on, baby," he said, "look what I got for you," and he pretended to open his fly.

She screamed and ran through the door, with Murph after her, yelling: "Come on, toots, look what I got for ya."

The custodian caught Murph in the lobby and gave him his lumps. After that he left school and a little while later he was sent away for robbing a candy store. The teacher couldn't do a thing with the class; big kids swore at her right out, and had her bawling almost every day. At the end of the term she hated us so much that she didn't come to our graduation and I understand that she quit teaching school.

Of course, high school was different. The teachers were better and there were girls: three thousand girls—girls and parties and dances.

I walked on up Madison Avenue, turned east and continued uptown, hardly conscious of where I was going. After a while I stood in front of the school, John Jay High School, where I was a student for three years before I quit and went to work for Langley. The school looks like Independence Hall in Philadelphia, except that it's bigger.

I sat on a bench in a little park, looking up the hill at the school, with the sun on the big windows and an American flag flying from the gold-eagled pole on top of the bell tower that never had a bell. Girls were coming down the long, curved walk, in groups of four and five, and I saw a girl who looked familiar. When she was closer I recognized the kid I had watched through Greene's window: the one like a nun. She had black hair, and widespaced innocent eyes under a broad, smooth forehead. She had a soft-looking white throat and a moist, red mouth. She had a guilty, half-scared look, as if she expected someone to hit her, or take something away from her. She looked as though she had dreams she was afraid to tell the priest about, dreams that made her hot and embarrassed when she remembered them in the morning.

I stood up and waved to her, making *come here* with my hand. She left the others and came to me.

"Hello, Mattie," she said. "I heard you were back in the neighborhood."

"Hello," I said, and stood like a fool; I guess she realized that I didn't know her, or expect her to know me.

"You don't remember me?" she said. "Gina Tragorna, from Eighty-fourth?"

"Oh, sure," I said. "Sure I remember you. Gina Tragorna. You look different."

"Yeah," she said. "You look different, too, Mattie, in that suit."

I had known her brother, a big Hunky kid who had gone into the Marine Corps.

"How is Pete?" I asked. "Good old Pete."

That was it, Pete Tragorna, a husky Hungarian kid who played on the John Jay first team while I was on the second. I hadn't known him very well.

"Peter was killed at Iwo Jima," she said. "I thought you knew that."

"No," I said. "No kidding?"

"Yes," she said. "A long time ago."

"Gee, kid, I'm sorry."

"Yeah," she said. "It was too bad."

I looked down, into her black eyes; she looked back for a second, then flinched and let her eyes drop so they stared at the place my suntan tie was tucked into my suntan shirt.

"Are you coming back?" she said.

"Huh?"

"Are you coming back to school?"

"Yeah. Yeah sure. I guess so."

"I'll be seeing you then," she said.

She held out her hand, under her books, and I squeezed it.

"Sure," I said. "Sure you will."

I watched her walk back to her friends, who waited in a giggling huddle, watching her rump go pump-pump-pump and her clean bare legs in their bobby socks, firm and pink so that the skin looked smooth and shiny as silk. Then I remembered what Murph had said. "Jailbait," he called her. San Quentin Quail. I thought of a crack I had heard in the Army:—*if they're big enough to bleed they're big enough to butcher*, and I had to laugh, standing there, watching the kids come out of school. I crossed the street to a candy store and called the school from a telephone booth, making an appointment with old man Kieran, the tough Tammany principal.

"You want to *en*-ter the school?" The clerk spoke with a Brooklyn accent.

"That's right," I said. "The name is Dolan. D-o-l-a-n, Dolan."

I walked out of the candy store and took another look at the big red brick school, with the concrete stadium beside it even bigger than the school. The building was ten years old, but it looked new, powerful, prosperous. Well, I thought, watching the janitor take in the flag, school would be better than a dead-end job for thirty-five dollars a week; the government gave you sixty-five a month, there was nothing to do, and there were other girls, lots of them, if Gina Tragorna didn't work out.

PART II

CHAPTER ONE

N THE MORNING I put on one of my outgrown civilian suits and went to the school to talk to Kieran.

"Yes, Dolan," he said. "Shake hands."

His hand was dry as a dead leaf, bony and strong. He is the kind of thin-faced Irishman you see around the Municipal Building, cut from the pattern of Jimmy Walker, smart, tough, and tricky as a priest. His face is red from massage and whiskey and he wears white shirts with stiff collars. Blue suits. He can be mean as a cop when he pleases. With me he was nice.

But he didn't want me back.

"Why don't you go to a private school? De La Salle, or Fordham Prep?"

"I'm a Protestant."

"Oh?"—as if he didn't believe it.

"Sure," I said. "County Antrim."

He laughed; with those people, being Irish is like belonging to a club.

"You know, Dolan," he said, "I think that the government would pay tuition at a private school even for a heretic from the Six Counties."

I grinned, playing his game.

"Yes," I said, "but I'd like to finish here, sir, where I started."

The "sir" impressed him; it is an old trick. Call a police sergeant *lieutenant,* call a lieutenant *captain,* always promoting him one grade, because he has that on his mind, never two, because then he'll know you are trying to flatter him. Calling Kieran "sir" made him think the Army had taught me manners. He hesitated, examining me with his blue metallic politician's eyes, then pressed a buzzer to call the clerk.

"Get me the card for Matthew Dolan." He looked at me. "That's right, isn't it? Matthew Dolan?"

"That's right, sir. From East Eighty-seventh."

"A Yorkville boy," he said, as if coming from Yorkville was like going to Yale. "I'm from the neighborhood myself."

He didn't have to tell me that. The Kieran family is well known in Yorkville. There were twelve children, split into three groups. Four went into the Church, two priests and two nuns. Four had jobs on the City payroll, three school teachers and a cop. Four had gone into the rackets and one of them was dead, shot in the chest by his own brother during a stick-up on the West Side.

He might have been something in the rackets himself, the way he sat facing the window with his fingertips pressed together, looking tough and hard and competent. He got the job through politics but he knew as much about running a school as anyone promoted for merit.

Through the washed window behind Kieran you saw a row of apartment houses, women grouped at the entrances, sitting on camp stools, minding babies, nodding across the bobbing carriages as they gnattered at one another. Inside, you got the school smell, of chalk and cedar shavings from pencils, of girls and enormous toilets, of varnish and floor oil and the sawdust they sprinkle on the floors before they sweep, of books and of thousands of reams of paper. And you got the sense of being up on charges, there to explain something bad you'd done. There was an expensive, City-owned clock, ticking away, somewhere in the outer office. I felt uncomfortable, the way you feel when the police take you down to the station house to scare you, just making you sit on a bench, listening to the cop-clock tick, wondering what they are going to do; then, when they think they've scared you enough, they turn you out onto the street.

After a while the clerk came back and handed Kieran my record card. He studied it, then looked at me. During my three years in the school I had an average of ninety-three.

"Why did you drop out of school?" he asked. "Why didn't you go on, to college?"

"Well, sir," I said, "my brother went into the service early and I had to help out at home."

He nodded and looked at the card again.

"My inclination was to turn you down," he said. "But I think we'll take a chance."

"Thank you, sir," I said.

"There are a few other veterans in the school. Younger than you, though. Navy boys."

I nodded. I knew them; kids so crazy for a uniform they had shipped in the Navy at seventeen. They thought you needed a uniform in order to get girls. I stood up.

"Were you overseas, Dolan?" Kieran asked.

I thought it would suit him better if I said yes.

"Yes, sir," I said. "With the paratroops. Eighty-second Airborne."

It was the right answer.

"A fine division," he said. "One of the best."

We shook hands and he told me to see Miss Webber, on the fourth floor.

"She'll give you your program," he said. "I'll call her."

"Thanks," I said. "Thank you, sir."

He waved at me with his thin, dry hand; I think he knew he had made a mistake.

Webber had short hair, turning grey, a thin, intelligent mouth and bright blue, Dutch-looking eyes. There was a blue art-vase on her desk, holding a bouquet of late flowers. She looked up from her book and nodded at a chair: *Sit down, Dolan,* then went on reading. I sat down and watched her read until the clerk brought my record card. They didn't trust me to carry it, for fear that I'd change the marks.

Webber put her book away, took a printed form from her desk, and wrote my name at the top in square-block library printing. Then we talked and agreed upon subjects. She filled in the boxes and signed the card, blotting it before she handed it to me. I said: *"Thank you,"* and started out, but she called me back when I reached the door. I turned and walked back to her desk. She offered me a cigarette.

"Thanks," I said.

I held a match for her, wondering what kind of good advice she was going to give me with the cigarette.

"Why are you coming back here? Too lazy to work for a living?"

"To get an education," I said. "I'm thinking of going to law school."

How could I tell Miss Webber that I was going to open a saloon as soon as I was twenty-one; that until then I was just using up air, just waiting for time to pass?

"Let me give you a piece of advice."

She put out her cigarette angrily, looking at me instead of the ashtray.

"Keep away from the young girls."

"What do you think I am?" I said.

She laughed.

"I'm an old maid, Dolan," she said, "but I know more than you give me credit for. You've been in the Army and out working, making money, having things your way. You're nineteen, almost a man. You've been with prostitutes and Victory Girls, and with all those women in the war plants. Leave these children alone."

"Look, Miss Webber—" I started to say.

She interrupted me.

"Last year, Dolan, we had thirty-four girls pregnant. Thirty-four that we know about. The soldiers, during the war, gave us a lot of trouble. They were gone before we could find them, shipped out, some of them dead before the girl knew what had happened."

"What's that got to do with me? I'm not a soldier any more. I'm a student. From today on."

"You're here," she said. "We can put our hands on you. So leave the young girls alone. They've had a bad war, too."

I was angry enough to spit in her face, but I stood there, saying nothing. She believed in direct attack, the way most school-teachers do, not giving you a chance to answer, hardly giving you a chance to think, just throwing words at you.

"That's all, Dolan," she said. "I disagree with Mr. Kieran's decision, but he's the principal. I just work here."

"Okay, save it," I said.

She looked up quickly, like a regular officer.

"Don't be impertinent, Dolan," she said. "Just go on to your classes."

In the corridor, outside her office, I looked at the program card: *English—Spanish—History—Math—Music Appreciation.*

For a moment I was tempted to tear up the card and walk out into the sun, where I wouldn't be lectured by old maids—to just hang around the neighborhood with the boys, or, maybe, to go away: *California.* Or Florida, where the money ran down the gutters. Then I thought of the personnel man and the thirty-dollar job he wanted me to take, and I thought of Fred and his promise to back me in business when the time came. I put the card in my pocket and walked down the corridor, looking at the numbers on the doors.

I walked across the field to the big man who wore a sweat-shirt and a baseball cap. He was a new coach; Raftery, the old one, had been killed on the Rhine. I stood for a second and waited; the scuffed-up grass smelt fresh and good.

"I'm Dolan. Mattie Dolan. What do you do to try out?"

For a moment I thought he was annoyed, then he looked at me and grinned. Most of the players on the field were lighter, two, three years younger; those who had weight were slobs, red kids, all blubber and sweat. There were about thirty on the field, tossing a dozen balls around, waiting for practice to begin.

"My name's Garry," he said, giving me a hand that was square and hard as an inch plank. "Ever play before?"

"A little."

"Where?"

"Here, for a while. And in the Army."

He looked around; no one was near us.

"Don't say anything about the Army," he said.

"Okay."

I drew a suit and came back on the field. The springy turf, under my cleats, felt familiar and pleasant. It was a nice, pre-fall day, cool and clear, so that the concrete edge of the stadium stood out sharply against the sky. I moved up the line, spat on my hands, charged hard and hit the dummy. Garry, watching me, jerked his thumb: *okay!*

"That's the way, Dolan. Hit 'em hard!"

"Kill or be killed, eh, sir?" I said.

That was a slogan our Army picked up from the British Commandos. Garry recognized it, smiled and said, "Kill or be killed, Dolan. But, remember, this is football, not unarmed combat."

I felt good. Against these kids I knew that Garry thought I looked like the big time. We had a coach at Fort Benning who had played for the Bears and another who had played for West Point. Fellows on the teams at Benning had played industrial ball, in coal towns, places like that. There were some ex-college players and some sand-lot toughies, all good, and fellows playing on the good army teams were playing for more than money. They were playing to keep out of combat. Against that kind of competition I was never more than fourth string, but I learned. I learned a lot.

We tackled the dummy for half an hour, then chose up sides. My side received a bad kick dribbling up the field. One of our ends scooped up the ball and I cut out in front of him. A kid on the other team crossed after the end and I blocked him out, clean and hard, into the middle of next week. By the time I got up, the end had scored. The kid I had hit was still on the ground and I started to help him up. A guy on his side said: "Leave him alone, you mugg." Then he said to another kid: "These lousy army muggs. Think they're wise guys."

Jesus, I thought. You couldn't win. The combat guys called you boy scout because you weren't sucker enough to get shot at and these punks, who had been asking the teacher for permission to go wee-wee while I was making good money at Langley, acted as if you were a bum.

We played two twelve-minute periods, no scoring allowed, after the first touchdown our end made. I was surprised to be in such good shape, and I tried hard, showing off a little. After he blew the whistle and told us to quit, Garry walked over and slapped me on the back. I was breathing hard, a bit winded, but good for forty minutes more.

"That was a nice block," he said. "Nice going."

"Thanks," I said. "Some of the kids didn't seem to like it."

"Forget that," he said. "Fresh kids. You start with the first team on Saturday. Right half; okay?"

"*Ooo*-kay," I said.

A dozen girls had been watching practice from behind the sideline rope. I walked up to Gina, sweating a little, with my hair mussed and my helmet in my hand, just like a college player in the movies.

"Hello, kid."

"Hello, Mattie."

"Walking home?"

"Oh, yes."

"Wait for me," I said. I reached across the rope and squeezed her hand. You would have thought I handed her a ten-dollar bill, the way she smiled up at me. "Wait here while I take a shower. I'll be out in a couple of minutes."

"Okay, Mattie."

I took a hot soapy shower and combed my hair in front of the mirror screwed to the back of the locker door. I looked good after the workout and I felt good too. I stepped on the big Fairbanks scale, naked, and jiggled the brass weights. One eighty-nine and a half: a good weight for my height.

The other girls had gone home but Gina waited where I had left her. I took her books and she put her hand through the crook of my arm. We walked downtown toward the neighborhood. When we got to Eighty-sixth and First I said, "How about a glass of cold beer?"

"Gee, Mattie, I couldn't," she said. "My mother would kill me if she smelt liquor on my breath."

"Beer isn't liquor," I said. "It's food. Haven't you ever had a drink?"

"I had a wine once," she said. "At a wedding."

"How old are you?" I said.

"I'll be sixteen," she said.

"Come on," I said. "Have a beer. It's a free country."

"Gee, I can't, honest," she said.

We were standing on the corner at the foot of the hill and the sun was shining through her black hair so that the fringe had a golden halo on it. Her moist, red mouth was turned up to me, opened a little, with her teeth showing, white and clean.

"Come in with me anyhow," I said. "You have a coke or a gingerale."

She looked up and down the block.

"Okay, Mattie," she said.

We went into a sour-smelling dark saloon with a sham-rock painted on the front window and an angry-looking black

Irishman in a dirty apron behind the bar, loafing on his elbows, looking out the window. It was dark in the place but not dark enough.

"I'll have a beer," I said.

The bartender shook his head without bothering to straighten up. I took my discharge button between my thumb and finger and almost rubbed it against his nose.

"I'll have a beer," I said.

"I can't serve her," he said, nodding at Gina.

"She's having coke," I said.

"Not in here, she ain't."

"Whaddya mean?" I said.

"She don't get nothing in this place. We got a license to think about, sonny."

I stood there, feeling cheap.

"Ah, ya muzzler," I said.

I felt like slugging him, the way he stood there, leaning on the back-bar.

"On your way," he said.

"Come on, kid." I took Gina's arm. "Let's get out of this dump."

We went to the Greek soda fountain on York Avenue. I ordered two cokes.

"Can I have a soda?" she said.

"Sure," I told her. "Anything you want."

"Chaw-kolit," she said.

I changed the order.

"Anything you want, kid. You're the boss."

I touched her hand; the skin was warm to the touch, fresh and warm.

"Gee, Mattie," she said. "It's nice of you to treat me, honest."

"A pleasure," I told her.

But it wasn't a pleasure. I felt like a punk kid, sitting in the back of the soda fountain on a rickety wire chair, with the candy smell and the soda smell and all the kids sitting around on chairs and on the whirling stools at the marble counter, with their books on the sticky table tops, giggling, giggling, giggling, and the god-damned juke box sounding off the same dumb tune four times in a row, and two girls trying to dance together on the slippery tile floor, until the Greek came over and told them to go sit down, and asked them couldn't they read the sign on the wall: NO DANCING.

I walked Gina home to Eighty-fourth Street and thought of taking her into the hallway, where I could love her up a little, then decided to play it smart and wait.

"Gee, kid," I said. "I go for you. Who do you hang around with? Tell me his name and I'll kill him." I grinned and handed her the books.

"Gee, Mattie, I don't go with nobody."

"Honest?"

"Honest, Mattie. I don't hardly bother with the fellas at all."

"Not even me?"

"Well, with you, that's different."

"What do you mean, different?"

"Well, I know you from before," she said. "And you were in the war, a veteran. Like my brother."

"So that's settled, huh?" I said. "You and me?"

"Okay," she said. "But we got to be careful. My old lady is awful strict. Only that you were a friend of Pete's she might not mind so much."

"Sure," I said. "Pete was my buddy."

"And listen, Mattie,—" she said, touching my hand.

"Yeah?"

"I don't go the limit," she said. "Maybe you don't like that."

"Aw, what do you think I am?" I said. "I told you I go for you, didn't I?"

"Will you come up to the house for dinner?"

"Sure," I said. "Why not?"

"I'll tell them you were a friend of Peter's. They don't let me go with fellows."

"How come? Aren't you human?"

"My mother's strict. My father's not so bad, but my old lady's strict."

I remembered watching the old lady slap her, the day I saw her through Greene's window.

"What the hell," I said, "you have the right to go out with somebody."

"If they know you were a friend of Peter it will be all right," she said.

"Sure," I said. "Sure it will."

I kissed her on the tip of her nose and she blushed.

"So long, Mattie," she said. I watched her hurry up the stoop and disappear into the hallway of the house.

Jailbait, Dolan, I said to myself. *San Quentin Quail.*

I started to whistle, walking away, the dumb tune that had been on the juke box back in the Greek candy shop. I stopped at Greene's and went in for a beer. There was the Wop, sitting on a stool, with Murph beside him, leaning on the bar.

"Hello, schoolboy," said the Wop.

"Save it," I told him. Then I said to Greene: "Three beers."

"Look who's buying," said the Wop.

"Shut up, Wop," Murph said. "Lay off Mattie. He's my friend. My buddy. If he has the idea to go to school, that's his business, so you shut up."

He put an arm around me and squeezed. I caught his breath, stinking with whiskey. He was half loaded, in the afternoon.

"Is that right, Mattie?" he asked. "You're my friend, huh? My buddy."

"Yeah, Murph," I said. "Drink your beer."

"Sure, pal," he said. "Watch me."

He lifted the glass and drank the beer without putting it down.

"You tank," said the Wop. "You Irish tank."

Murph grinned, wiping his mouth.

"I may not be much of a whiskey man, but I sure can put away the beer."

We had two beers and I started to go.

"So long, bums," I said.

"So long, sucker," said the Wop.

"So long, pal," said Murph.

At the doorway I stopped, then turned around and walked back to the Wop.

"Listen, Wop," I said. "Remember that dark Hungarian kid? The one I said looked like a nun?"

The Wop turned on his barstool.

"Sure," he said. "Gina. What about her?"

"Nothing," I said, "except that I have ten dollars that says I can make her a week after she's sixteen."

The Wop laughed, that mean Italian laugh.

"You're nuts," he said. "She's a good kid. Strictly no dice. Newman Club."

"Put up or shut up, paisan'," I said. "It costs money to talk. Ten bucks."

"Okay," he said. "I'll take the bet."

We shook hands on it.

"Spring for another beer?" asked Murph.

"Sure," I said. I put the money on the bar. When the beer came I lifted my glass and touched it to the Wop's.

"You're going to lose that dixie," I said.

He laughed, showing his white mean teeth.

"Heh-heh-heh. We'll see about that."

I drank the beer and went home. I felt good, confident, as though I could lick anything in the world—partly the beer, partly the fact that being with Gina had worked me up, and partly because I knew that the Wop was a sucker, a sure loser. He never won a bet in his life.

CHAPTER TWO

"You take a little wine?" said old man Tragorna. "She's sweet. Tokay. Hungarian wine."

"Sure," I said. He handed me a glass. The wine tasted like grape juice, sweet as cream soda, with no bite to it, but I drank it and pretended to like it. Gina sat on a straight-backed chair, watching me and her old man, her hands folded on her lap. She was wearing stockings instead of socks, cheap rayon stockings that didn't do anything for her legs. We sat in the front room while the old lady was busy in the kitchen.

The apartment was smaller than ours, but clean. That's one thing I give old lady Tragorna. She was clean. I don't think she had smiled in fifteen years, or laughed ever in all her life, but she was clean. It was a passion with her. They had lace curtains at the windows, cheap stuff made by machine, but the old lady washed them every week and carried them up to the roof to dry in the sun on wooden frames. You would have thought she intended to wear them next to her skin like underwear, the care she took of those curtains.

The rug was worn the way ours was, but swept so clean you hesitated before you dropped your ashes on the floor. The kitchen was clean, too, with copper pots from Central Europe polished and hung in a row over the stove. The floor was scrubbed every day, so the boards were white as the deck of a ship.

One thing that licked her was the roaches. She tried hard, so the kitchen stank from poisons she bought to kill them with, but in those old houses it's no use. You drive them upstairs and the other family puts out stuff and drives them right back down again.

The front room was like ours, small and dark and crowded with stuff, but clean, the way ours never was. There was a picture of Christ in a light blue bathrobe, holding his red heart in his hands, and the heart was outlined with phosphorus paint so that it glowed in the dark. Underneath the picture you read: *Sacred Heart of Jesus*. Across from Christ, in a carved gilt frame, was a picture of Gina's old man in his good clothes, taken a long time ago, with a stiff collar and a heavy gold chain he must have rented from the photographer. On another wall was a picture of Pete, dressed in his greens and wearing a cap that looked stiff enough to bounce a quarter on, the way Marines are supposed to do. It was a retouched picture, one of the specials they sold to servicemen. Tucked into a corner of the frame was a smaller picture, a snapshot, showing Pete in a jungle suit, wearing a helmet and looking rugged, with an M1 slung on his shoulder and the pockets of his suit heavy with grenades. Tucked into other corners of the frame were half a dozen religious cards, printed in Easter-egg colors.

"That was joost before Peter was kill," the old man told me, getting up to point. "One week."

He crossed himself and sat down, then got up again as though he had sat on a pin. He picked up the bottle.

"You need more wine. I fill 'em up."

"Thanks."

He was a small, shy guy, thirty-seven or thirty-eight years old, with a black mustache and small hands, hands that didn't go with his face, which was weathered, or his body, which was small but tough. The big knuckles on both of his hands were broken as though they'd been stepped on. He saw me looking at them and smiled.

"Case," he said. "Packing case. Fall on my hands, boom, like this."

He showed me the way his hands had been broken. He went out of his way to please me and I felt a little uncomfortable with him. Gina just sat with her hands on her lap, looking at me, proud of me.

"Mattie was a soldier, Pop," she said. "Just like Pete."

The old man nodded.

"Pete was a good boy," he said. "A good Marine. Very brave."

"Yeah," I said. "They were a rugged outfit."

Personally, I thought they were jerks, dumb enough to believe their own publicity, but there was no sense in saying so to old man Tragorna.

"Come on, dinner!" the old lady called, and we all got up.

We ate in the kitchen, Gina and I on the sides of the table, the old man and the old lady at either end. The food was good—pot roast made a funny foreign way, heavy gravy, red cabbage cooked with sour apples. The gravy tasted sweet and sour and there was a clove taste underneath.

"You went back to school, Mattie?" the old lady asked.

"That's right," I said. "Finish my education."

"Good," she said. "Peter, he was going to college. Fordham."

"He plays on the football team, Ma," said Gina.

The old lady examined me, looking across the iron pot that held the meat.

"Why?"

"What do you mean, why?"

"Why you play football?"

She had an accent thick enough to mention, but not as awkward as the old man's.

"Aw, Ma—" Gina said.

"Na, na," the old lady said, cutting Gina off. "I ask him. Why you play?"

"Gee, I don't know," I said. "Something to do, I guess."

"For Gina, school is enough to do. I want she should finish the commercial course." She looked around the kitchen. "Not to live like this."

CHARLES GORHAM

"What's the matter?" the old man said. "Is no good?" He had a mouthful of food and after he spoke he wiped his mouth and smiled.

"For you, good enough," said the old lady. "For me, good enough. But for her," nodding at Gina, "not good enough."

Foreigners are all that way, Hunkies and Wops and Polacks and Jews—they sweat and slave and do without, all so the frigging kids can study, get to be doctors and lawyers and dentists. Old lady Tragorna was modest. All she wanted was for Gina to wind up as somebody's secretary, working in an office instead of a kitchen. That was enough of a lift for her; she worked out, a few days a week, for Jews who lived on the West Side.

"Yeah, it's a great thing to have an education," I said. "I met a girl the other day. Secretary. Fifty a week."

"See, you!" the old lady said, jabbing at Gina with her fork. "See, so smart? Fifty a week."

"Yeah, it's a great thing," I said. "My brother Rusty's going to law school. Be a lawyer."

That impressed her.

"So?" she said. "And you....?"

"Gee, I don't know," I said. "I'll see when I finish high school. Maybe law, maybe a doctor. I haven't made up my mind."

We finished dinner with a sweet cake that came from a Bäckerei on Eighty-sixth Street, German stuff, rich with whipped cream and almond paste. Then we moved back to the front room and the old lady gave us coffee, strong and black, in cups with pink roses. The old man produced another bottle and poured three drinks into small glasses.

"Slivovitz," he said, proud of the stuff. "Hungarian brandy."

It was sweet and fiery at the same time, prune juice and neutral spirits, nice with the coffee. When we finished, the old man looked at his wife and nodded; she shook her head. After a while they got up and I heard them through the bedroom door, talking in whispers, thinking they were private.

"*You think it's right?*" the old lady whispered. "*Leave them alone?*"

"*Yeahsure,*" the old man said. "*He's a good boy, friend of Peter. He's gonna be doctor. You heard him.*"

Gina, listening, blushed and looked away. The old man came out of the bedroom, wearing his hat, Hunky style, straight and square on top of his head.

"So," he said, "we go out for a little."

He offered his hand and I shook it, feeling the broken knuckles.

"For an hour," the old lady said. "Hour and a half. We go for a walk."

After they were gone, Gina said, "See, I told you she's strict."

"Forget it," I said.

She stood up.

"Will you help me with the dishes?"

"Sure, why not?"

I had another taste of the old man's brandy, then followed her to the kitchen. She put on a clean flowered apron and poured soap-powder into the dishpan, running water on top of the soap, stirring it up with the dishmop, being very precise and efficient. She was working a gag that all dames use: letting me see how smart she was and useful around the house. I would have made a bet that the next time I came there to dinner she would be in charge of the cooking with the old lady helping but not saying so.

"He's a nice guy, your old man," I said, knowing that she liked the old man best. "What does he do? What's his racket?"

"He works on the docks on the West Side," she said, handing me a dish to dry. "Longshoreman."

"With those hands?"

"He's small but he's very strong," she said. "But lately he's been sicklike, with some trouble in his chest. Last winter he had the pleurisy, and since then he coughs all the time."

"Tough," I said. "He's a nice guy."

We finished the dishes and stacked them away. They were thick ivory-colored plates, with thin, dark veins, and you saw that there had been a gold edge around them. Over the stove on a wooden shelf sat a row of white porcelain jars with foreign lettering on them in blue: *Zucker, Reiz, Feigenkaffe.* There were a coffee-grinding machine that you worked with a long crank, a pepper mill, and a large glass jar of sweet Hungarian paprika. The old lady seemed to stick to a lot of ideas brought with her from Europe, in spite of the fact that she was so eager for Gina to be an American girl who could do shorthand and typing.

There was an old oak upright piano in the living room, with brass candlesticks bolted to the sides. On top of the piano was a china figurine, German looking, broken once and skillfully mended. The piano was closed and looked locked.

"Can you play it?" I asked.

"No," she said. "Not much. She made me take lessons four years, but I gave it up."

"Can't you play anything?"

"Not much."

"Go on, try it," I said.

She got the key and opened the piano. The keys were yellow as old teeth, but washed clean. She found some music and played from the notes, sitting up straight like a kid in school, arching her wrists and trying hard. It sounded as though someone stood behind her, holding a whip to make her play.

"Let it go," I said. "Let it go."

"Yeah, she made me take up piano," Gina said. "I hate it, honest."

"The piano's all right," I said. "If you can play it."

"I guess so."

I sat down and boogied a tune: "You Got to Accenshuate the Pos-itive," banging the bass like Pete Johnson.

"Gee, Mattie!" she said. "I didn't know you could play the piano."

I finished the piece and closed the piano.

"I can't," I said. "Just a little by ear."

"Where did you learn that?" she said.

"In the Army," I said. "A fellow taught me."

I got up from the piano stool and sat in an armchair. It was dark outside, and you heard the noise of the street coming up the airshaft: the sound of a heavy bus taking the hill in first gear, the engine noise rising, rising, until you thought it would explode; the sound of some impatient bastard leaning on his horn behind the bus; the sound of a radio, low but strong, coming from one of the other apartments; the sound of somebody's old lady, calling from a window down to the street: "*Fran*—SISS-S-S! ! ! ! ! *Fran*—SISS-S-S! ! ! ! !" and a little later the voice of the kid: "AW—*right*. AW—*rightinaminute*."

In the dark, with just a couple of lamps, the Tragorna front room didn't look so bad. Gina, across from me, looked pretty and younger than usual.

"What do you do with yourself, kid? Now that you quit trying to play the piano."

"Gee, Mattie, I go to school. You know that."

"I mean for fun. For recreation."

"Oh," she said.

She sat, thinking for a minute. It occurred to me, watching her, that she was a year behind in school.

"Gee, I keep a scrapbook," she said.

"Let me see it."

"Aw, gee, Mattie, you wouldn't be interested."

"Let me see it," I said.

"Okay, Mattie," she said.

She got the book, a big cheap scrapbook with a white, embossed imitation leather cover, padded with felt like an old-fashioned Bible, labeled in gilt: *Snaps and Scraps*. The pages were covered with photographs: a few originals of movie actors, press-agent shots with faked-in autographs. Most of the pictures had been clipped from the movie magazines. There were dozens of Sinatra in the middle of the book, and an old ribbon badge that said FRANKIE.

"I don't like him no more," she said.

"No?"

"No, I like a fella to be manly."

Toward the back of the book, on white pages, she had a collection of newspaper clippings from the *Jayhawker*, our school paper. I leafed through them, then noticed that there were football stories from Forty-one and Forty-two. Where my name was listed, with the substitutes, she had underlined it in red. There were group pictures of the squad, and my head and shoulders had circles around them. I looked young; a punk kid, thirty pounds lighter. At the end of the book there were new clippings, from the last few weeks; one, from the school edition of the *Journal* showed me in football clothes, a big, three-column picture.

"What's all this?" I asked. "All this old stuff from before?"

"Aw, Mattie!" She took the book and closed it. "It's nothing, only a book I keep."

"How come all that old stuff about me, from before the war when you didn't even know me?"

"I just kept it," she said.

"Yeah. But why?"

"I always used to go for you. When I watched the practice, when Peter was on the team."

"What the hell," I said. "You were twelve—thirteen."

"I used to wait for Peter," she said.

"Yeah," I said. "Poor old Pete."

I got up and looked at the picture of Pete, then touched one of the candy-colored cards.

"What are these?" I asked.

"Prayers," she said. "Perpetual prayers for Peter."

"You go for that crap?"

"Mattie!" she said. "Don't talk like that."

"Listen, kid. When you're dead, you're dead."

I sat down on the couch where she sat and put my arm around her, then took her chin in my other hand and turned up her mouth and kissed her. She kissed back for a second, then pulled away.

"Don't, Mattie. Please."

"Okay," I said. "Have it your way."

I leaned back on the couch, looking at the ceiling. She bent over and kissed me on the forehead, then smoothed back my hair.

"You're sweet," she said.

"Yeah," I said. "Sweet like sugar."

"What are you going to be?" she asked. "When you get out of school next year?"

I sat up.

"Next year, I don't know. But the year after that I'm going to open a saloon."

"Honest?"

"Sure," I said. "It's the best business."

I got up and crossed the room, poured myself a drink of Hungarian brandy. It didn't make me drunk, on top of the food, but it made me feel warm and good and it gave me a lot of confidence. I sat on a straight-backed chair, reversed, with my arms folded across the back and my chin resting on my arms.

"Sure," I explained. "With a good saloon you can't lose. It works on percentage. P.C.T. I'll hire a pair of bartenders who understand the racket. They can steal from the public all they want to. But not from me."

"Mattie!" she said, pretending to be shocked but really impressed by what I was saying.

"It works by the bottle," I said. "The house wants a set percentage and it doesn't care how the man behind the wood makes it. Just so he makes it. There are lots of ways to work it. For instance: a couple comes in and orders Tom Collinses. The bartender mixes the first one strong, plenty of gin. After that he tapers off. By the third or fourth drink the customers are drinking lemonade, but they don't know the difference....

"Or with Manhattan cocktails. Unless he watches you make it, the average guy can't tell if a Manhattan's made with whiskey or rum. On account of the sweet vermouth. So, when they're going to a table, you make the Manhattans with rum. It's all percentage. P.C.T."

She was sitting up straight, looking at me, trying to decide whether I meant all this or was just giving her a rib. I was talking partly to hear myself talk, and partly to get a rise out of her.

"Take politics," I told her. "Where do the voters of the neighborhood hang out? In saloons. So who has political influence? Guys who own saloons. Look at Old Lady Condron. Look at Daly. Look at Moriarty, over on Third. Look at Jimmy Kelly, down in the Village. All saloonkeepers." I grinned at her. "Stick with me, kid. Someday I'll be district leader, running all of East Yorkville."

"Aw, Mattie," she said. "You're crazy."

"Oh, no," I said. "My old man is crazy. Yes. My brother Rusty is crazy, trying to be a shyster when what you want to be is the guy that hires the shyster. My old lady is crazy, the dumb lush. But not me. Not Mattie."

"Aren't you going to get a job or anything when you quit school?"

"Jobs are for suckers," I explained. "Who ever got anywhere working at a job? Your old man?" I looked around the apartment; I could see that I had hurt her feelings. "My old man?"

"Aw, Mattie ...."

"Suckers," I said. "Sure losers."

I got up and looked at my watch. It was nearly eleven and I wanted to miss the old man and old lady.

"You got to go?" she said.

"Yeah," I said. "Your folks'll be back."

Standing in the doorway, I kissed her good night and let my hand fall to her breast, holding it there for a second, feeling her body tighten up in my arms.

"Good night, kid," I said.

"Good night, Mattie."

At the foot of the stairs I waited in the quiet until I heard the door close slowly, as if she hated to see me go.

CHAPTER THREE

Cohen turned away from the blackboard, chalk all over the tail of his coat, holding a rubber-tipped pointer in his hand. He was a small man with gold-framed glasses and hair that shed dandruff. He wore a key on his watch chain and always had chalk in his fingernails.

"We study it, Dolan," he said, "because it happens to be in the syllabus."

"So why not change the syllabus?" I asked.

Cohen shrugged his shoulders.

"I only work here," he said. "Take it up with your state senator."

Then the bell rang and I picked up my books, moving through the crowd in the hall on my way to the next class. Everything was done by the bell, the way it is in a prison. Fifty-five minutes of listening to one of the jerks sound off: BELL; five minutes to move along: BELL; fifty-five minutes of another one spouting about another subject in the same tone of voice, then: BELL. Nine until three: BELL, BELL, BELL, and eat in the lunchroom upstairs with a chowline longer and tougher and meaner than any of those at Fort Benning, Georgia.

The teachers were jerks, working for fifty dollars a week and a pension, smelling of chalk and bad breath, dead, dead as my old man. And the subjects were deader than the people who taught them, even the subjects that should have been good.

For instance, History.

We spent a week on Metternich, and in spite of Cohen I got a good idea of what went on at the Congress of Vienna. It was just the way Shultz, say, organized the Bronx and the West Side. There were two or three hundred petty crooks and beer peddlers working on the Heights and up in the Bronx. Shultz moved in with an organization and explained the whole situation before his boys cracked a skull.

"You go partners with me," he said, "and give me half of what you take. I'll guarantee to triple your business inside of a month." Smart people went partners with Shultz, and he did triple their business. Other people retired from business, for good. The idea was that the organization, with a smart operator heading it up, was stronger than a lot of little guys, led by third-rate punks.

That's what Metternich had in mind.

I asked Cohen why we bothered with Metternich, who operated so long ago, and he argued that the reason for studying history was that you understood what is going on now better if you knew what had happened before.

"So why not study Shultz?" I asked him. "He happened before. And it's more to the point. The kids will understand it better. At least they heard of the Bronx."

"Shultz was a gangster," Cohen said.

"So what was Metternich?" I asked. "Shultz was a public benefactor."

"Oh, Dolan, go away—"

I think I could have convinced Cohen, but just then the bell rang.

Take Mathematics.

Algebra is easy and pretty good fun, but why study it when, in business, you will have a cash register and a bookkeeper who comes in once a week to do your books and help you beat the income tax?

Take Chemistry.

What is the sense of wasting your time making up bad smells in a laboratory when, if you want something in that line, you can go to the drugstore on the corner? My uncle Fred never took chemistry but he told me that during prohibition he used to make gin, whiskey and rum, so that the customers liked it well enough to pay ten dollars a bottle for it. I'll bet that none of the jerks in the John Jay Chemistry Department could make anything you'd pay two cents a gallon for.

Take English.

Half the kids in John Jay have trouble getting through Little Abner. In fact, a lot of them ask other kids to help them, and half of it is pictures. So what is the sense in giving them something called *Idylls of the King,* and something called *The Daily Theme Eye,* when they can't even read the *Daily News?* Why not teach them to read the *Daily News?*

"Why do we study this useless stuff?" I once asked Cohen after class.

"It's part of your education, Dolan," he said. "Just all part of your education."

"What's an education for?" I asked him. "To help you get ahead, right?"

"In a way," he said.

"So how is this helping anybody? All it does is give jobs to chumps willing to work for fifty a week because they get two months' vacation. And it gives the kids something to do, keeps them off the streets."

"Maybe that's a good thing, too," said Cohen.

"Listen, Cohen," I told him, "school is all right if you're going into some racket where the law requires it—law, maybe, or medicine. If you're going into business it's a waste of time. I learned more on the streets than I'll ever learn in this place. A whole lot more."

I picked up the black-bound book that rested on Cohen's desk; it wasn't a high school text, it was something he was reading on his own. The title was stamped on the black with gilt: *Urban Economic Problems.* There were three authors. I leafed through the book, with its tables and charts, then dropped it to the desk with a bump that made Cohen start.

"I'll bet I know more about the urban economic system than all three of the guys who took ten years to write this book. There's only one thing to know about the urban economic system: *don't be a sucker.* That's all there is to it, and you can learn it on the streets, faster and better than from this book. And you will remember it longer."

"I don't doubt it," he said, brushing chalk dust from his coat. "I don't doubt it at all, Dolan."

He stood up and I brushed his back.

"It's all over you," I told him. "You look as though you'd taken a bath in chalk."

"Thank you, Dolan."

He hiked his coat up over his collar and straightened the glasses on his nose.

"Thank you."

"Save it," I told him. "You're welcome."

Then the bell rang.

CHAPTER FOUR

O ne night I came home late, at four o'clock in the morning, three beers inside of me making me feel confident. Rusty was reading in the front room, wearing a pair of horn-rimmed glasses that I hadn't seen before. He took off the glasses and said: *"Hello,"* then rubbed his eyes as if they burned. He was tired. His tie was pulled down and his collar was opened. He looked more like a freight-yard clerk working overtime than an ex-lieutenant who meant to be a lawyer.

"Why the cheaters, Rusty? Are you going blind?"

"Just strain," he said. "I ruined my eyes on the Gee-box, during the war."

"What's the Gee-box?"

"Radar scope," he said. "It's a navigation thing."

"Yeah? If it's service connected, you can get a pension. Vince Rhattigen, the Legion commander, explained all that to us. It's easy."

"I'm not looking for anything from the Legion."

"Don't be a chump. It's money, isn't it?"

I sat down; under the hard top light you saw the lines in Rusty's face, some from the war and some from books like the one opened in front of him.

"What are you looking for?" I asked.

He pushed the book away from him and put his glasses on top of it. Looking at him, under the light, you never would have guessed he was my brother. Not because I'm dark and he is red-haired. There was a total difference between us, as if we came not only from different parents, but from different cities, different countries, different worlds. Yet he and I had slept together, eaten together, cruised the Yorkville streets together, all our lives, since we were born, up until the day he went into the Army.

We sat on opposite sides of the round oak table, looking across it at one another. It was cold outride and the windows were fogged. From the bedroom came the rhythm of the old man and the old lady, breathing together peacefully in sleep. The fact that it was early morning and entirely still in the house seemed to give importance to the conversation.

"I don't know," said Rusty. "I'm reading these books to find out. Not what they have," he said, indicating the bedroom door and the heavy steady breathing. "And not what people like Fred have either."

"What then?" I said. "You don't want to be poor, you don't want to be rich. What do you want?"

"For one thing, I want to be a lawyer. It's something. It's status. Then, someday, I'm going into politics."

"On what, Rusty?" I asked. "I know something about politics. You don't get elected on your good intentions. You get elected by working with the boys. The organization."

"There are other ways."

"How?"

"Having a program that means something. Being honest. Being—oh, hell! Mattie, let's drop it. Let it go, let's not argue."

"Rusty, you're wasting your time. Let me tell you a few facts."

He picked up his glasses; we hadn't moved from the table, but I had the sensation of having Rusty pushed into a corner. He felt it too.

"Go ahead," he said.

"Look at the Jewboy on Second Avenue who went to law school. St. John's. He went and he graduated. He passed the Bar. If he goes into court the judge calls him counselor. On paper, he's a lawyer."

"So?"

"So does he have an office? Does he make a dime? Like hell! His old man has a butcher shop with a sign on the window: SAUL *WINOGRADSKY—Kosher Butcher.* Down in a corner of the window, small, in new gold leaf, you can read: MILTON WINOGRADSKY—*Attorney-at-Law—Notary Public,* with a little red seal in the middle, like the seal Miltie will stick on a piece of paper for you, if you give him a quarter."

Rusty folded his glasses with a click.

"What's that got to do with me?"

"Everything," I said. "If Miltie, who is probably smarter than you are, being a Jew, went to school for seven years to learn how to stick a red seal on a tax form, where do you come in?"

"Oh, Mattie, for God's sake! Stop acting as if you knew it all."

"I know it all," I said.

I walked to the window and pulled back the curtain. It was dead quiet outside, as if the new cold brought the quiet with it. Then, far away, we heard a horse clopping on the roadway, the sound of his hooves metallic and sharp, getting closer, each sound clear, then dying away again. I let the curtain drop back into place.

"What are you going to do, Rusty?" I asked. "Hang out your shingle on the back of the old man's cab?"

Rusty sat with his feet on the table, one hand shielding his eyes, talking without looking at me, his voice a monotone, as if he repeated something he'd memorized.

"Look, Mattie, I'm a different guy now," he said. "When I went into the service I was a jerk, a punk kid, good enough to be a shipping clerk or to work on a truck or maybe, with luck, to get on the cops or in the fire department. I was nothing, just a lump."

"Why are you different?" I asked. "Because you read a book?"

He shook his head.

"No, Mattie. I read the book because I'm different. I'm a man now, not a god-damned animal."

I laughed.

"So the Army made a man of you! That's a good one."

"No, but getting out of the neighborhood did," he said. "Being treated like a human being did." He took his hand away from his eyes and looked at me. He wasn't in the corner any more. "But you're too damned smart to understand me. You don't believe in working for anything."

I picked up his book, riffled the pages and put it down.

"The things you work for, you don't get," I said. "You're too busy working for them. The way to get the things you want is to take them."

"The way Fred does, I suppose."

"Not exactly. But that's the idea."

"Fred is going to wind up dead."

"So are you. So am I. What of it? Fred has a good time. He enjoys life."

Rusty stood up, rubbing his eyes.

"To hell with Fred. I'm going to sleep."

We stood in the quiet room for a minute without saying anything. I don't know what Rusty, standing there, thought of me. I thought that he was a fool because he imagined that going to college would make him one of the people on top, when all the difference it would really make would be that he'd say *"yes, sir,"* and *"no, sir,"* to a big-boss lawyer, instead of to a fare getting into his cab, or to the boss on the loading platform if he drove the truck he had talked about. There was nothing, really, for us to discuss, because we couldn't find any point of agreement with which to begin the conversation. School, for me, was a way to kill time that the government was willing to pay you for killing. School for Rusty, Columbia College, was becoming a religion. He seemed to believe that somewhere, in those thick books he read all night, he was going to find an angle, a password that would turn him from a nobody into a somebody. But Rusty, I knew, was one of the people you take things from. He never would learn, from a million books, how to be the one who did the taking.

"Good night," he said.

"Good night, Rusty."

"Aren't you coming?"

"Later."

When he was gone I went back to the window and leaned against the frame. Watching the darkness and the yellow light that came up the courtyard with difficulty, made me feel totally alone and it occurred to me, staring into the darkness, that in all the world, among billions of people, radiating over the earth's surface from that point of light at the foot of the court-yard, there wasn't a person who cared whether or not I lived or died, except Gina, a simple-minded child, and, maybe, the old lady, sometimes when she was drunk or sentimental. Why should I care about them, all those billions of bastards out there in the dark, when not one of them really cared a good goddamn for me?

I walked back to the front room table, picking up Rusty's book: *The Rise of American Civilization.* I looked at the dense fine-type pages and wondered whether, in that book, there was any mention of a slob like Murph, any mention of a guy like me, and I wondered whether Greene's bar, and the colored houses near the camps down South, and the wild crazy wartime bars we used when we worked making planes at Langley were part of American Civilization, according to this book of Rusty's, writ-ten by someone named Charles Austin Beard. I closed the book and dropped it with a thud. Then I picked up Rusty's glasses and tried them on. For a moment, after I took them off, I was blind and dizzy as though I'd bumped my head. If Rusty needed those, I thought, his eyes must be really bad, bad enough to get him a thirty per cent disability pension—forty dollars and fifty cents every month for the rest of his life. And the damned fool didn't want it.

In the bedroom, he was asleep, crossways on the bed with one shoe on. I unlaced the shoe that was on and worked it off his foot. Then I swung him around on the bed and pulled the quilt over his shoulders. He was dead to the world.

I got into bed beside Rusty and lay there in the black room, thinking, thinking about myself, until the black turned to grey outside and the clanging, early morning noises came up the courtyard from the street. I got out of bed, not having slept, and went into the kitchen to make some coffee. The old lady, wearing a wrapper, sat in her place at the kitchen table. There was a bruise on the side of her face where I guessed the old man had hit her. The yellow light caught the side of her face. You saw that the flesh was puffy beneath the unhealthy calsomined skin, and the skin was rough on her cheeks, under yesterday's faded rouge. You saw that her hair near the roots was dark, giving away the brass-blonde treatment bought at the German beauty parlor. From a distance, when her blood was quickened by whiskey, she still looked like a woman. In the vicious light of the sun that morning she looked washed up and wrung out, something you would look at and throw away.

"What's the matter, Ma? Couldn't sleep?"

"No, Mattie. Couldn't you?"

"No."

I went into the bedroom and found my wallet; there was a hundred-dollar bill in it that Fred had given me. I went back to the kitchen and dropped it on the table.

"Here, Ma. Buy yourself a railroad."

Folded, she thought it was ten dollars.

"Thanks, Mattie."

Then she picked it up and her breath caught.

"*Praise-be-to-Christ-who-died-for-us-all!* Mattie, did you steal it?"

"It's clean, Ma. Clean as a pistol."

"D'ja get it from Fred?"

"Maybe."

"You're a good boy, Mattie. A good boy."

"Sure, Ma," I said. "I'm a good boy. I'm a winner."

A few nights later, bored with the neighborhood, I went to see Fred. I sat in his comfortable living room and watched him take a good cigar out of its sealed glass tube. He threw the tube in the wastebasket. It looked too valuable to throw away.

"If you need a dollar," he was saying, "don't forget to ask for it. I'm no mind reader. The only way I know you're broke is if you tell me."

"Okay."

"You're doing all right," he said, squinting at me through the blue expensive smoke. "I saw you last week against Evander, when you scored three times. You're doing all right."

I nodded.

"I'm sure of making all-city half, I guess," I said.

"That's the stuff."

"But the kids are beginning to lay for me. Kids on the other teams. They forget the game and go after me. Every game, I'm marked."

"Are you worried?"

"No, I'm not worried. I can take care of myself. But I don't like it."

He laughed.

"Since when are you supposed to like to play football? It's not a game, it's a business."

We talked football. It was eight o'clock and I was hungry. After a while Fred said, "Come on, kid, let's go and eat."

He called the garage and we went downstairs, standing under the canvas canopy, waiting for the Cadillac. That year no one could get a car. Even the cops were driving old jalopies. Fred had a Forty-two Cadillac with less than five thousand miles on the clock: a block-long, cream-colored car, custom built, with a lot of brightwork, the kind that makes doormen snap to attention. Fred gave the colored boy a dollar and we got into the car. It smelled of new leather and of strong perfume, from some woman Fred had taken out.

We drove downtown to one of those streets with funny names, south of Washington Square, and stopped at a place that looked like a dump from the street. Inside it was a movie set—plaster and gold and wine-colored velvet, with a velvet rope on a brass hook to keep the people in line from crowding. A dozen people waited for tables, impatient behind the velvet rope, stretching their necks to curse at customers who were taking too long over coffee. The Greek headwaiter recognized Fred and trotted up, holding half a dozen menus that were as large as the *Daily News.*

"Mr. Fred!"

"Hello, George."—with a big grin, holding the money under his hand.

"I have your table."

"Aw, now look," said one of the men standing in line behind the rope, "we've been—"

But the Greek cut him off, wagging a finger.

"Sorry, sir," with a flash of teeth, "Mr. Fred reserved this table. Two days."

We sat down and waited for the steak. It was three inches thick, broiled over charcoal, spurting rich red juice when you cut it. The steak, for two, must have weighed four pounds. And that fall the butcher shops had cardboard hams on the hooks in the windows; if the butcher gave a woman a thin lamb chop he wanted to get stayed with for doing her a favor. But in this place there was all the meat you could eat, porterhouse steak flown East from Kansas City, not meant for the neighborhood markets. All you needed was the price. The bill was fifteen dollars.

"Did you really reserve this table?" I asked.

Fred shook his head, then swallowed a mouthful of steak. He smiled.

"I'm just known here, that's all. I did business with them during the war."

I don't think Fred ever had to reserve a table or a woman or a seat at the fights. He just got what he wanted, wherever it happened to be, and why should he have bothered to call up, when, most of the places he went, he was known?

He drove me home in the Cadillac and gave me some money when he said good night.

"Don't let the peasants get you down," he said. "Just keep hitting them hard enough to hurt."

"Okay, Fred," I said.

I climbed the smelly stairs and went into the dark, smelly apartment. What was left of dinner was on the table: potato salad and fried bologna. It looked like one of the meals Rusty fixed for the old man, after they'd waited for the old lady and decided to give her up.

CHAPTER FIVE

We played Clinton on our field, a big game on a nice day, with all the seats in the stadium filled. The Clinton coach, in the locker room, must have told his team before they came out: "Watch that Dolan, that big fellow. Don't give him a chance to get started. Ride him, rattle him, try to get his goat."

They did their best, but I scored twice. All through the first half a sixteen-year-old kid named Liggon, one of their backs, tried to get me mad enough to hit him, so that I'd be put out of the game. After each play he would say: *"Hello, Pop. Geting tired?"* or *"Hello, ringer!"* or: *"How much do they pay you, Dolan?"* or: *"Do you have to go to class, too?"* After one play he sat on the grass, looked at me and smiled. *"Dolan,"* he said, *"tell me frankly, can you read?"*

He looked like the kind of kid who wore glasses; he weighed about a hundred and thirty pounds and played ball entirely on his nerve. He was a fresh, nervy kid.

Halfway through the third period we led Clinton by three touchdowns. We kicked off to them and Liggon took the ball, cutting toward the sidelines, and I crossed after him, fast. I hit him off balance, just after he stepped outside, and the impact carried him into the concrete wall at the foot of the stadium. The whistle blew and I got up. Liggon was still, on the ground, with a dozen people around him. His face was as white as paper. I started to walk toward him.

"Mattie!"

It was Garry, our coach.

"You'd better go to the showers, Mattie."

"How come?"

"You'd just better, that's all."

I had a shower, then dressed, and sat on a bench in the locker room, smoking cigarettes. The crowd in the stands had been lively before, talking it up, cheering and singing, but I didn't hear them now. After a while, in maybe half an hour, the team came in and started to undress. No one spoke to me.

"What was the final score?" I asked one of the kids who was taking off his pads. He looked at me and turned away.

"Okay, punks," I said.

I stood up and dropped my cigarette to the concrete floor, stepped on it and squashed it with my heel until the tobacco came out of the paper. I walked out of the locker room. I met Garry, coming down the ramp, carrying half a dozen helmets.

"Who won?" I said.

"What?"

"Who won the game? What was the score?"

He shifted the helmets to the other hand.

"Why did you hit him so hard, Mattie?"

"Isn't that the idea?" I said.

"His back is broken," Garry said.

I stood on the hard concrete slab, looking at Garry, understanding the fact that Garry was frightened, really scared, and scared of me.

"Where did they take him?" I asked.

"Bellevue," said Garry.

"Jesus," I said. "I'm sorry, Buck, no kidding."

Garry nodded.

"Is he going to die?" I said.

"I don't know," Garry said. "I guess so."

"Jesus, Buck," I said. "I'm sorry. No kidding."

He touched my arm.

"Sure, Mattie. Sure you are. I know that," he said.

I nodded toward the locker room.

"I guess they're pretty sore at me? The other fellows on the team?"

He looked at the closed locker-room door.

"Yes, Mattie. I guess so. I guess they are."

He walked down the ramp, toward the door, swinging the varnished helmets.

"Buck!" I called.

He turned around.

"Who won?"

"We won," he said. "Twenty-one nothing."

"That was the score when I left the game."

"Yes," he said. "That's right, it was."

He went into the locker room. I walked across the empty field, kicking the divots gouged up by the cleats, watching the toe of my right shoe as I kicked the clods away from me. Gina was waiting at the main gate. She wore a blue and orange badge: JOHN JAY. I unpinned it and threw it away.

"I'm sorry, Mattie," she said.

"What?"

"I'm sorry about that fellow, Mattie. For what happened."

I turned, facing her.

"BE SORRY FOR SOMEBODY ELSE! Yourself, maybe."

She stepped back, afraid of my temper.

"Go on, Gina," I said. "Go home, I want to be by myself, that's all."

"Okay, Mattie," she said.

I kissed her.

"Don't be mad at me, kid. Don't be sore, huh?"

"Gee, no, Mattie, honest."

She walked away, by herself. I stood on the corner, near the stadium, in the shadow of the concrete wall. Then I started to walk west, away from the school. A crosstown bus was loading at the curb, so I got in and rode through the Park. On the West

Side I got out and walked downhill to the River. I sat on a bench in Riverside Park and watched the sun go down. It took a long time to get dark.

Across the River, on the Jersey side, I saw the bright lights of an amusement park, with the ferris wheel going *under*andover, *under*andover, like the slow flywheel of a powerful engine. On the West Side Highway, near the River bank, a million cars moved north and south, with their low lights on, and you heard them purr like a million cats. Once in a while a wise joker cut out of line with a blast of his horn and you saw him weave through the other cars like a smart back on a broken field.

Behind me it was dark in the trees, but behind the dark was the whole City, changing over from day to night. You could feel the City more than you could hear it, and it made you feel comfortable and somehow safe, just knowing it was there: seven million people, eating and drinking and sleeping and dying, getting laid and getting their lumps. Somewhere, right at this minute, in Bellevue or the Medical Center, St. Vincent's or Doctors' Hospital, somebody's baby was getting born. I tapped the wood of the bench with my finger and thought: just when I tapped that bench, I'll bet, a kid was coming out of his mother, and I thought to myself, looking at the river: *I'll that kid is a sure loser*—the one I tapped out on the bench. A loser like Liggon, the poor bastard, down there in Bellevue with a broken back, or a loser like Garry, who would be in trouble if Liggon didn't get over it.

I was restless, eager to be moving, tense and expectant, with nowhere to go, the way we felt often on summer nights in the South, at Fort Benning, when we'd get dressed in clean suntans, shave and slick up and go into town even when we didn't have any money, just to walk, walking nowhere, just looking, looking around for something to do.

I got up and climbed the hill, through the dark of the trees, walking fast to get out of the Park, away from the quiet and the lonely feeling. I walked back to Columbus Circle and stood on the curbstone. The lights on the Circle were red and green, like a honky-tonk in a tank town. Barkers and pitchmen worked the curb and in the mean little shops around the Circle they were selling statues of the Statue of Liberty, kewpie dolls with big pink bows, souvenirs and postcards, or: *Your Photo While U Wait—5 Min.*

Across the Circle, in the safety zone, nuts were setting up flags and boxes, nuts and communists getting ready to do their spiel and take up their collections. A tall, thin man in under-taker's clothes climbed to his platform and took out his watch. He put the watch on the railing of his stand, and remarked in a voice they must have heard in Brooklyn: *"If there is a God I give him sixty seconds in which to strike me dead."*

The crowd stood with its mouth open, waiting for the under-taker to drop dead, ticking off the seconds he stood there, watch-ing the sky with his hands on his hips. When the minute was up he put his watch away and said: *"That disposes of God Almighty!"*

"Ah-h-h, you stupid muzzler!" I yelled.

I turned down Broadway and walked deliberately into the bright lights of the Square, just one of a million people, bumping shoulders and saying: *"Excuse me!"* seeing each of the million faces colored by the lights of the big marquees, people going and coming from movies, touts in cheap, brand-new clothes, swing-ing watch chains in front of drugstores, suckers themselves, on the prowl for suckers, sure losers, and cannibals, eager to eat one another, ready, maybe, to eat themselves. At Times Square I turned into a United Cigar Store on a corner and used the worn-out phone book.

New York, City of
Dep't. of Hosp.
"Bellevue *Hos*pital!"

"I want to find out about a boy named Liggon. He came in this afternoon."

"A patient?"

"Yeah, sure. A patient."

"Are you a relative, sir?"

"Sure, sure I am. I'm his brother."

"One moment, please."

I waited, tapping on the glass panel of the door. After a while a man's voice told me that Liggon was still unconscious, that the case was marked critical.

"What are his chances of pulling through?"

"About fifty-fifty, I guess. Just about that—fifty-fifty."

I hung up and walked out into Forty-second Street. There was a sickening smell of syrup coming from an openfront popcorn place, and the street was filled with slab-faced people, furtive people, coming and going, women gashed with lipstick mouths, men wearing cheap, turn-down hats not meant to stand the rain. I stood, leaning against the building, wondering whether I looked like the rest of the people crowded into the block. After a while I bought a paper. There was nothing in it about Liggon. I got into a taxi and rode uptown and went into Greene's instead of going home.

"There he is," said Murph. "There's Mattie, the murderer."

"What do you mean, you bum?" I asked.

"Heh-heh-heh!" laughed the Wop. "We heard about it, all right."

"Yeah," said Murph. "Your girl friend, little Tragorna, was telling the kids all about it. How you broke the guy's back."

"What does she know?" I said. "The guy's got a fifty-fifty chance, they said."

"Jesus," said Murph, turning around, resting his elbows on the bar, "nobody has a better chance than that."

"Heh-heh-heh!" laughed the Wop.

I bought them beer, for something to do. At midnight I walked to the newsstand on the corner of Eighty-sixth and First, looked at the stack of mint-fresh copies of the *Daily News*, then decided not to buy a paper.

CHAPTER SIX

read the marked story in the *Times,* read it again, then handed the paper back to Kieran. It was Monday morning.

"Honest, Mr. Kieran," I said, "I just tackled the guy. I didn't mean to hurt him."

Kieran sat in his swivel chair; what you noticed was the starched white collar resting against his rough red neck. He looked like a tough police magistrate.

"I don't think you meant to kill him, Dolan. But I wouldn't want to bet on the fact that you didn't mean to hurt him. I've talked to other boys from the team; they say you're what they call a mean player. Not dirty, but mean."

"I play according to the rules," I said. "Is it my fault that I'm better than they are?"

"That's what they say, Dolan. You don't break the rules more than anyone else. You're just mean."

"I just tackled him," I said.

He nodded and sat for a moment, tapping his desk with an automatic pencil, watching the lead make marks on the blotter. Then he picked up the morning paper, opened to the sports page. There was a picture of Liggon and one of me, and a column-long story, most of which was a quote from the De Witt Clinton coach. Reading the story you might have thought I had played on a penitentiary team, instead of at Benning for the U.S. Army. The coach called me a ringer and over age, a professional and a street-bred hoodlum. He said the Army had made me a killer, and that combat had made me ruthless. He said that the fellows on my own team hated my guts and had told him that I went around saying "Kill or be killed."

"That's just a joke," I said to Kieran, putting the paper on his desk. "Kill or be killed. It's just a gag. Something we used to say in the Army."

"Maybe," said Kieran. "In any case, I want you to turn in your football suit before you go back to your classes."

"You mean I'm kicked off the team?"

"Not kicked off," he said. "You just can't play any more, that's all."

"Why not?"

"Because you don't belong here, Dolan," he said. "You don't belong in this school. This is a public school, for children. You're not a child any more."

"Where do you think I belong then?" I asked him. "I'm entitled to an education, just as much as anyone else."

He stood up.

"I don't know where you belong, Dolan. But it isn't here, in this school. Turn in your uniform before you go back to your classes."

I looked at him, standing there in his good blue suit: cop, judge, jury and jailer.

"You ask Garry about it," I said. "All I did was what he told me to do."

"Mr. Garry is up on charges, Dolan. He won't be coaching here any more."

I stood, holding my books by their strap, trying to think of something to say.

"That's all, Dolan," he said. "You're excused."

I stood in the corridor, outside the office, holding my strapped books in my hand. The bell had rung for the period change and five thousand kids were trooping through the halls. Groups of them glanced at me and whispered; everyone was talking about it. After a while I saw Gina, with four girls from the Newman Club. I walked over and took her arm, drawing her away from the others.

"Come on, kid. Let's sneak out."

"Gee, Mattie, I can't, honest. I got a class. Book-keeping."

"You'll never miss that," I said. "Come on."

We went out the back way, avoiding the kids from the traffic squad who were supposed to guard the doors.

"Let's go to the Park," I said.

"Okay."

We sat on a bench on the Promenade, high above the East River, looking across at Queens and the Island, watching the boats go upstream and down, tugs pulling barges loaded with brick, Department of Sanitation scows carrying garbage out to sea, gulls busy around them, making a frantic, mewing noise. An excursion boat built fat like a pigeon was going out, loaded with people, a hundred flags flying from the halyards, the three-piece band on the fore-deck playing a lively Polish tune. Some kind of political outing. Behind the boat, riding out of the water, was a Police Department launch, with a green flag stiff as a board in the slipstream: PDNY and a fat cop sitting in the cockpit, steering the boat and running it fast, as if he owned the River and the City and the whole damned world. It was a warm fall day, pleasant as summer in the sun. I sat back on the wooden bench, staring at the river, ignoring Gina.

"What's the matter, Mattie?" she said.

"I'm going to quit," I said.

"What do you mean?"

"I'm going to quit. Take a powder. Blow. Vanish. Resign. Desert. Whatever you want to call it. I'm going to quit, that's all."

"You mean school?"

"I don't mean I'm going to quit living."

She sat, looking at the docks on the other side of the river.

"On account of that fella that died?"

"No," I said. "Not on account of him. On account of me. I'm fed up with it. Sick of it. It was a mistake in the first place, going to school."

"What are you going to do, Mattie?"

"Nothing."

"Nothing?"

"That's right. Just nothing. I'm going to get on the Fifty-two Twenty Club, and just look around. I'll get my own education, just looking around."

"I guess I won't see you any more," she said.

"Why not? I live right around the block. I'll see you more. More than ever."

"Honest?"

"Sure."

I put my arm around her, then kissed her, harder than I had before, kissing her so that she understood what I meant. She pulled away, blushing, and her breath caught in her throat.

"Don't, Mattie."

"What are you saving it for?" I said. "The Junior Prom? You can't get anything for it in pawn."

She avoided looking at me, and stared at a coal-chute across the river.

"I told you I didn't do that," she said. "I don't mind if you kiss me, but not like that."

"Why?"

"They say a fellow loses his respect."

I laughed.

"Where did you hear that?"

"In the Newman Club."

"Is that what you talk about? Things like that? When you're supposed to be talking religion?"

"No. Only sometimes, you know, we talk about things."

I gave her a cigarette and lit it, then lit one for myself. She took short little amateur puffs, blowing the smoke away.

"I suppose you went out with lots of girls in the Army, huh, Mattie?"

"Sure. Millions. Live ones, too."

"Do you love me, Mattie?"

"Sure," I said. "Sure I do."

"I love you too," she said.

"I'm sorry, Gina," I said. "I didn't mean to be rough with you."

"That's all right, Mattie," she said.

I kissed her, just on the lips.

"I got to go," she said. "I don't want to miss two periods."

We stood up.

"Aw, Mattie!" she said. "You tore my dress!"

There was a little rip in the V of her dress.

"Forget it," I said. "I'll buy you a new one."

She stood, tucking in her chin, inspecting the torn seam.

'If my mom sees that, she'll sock me."

"You mean she *hits* you?"

"Sure," said Gina. "I told you she was strict."

"I'd like to see my old lady clout me," I said. "Or my old man. Now or anytime."

I took her back to the school and forced one of the doors that led into the building from the delivery court. A traffic squad picket wearing a blue and orange armband ran up with his notebook in his hand. I caught the lapels of his coat and held him while Gina ran to the stairwell. When she was safe I let him go.

"Oh, it's you, Dolan," he said, as if its being me made it all right."

"Mr. Dolan," I said. "Mr. Dolan to you. I'm through with this place."

I went to the square a block from the school and sat down on a park bench, with my books on my lap. I smoked a cigarette, lazily, and looked at the school, looming on the hill. The sun shimmered on the big windows, bouncing off the glass like flames, so that for a second I thought the place was on fire. I was glad Kieran had been hardboiled with me, because being mad at him made me forget about Liggon.

When I finished my cigarette I took the leather strap from my books and tore out all the flyleaves, because my name was written on them. I tore the flyleaves into little pieces and watched them flutter away. Then I saw a wire-mesh basket that they use for burning trash. I carried the books to it and dropped them in, one by one: *Modern European History,* heavy as a brick, on glazed paper; *Advanced Algebra,* a new copy; *Shakespeare's Twelfth Night* by E. van E. Van Evingham; Chemistry, Spanish— the whole works. I thought of keeping my looseleaf notebook because I bought that myself, then I figured: *what the hell?* and dropped it in on top of the textbooks. I touched a match to the bottom of the basket and stood watching the books burn. *Dolan, there goes your education.*

"Burn, you bastards, burn!"

I spat into the flames.

When the books were burnt I walked out of the square and turned uptown. There was money in my pocket, plenty of money, and all my time was my own. I had a drink in a strange saloon, then took a taxi to the neighborhood, going into Greene's in the afternoon, looking for Murph and the Wop.

PART III

CHAPTER ONE

I N MY SLEEP, I was dying of thirst. My mouth was dry to the touch of my tongue and I seemed to be in a rocky place, breathing dust instead of air. I felt dizzy, as though I'd been whirled, strapped, at a great rate of speed in the patent machine the medics use to find out how many G's you can take: how much gravity is needed to kill you.

Far away, outside of sleep, I heard the sound of an iron chain dragging over a concrete pavement, bumping over cobblestones, ending with the anger of an ambulance bell that made me wide awake. I was at home, in bed, and a shaft of sunlight came through the window, striking my eyes and blinding me. I got out of bed and went to the window, looking down into the street. It was a burglar alarm going off behind the lattice-barred door of the furrier's shop on the other side of York. I couldn't see the crowd, but I knew what it was: neighborhood kids breaking in while the old Jew was down at the market.

I was naked and my grey suit was folded neatly on a chair. Someone must have put me to bed. Rusty? Maybe. Or Murph? Maybe even the old lady, if she was sober enough to see me.

I went into the kitchen, wearing my shorts, and saw beercans on the kitchen table, triangles punched in their tin tops. They were empty.

There was no more beer in the house, so I opened a can of tomato juice and drank it. It was warm and slippery. I scooped the sodden grounds from the pot and made fresh coffee. I was dizzy and vague and uncertain about the time of day and the day of the week. I found the old man's *Daily News* and saw that it was Thursday; three days I'd been cruising with the boys, drinking the way a man drinks when he has something on his mind. I remembered buying the bar in Greene's, drinking there for a long time, making an old, old friend of Murph, and I remembered the walking tour, hitting all the bars up and down Third Avenue. I washed my face and looked through my clothes. I had forty-eight cents. Four dimes, a nickel, and three pennies. I sat on the edge of the bed, sick, and tried to remember how I'd spent the money, the thick wad of green money that had been in my wallet when I started out, after I burned my books in the park and went to Greene's to look for the fellows.

"The hell with it."

I shaved and combed my hair and since I was broke I decided to get dressed up in a suit. Money was another problem.

There was nothing much in the house to hock. Rusty owned one good suit: a special from Bond's, worth thirty-five dollars, good for three or four in pawn, and a lot of trouble from Rusty later. The old man had a blue serge, bought with WPA money. The old lady didn't have any mink.

I stood in the bedroom, thinking.

Then I dragged Rusty's footlocker from under the bed. His medals were in the top tray, in blue boxes lined with satin, and the names stamped on the outside in gold: *Air Medal, Purple Heart, Distinguished Flying Cross, Silver Star.* In the boxes, tucked under the medals, were the typewritten citations. I took the Silver Star out of the box, then read the citation: "...the actions of Lieutenant Dolan on this occasion reflect great credit upon himself and the Armed Forces of the United States." Signed by Jimmy Doolittle.

What Rusty did, you found out, if you read behind the GI language, was put out a fire in his airplane.

I closed the box and put the medal in my pocket. Then I latched the footlocker and shoved it back under the bed. I hoped that Rusty didn't amuse himself by admiring his medals when he was alone.

I walked across town to Third Avenue and went into the hockshop, a narrow store with a high wooden counter. There was the smell of mothballs and of boxing gloves. I pushed the medal toward the Jew through the cashier's grille in front of his desk.

"How about five?" I said, pointing to the speck of silver in the center of the bronze.

He picked up the medal and held it in his hand, then laughed through the screen at me.

"Listen, sonny. For fifty cents I'll make you one."

He was a nasty, thin-faced Jew about thirty years old. His father owned the pawnshop.

"Lay off the con," I said. "How much?"

"Nothing."

"How come? It must be worth something."

I was thinking of the satin-lined box and the gold stamping on the outside.

"Look."

The pawnbroker reached into a drawer and took out a printed list.

"Give a look," he said. "This is what they cost new. Yours is second hand."

It was a Quartermaster Corps list, giving the prices they charge for medals, if you lose one and want to replace it. *Silver Star:* 68¢, *Purple Heart:* 54¢, *Air Medal:* 48¢, and so on. The only medal worth more than a dollar was the Legion of Merit, something they give to generals and mess sergeants.

I pushed the list back to him; he was right.

"Okay. How was I supposed to know?"

He laughed.

"I know the boxes they come in that makes them look like jewelry. I keep this list here to show guys like you, hard to convince. We get ten, fifteen guys a day, trying to raise a couple of dollars on this junk."

He picked up the medal and weighed it in his hand, then folded the ribbon across the bronze and handed it to me through the cage.

"Okay," I said. "Thanks anyway."

I was at the door when he called me back.

"Hey, sonny! Come here."

I walked back.

"Yeah?"

"That's a nice watch," he said. "I could give you maybe something on your watch."

I looked at the watch on my wrist.

"Are you crazy? I wouldn't hock that, you dope."

I put the medal in my pocket and walked west on Eighty-sixth, cutting downtown as I crossed, then walking through the Park drive until I came out on the West Side. It was a cold bright day, and you knew that it was almost winter. The windows of ginmills were coated with steam, filled with people drinking to keep warm. People hurried with their heads down, hands in their pockets, walking fast.

I went into a bar on Seventh Avenue and ordered a beer. Forty cents: four beers. Fifteen minutes to a beer and I could sit in the warmth for an hour. Forty cents an hour.

It was one of those Broadway bars, cheap modern fixtures, with a heavy coat of varnish hiding the gumwood grained to look like light mahogany. It was a fast-money bar, operated for the transient trade, no regular clientele. But the beer was good, cold and clean as if the pipes were kept right. I sipped the first beer, taking my time, and waited until fifteen minutes had passed, by the sweep-second clock on the wall, before I asked for the second. I took Rusty's Silver Star from my pocket and put it on the bar beside my beer glass...a chunk of bronze with a dime's worth of silver soldered to it, plus two inches of red, white, and blue ribbon. What a chump I had been to think it might be worth anything in pawn.

"Not worth much, is it, soldier?"

He was a prosperous-looking man of thirty, wearing a soft blue overcoat and a hat worth twenty-five dollars.

"You're reading my mind."

I picked up the medal and put it in my pocket.

"That, with a nickel, will buy a cup of coffee."

He laughed, to be polite.

"Where did you get it?" he asked.

"Europe."

"Infantry?"

"Air Force," I said. "I was navigator of a B17."

I thought that if Rusty was smart enough to be a navigator that I could have been two navigators.

"Oh," he said. "I was in the Pacific. Navy."

He was a Navy type: neat, college looking, careful about the knot of his tie, good complexion, custom haircut.

"Rough," I said.

"Not for me. I was at Pearl throughout the war."

"Even so," I said. "Those islands."

I guessed that he was strong on the veteran angle.

"And what did it get us?" I said.

He smiled: *Will you join me?* and nodded at the bar.

I thought it was best to play him smart, man-to-man, because he looked the type.

"Gee, sailor, I'd like to have a drink with you, but I can't buy back today. I'm about broke."

"That's all right. What will you have?"

I lifted the empty glass.

"I was drinking beer."

"Have a whiskey," he said. "Have a scotch."

"You don't have to do that."

"I'd like to," he said. He rapped on the bar with his ring. "Bartender. Two Johnny Walker. Black."

We had lunch together in the Men's Bar at the Waldorf, a nice place with a long, curved bar and a lot of dark oiled wood. They bring the bottle and leave it on the table, so that you think they trust you. There are tapes pasted to the sides of the bottles to tell the waiter how many you took.

"What do you do?" he asked. "What line of work?"

"Business. I'm in business with my uncle."

"I see."

We took our time at lunch. When we finished it was three o'clock.

"How would you like to come up to my place and see a blue movie?" he asked. "I have some that I think would amuse you."

"What's a blue movie?"

He laughed.

"You'll see."

He paid the check and left the waiter two dollars and change. His wallet was a thin pigskin case, new, with gold initials. There was a lot of money in the wallet and it occurred to me that he might be good for a touch later on—five dollars, possibly ten.

His apartment was on the East Side, First Avenue in the high Forties, an impressive six-room layout.

"Is your wife in?" I said.

"Wife?"

He stopped and turned as though he'd been stabbed. Then he laughed.

"I'm not married. I live here alone. Sometimes people stay with me."

I looked around.

"Nice place."

"Yes, it is," he said, pleased that I liked it. "I kept it all through the war."

There was a thirty-foot duplex living room, with casement windows reaching from low sills all the way to the ceiling. The furniture was modern, light wood without any varnish, rubbed with wax until it was the color of honey. The living-room ceiling, high up, was painted pale lemon yellow.

"Makes you think there's more light," he said. "Just a trick."

One of the bedrooms was used as a studio; it contained a drawing board, a battery of lights and a model stand. On a costumer placed in one corner hung several dresses over wire hangers with white cotton shields to protect the shoulders.

"I draw them," he said.

"Oh."

The other bedroom had cinnamon walls and a low, modern bed varnished black. There were pictures in old gold frames and in one corner, catching the light, was a white plaster statue: a young Greek turning his head, wearing curls that impressed you as fake, marcelled in the smooth white stone. A smaller bedroom had a single bed; it didn't look used, but seemed to be a guest room, belonging to no one, like a clean room in a hotel.

In what might have been meant for the dining room was a quarter-size screen and a movie projector and between them sixteen seats of the kind you find in expensive movies where they run revivals and foreign films—divans, low soft seats, with ashtrays bolted to the backs. It was all money, real money. The rent must have been five hundred a month and the furniture was worth at least fifteen thousand.

I understood, watching him mix drinks at his bar, what he was and what he wanted. Several ideas passed through my mind, all of them related to money. I have nothing against queers; if that is the way they enjoy themselves, why should anyone interfere? But I don't trust them because they spend every minute looking out for themselves, watching always for the doublecross.

"Would you like to see the movies?"

He was a little too casual, and a little too eager, handing me a scotch and soda. I think that he understood by then that I knew what he was, and he was waiting to see what my reaction would be—whether to slug him, or try to make him, or to be afraid the way some kids would be. I put him off his guard, being more offhand than he.

"Sure," I said. "I'm a movie fan."

We carried our drinks into the projection room; they were tall cylindrical glasses that recalled laboratory equipment, three-fourths filled with a strong mixture of expensive whisky and fresh, lively soda. The guy put his free hand on my shoulder, squeezing so that you could take it or leave it—tutti-frutti, or man-to-man.

"My name is Howard," he said. "What's yours?"

"George," I said. "George Murphy."

He took off his coat and folded it across one of the seats, then started the projector, feeding in a reel. When it was rolling, he switched off the lights and sat on the divan beside me. It was quiet and close in the room, with no sounds except the whirring of the machine and the beat of our breathing. The pictures were silent. Some of the girls were good looking.

"Do you like this one?" he whispered, with a hand on my thigh.

"Sure. Sure, it's fine."

He put on a new reel and said, "I have to take a leak, fella. You watch the picture."

I heard the bathroom door shut and a moment later heard the sound of running water. I sat for a second before I remembered that his wallet was in his coat, two feet from me in the dark. I didn't wait for the elevator, but went down the stairwell two steps at a time and hurried past the doorman to the street.

In the taxi, rolling uptown, I counted the crisp new money ... two hundred and thirty dollars, mostly in new twenty-dollar bills, sticking together when you counted them, as though the paper had been magnetized, smelling of the mint, inky and fresh. Rich people always have new money; maybe they throw the old bills away, or give them to the poor, I thought. I put the money into my own wallet, holding out five to pay for the cab. At Eighty-sixth Street I left the cab and walked east to the river embankment.

There was a thin, mean wind coming off the river and the water looked cold and deep, with the tide running out, making white furrows over the reefs near Welfare Island. The sky was clear, clean blue as if it had been swept by the wind, and the air was clear as glass, with almost no City haze, so that the opposite shore and the Island were in sharp focus and looked like a good full-color photograph.

I sat down on a concrete bench and took out the pigskin wallet, going through the stuff that was in it. There was a New York driver's license, made out to Howard Ambrose, and snapshots of Howard himself, wearing a naval officer's uniform: two stripes with an oak leaf over them instead of a line officer's star. There were photographs of Howard posed with a hard-looking Italian kid who had a mean mouth and a prize-fighter's neck. There was a snapshot of the kid alone, wearing boxing trunks and amateur's gloves, and on the back of that one Howard had written: *Guido, Golden Gloves, 1940.* There were photographs of Howard with an old lady who looked like a prop mother, and half a dozen membership cards for clubs I had never heard of. There was a check from Bramwell's Store, one of the upper Fifth Avenue places, for a hundred and fifty dollars. For a moment I thought of cashing the check, then said: *Dolan, don't be a chump.* Howard wouldn't do a thing about my borrowing his wallet. What could he do without letting the cops know what he was? If I cashed the checks there might be banks involved. Banks and the Fifth Avenue store. In the end all I kept was the money. The check and the license and the photographs, the club cards and the memoranda, I tore into little pieces and dropped them like a handful of confetti over the granite rail of the embankment. I found a small, flat stone and put it into the wallet, then scaled the wallet out over the rail, into the water. It floated for a second, then sank. I reached in my pocket and found Rusty's medal and threw that after the wallet. That was simpler than waiting for a chance to put it back in the footlocker. If he wanted another one he could get it for sixty-eight cents. I was mad at him and his god-damn medal for making me look like a chump, trying to raise something on it in pawn.

I walked back to York Avenue, feeling good because of the money, not minding the wind that seemed to follow me west from the River. I was just shot with luck, one of God's favorite people, broke this morning, rich this afternoon, ready for almost anything.

Gina sat on the brownstone balustrade, seven steps from the street, on the stoop, letting her legs dangle free so that her feet in their scuffed moccasins beat a tattoo on the scarred stone pillars. She looked like a kid again, clean-scrubbed with no rouge, her thick black hair falling loose, hiding her ears and the side of her neck, making her face look stupid and Polack-flat.

"Come down here, kid," I said, standing on the sidewalk, looking up, pressing my fists against my hips. With the new money in my pocket I felt like a banker who has just robbed the government of half a million dollars: all strictly according to law, boxed in with perfect protection.

Gina came down the steps.

"Hello, Mattie."

I took her chin in my hand and said, "What did she do? Wash your mouth with soap? Come on, let's get out of the street before she has us pinched for mopery."

"Aw, Mattie, I can't. I gotta go up for dinner in a minute."

"I'll buy you dinner at the Chink's. Tell the old lady you met a girl friend."

She looked up the wall of the brown-faced house to see if her mother was watching from the window. No one watched from any of the windows, except for one where a crippled old man sat with his arm on the window sill, pretending to be a railroad engineer, nodding away over his cane.

"All right," she said.

We had a long meal at the Chink's, lobster and shrimp and that pressed duck, chunks of meat without any bones, cooked with a rich almond sauce. In the movie, afterward, we watched the picture, holding hands.

"I saw you with those fellas," she whispered. "Murphy and that other fella."

"So what about that?"

"You were drunk, Mattie, no kidding."

"Whaddya want me to do? Wear a sign?"

She moved a little closer and I put my arm around her, loving her up a little while we watched the show. The snotty usher flashed his light right in my face and said, "Come on, break it up. No two in a seat allowed."

I took my arm away.

"That punk," I said, loud enough so that he could hear me. "He thinks he's a cop, the way he acts, all dressed up like a pansy bellhop."

He looked around, over his shoulder, thinking of coming back to argue. The long flashlight looked like a club. Then he decided that the customer is always right and trotted down the balcony aisle, with his backside showing in the aisle side-lights, moving fast under the seat of his skin-tight sky-blue trousers.

"Come on, let's get out of here."

"Aw, Mattie, we didn't see half the picture yet."

"Come on, let's go."

Someone behind me said: "*Shhhhhhhhhhhhhhhhhhh!*"

I stood up, taking my time, blocking the view of the screen with my shoulders.

"Come on, let's go."

In the street, under the lights of the theater marquee, I took ten dollars out of my wallet.

"Here, kid, for Christ's sake buy a new pair of shoes, huh? High heels."

"What'll I tell the old lady?"

"Does she have to see them? Wear them when you go out with me. You won't look so much like a kid."

"Where'd'ja get the money, Mattie?"

"Where'd'ja get the money, Mattie?" I imitated her dumb kid talk. "I EARNED IT, JERK! Working for a fellow."

"Honest?"

"Sure."

We walked home slowly in the bright street lights and the lights from the shops on Eighty-sixth—beer halls and bakeries, record stores and jewelers, all lit up, making the street look like a carnival camped for the night in some small town. At the stoop I kissed her and she broke away.

"I gotta go up, Mattie. Honest, she'll kill me."

"Go up," I said. "GO AHEAD! Go where you please. Go straight to hell for all I care."

I stood, alone in the street, with the garbage and ashcans under the streetlight, watching an evil half-starved cat waste his claws on the galvanized iron of a corrugated garbage can, scratching away, making a noise, patient and methodical, acting as if he had all the rest of time in which to scratch through the iron to the garbage. I walked to the lamppost and thought of kicking the cat, but instead I reached down and raised him by the loose skin on top of his neck, taking the lid from the garbage can and letting it clatter into the gutter, putting the cat on top of the garbage.

"Go on, sucker," I said. "Eat it."

CHAPTER TWO

A few days later, matching pennies in Greene's, someone called from the telephone booth:

"Mattie! Mattie Dolan! For you."

I picked up my stack of pennies and walked to the booth.

"It's the Metropolitan Hospital. Out on the Island. I think it's your old lady."

"Yeah?"

I picked up the phone.

"Dolan speaking."

A Jewish voice with an uptown accent told me the old lady was there on the Island, an emergency case.

"She was hit by a truck on Third Avenue. Knocked down," he said.

"Was she killed?"

"No, no. She isn't badly hurt. But she's very badly alcoholized."

"You mean she's still stinking?"

"I wouldn't put it that way," he said, "She's very badly alcoholized."

"Okay. I'll come and get her."

At Welfare Island a beefy nurse wearing a cap with a flat visor, looking like the guard in a movie insane asylum, wrote my name on a piece of paper.

"Why don't you keep your mother at home?"

She had a policewoman's voice; the cap and uniform made her feel important.

"What do they pay you for if it isn't to go around picking up lushes?" I asked.

She was the woman who rode with the driver because there weren't enough doctors to man the emergency ambulances. She got up and carried the slip of paper through the heavy swinging door.

A tall intern wearing rumpled white led the old lady into the waiting room. It was a big tiled room with varnished benches along the walls, smelling of hospital and of people, foreigners who hadn't bathed. There were a dozen people on the benches, holding slips and waiting to be called into the other room for treatment. They all stared at the old lady.

She had taken a tumble. Her face was bandaged and they had scrubbed around the cuts so that, without any rouge, her skin had a dead unhealthy look, like the skin on the soles of your feet. She looked old; if she had said fifty you would have believed her.

"Hello, Ma."

"Hello, Mattie."

We stood there, looking at each other.

"Is this your boy?" the doctor asked. He was thin, with horn-rimmed glasses.

"Yes, that's my boy. That's my Mattie."

"You'd better get her home, son," the doctor said. "See that she gets some sleep."

"How about some pills?" I asked.

He shook his head.

"I'm sorry. I'm afraid not."

I helped her to the elevator, the one that is built into the piers of the Bridge. She was still drunk, but she had been so frightened that she tried to pretend she was sober. She held my arm and I felt the change in weight as she weaved and staggered.

It was dark in the taxi, crossing the Bridge, because the light was cut off by the steel girders and pylons of the superstructure.

She sat back in a corner of the cab, hiding in the shadows, aching and sick.

"Honest, Mattie, I'm through with it. I've had my last drink."

"Yes, I know. Until the next time."

I lit a cigarette and drew on it, then handed it to her.

"No, son, I mean it. This time I'm through with it for good. I've had my last drink."

It was the pain talking; the pain in her face and the fear in her heart, because she remembered the heavy truck sliding toward her between the El pillars, and her own drunken feet, unsteady in the slush, slipping and throwing her into it.

"Sure," I said, "sure you have."

She raised up in the cab seat and looked at her face in the vanity mirror bolted to the curtain of the car. She put her hand to the bandaged side, then touched the part of her cheek that showed.

"I was pretty," she said. "I was the prettiest girl in the block."

"Yeah," I said. "I heard about it. So why did you marry the old man?"

She thought that over, then said, reaching a decision, "He was a Protestant. Like me. And he was different then, twenty years ago. He had a good job."

"Twenty-two years ago," I said.

"That's right, Mattie," she nodded. "Twenty-two years."

I helped her up the stairs and undressed her. There was a long, ugly scrape on her leg that the hospital had ignored, with mud and silt from the cobblestoned street smeared on the skin around it. I washed the leg clean with water from the tap, then went downstairs to the drugstore.

"Listen," I said. "My old lady's sick with some kind of rheumatism. Can you give me something, some kind of pills, to help her get some sleep?"

"Got a prescription?"

"Sure."

I slid ten dollars across the counter.

"And give me a bottle of iodine."

The clerk handed me the package, wrapped in stiff grey paper.

"There's nothing in that but iodine," he said, putting the ten in the register.

"That's right."

The pills were sodium amytol. I fed her one with a water chaser, then doctored her leg with the iodine. She was half asleep. I covered her with a blanket, then drew the green shades at the windows. I sat in a chair, watching her, until I was sure she was sound asleep. Her breathing was heavy and every few minutes she rolled in her sleep and groaned at the pain, but she didn't wake up. The room was filled with the smell of the iodine and with the smell of her stale whiskey breath.

I was sorry for her, because even drinking didn't help her any more.

I think she was afraid to stay sober for more than a few days at a time, because sober she saw what should have been her life, squashed out behind her, finished and done with, about as significant as a stepped-on cockroach.

She started to drink, I supposed, because one morning she looked into the mirror and understood that she wasn't pretty any more. Perhaps she started when the fellows, fellows on the corners and on the backs of trucks, stopped whistling when she walked by.

And whiskey is a wonderful thing when you start it.

When she got drunk, just a few years ago, she became a Queen on a few drinks, Duchess of the barroom, deferred to and admired, because of her hair, bright blonde then, and the fact that her figure hadn't started to sag. Sitting at the bar, in the barroom haze, facing the mirror ten feet away, with fellows feeding her flattery and booze, she must have forgotten the old man, twelve years older and a sour-puss, and forgotten the fact that whatever future she might have planned was a long way behind her at age thirty-four.

When she was high enough to go home with a fellow she'd met in a bar, someone her age, clean, wearing a decent suit, talking a crisp modern line, she would get a little something from living—just laying in bed with the young fellow, letting him love her in the dark, strange room, carried out of her own place and time by the lift of the whiskey and the young fellow's love, kidding herself, there in the dark, that she was someone else, a human being, and not Mary Grace Dolan at all, from East Yorkville, with a chump for a husband and two kids who often made a meal of mickies—Irish potatoes cooked in the gutter over a fire made of stolen wood.

Then, at four or five in the morning, she'd come out, into the street, far away from the neighborhood, ashamed and frightened of the coming daylight. She'd hurry home in the morning light, with the dawn coming out of the East River and setting the high windows on fire, turning the building stones rosy pink. She'd hurry home, racing the sun, ashamed and sick, and afraid she'd caught some disease, with her underwear wrapped in a newspaper, her makeup smeared or washed off with cold water from a rooming-house tap, hurrying, hurrying, hurrying, home, afraid that someone from the neighborhood would see her, looking up at the drawn blinds in the windows of all the tenement flats, suspecting a couple of hundred eyes watching her from behind the blinds.

We kids would hear her come in, closing the front door quietly, trying not to wake anyone. She'd go to the kitchen and we would hear her put the coffeepot on the stove. Then we'd smell fresh coffee through the apartment and hear the clink of the cups and saucers as she put them on the kitchen table. Then we'd lie in our bed, propped up on our elbows, almost holding our breath while we waited for the old man to get out of bed, taking his time, making a noise, cursing to himself as he stumbled, getting into his greasy trousers, missing the buttons on his blue shirt. Sometimes he beat her before he went out to pick up the cab and go to work. Sometimes he didn't touch her, or look at her, or speak to her, but just sat, holding his coffeecup and blowing on his coffee, staring at the wall and looking as if he wanted to kill either her or himself.

I sat, thinking of that, in the dark, close room that was dead quiet, except for the sound of her uncomfortable breathing and the occasional moaning that came when she rolled a little in her sleep. I got up and walked to the bed, then straightened the covers and tucked them in under her shoulders. I looked down at her bandaged face, indistinct in the darkness.

"Jesus, Ma," I said out loud. "Jesus Christ, you're a loser. A sure loser."

I put the sleeping pills into my pocket and tiptoed out of the room. I was surprised that it was daylight, midafternoon, in the rest of the apartment. I went out, down to the corner. When I came back, almost ten hours later, I looked into the bedroom and she still slept, and looked as if she hadn't moved at all, so that I bent and listened to be sure she was alive. I half woke her and fed her another sodium amytol pill; what she needed was a long, long sleep.

The old man sat in his chair, the one that faced the brick wall.

"She's gonna get killed one of these days, and a good thing for her. Serve her right."

I looked at him.

"Jesus," I said. "It can talk, too."

He paid no attention to what I'd said, but went back to reading his *Daily News*. After a while, having thought it over, he looked up from the paper.

"What are you going to do with yourself, now that they've kicked you out of school? Just hang around, like a bum?"

I stood, looking at him, and looking at his chipped black fingernails.

"That's right," I said. "For the time being, that's what I'm going to do. Just hang around."

CHAPTER THREE

We hung around.

We hung around Greene's if we had the money or if one of the last-war guys from the Legion was there to buy us beer. If we were broke and Greene's was empty, we stood on the corner in front of the White Cat Sandwich Shop, watching the women walking by, high-ass on their high heels, with dogs on leads or kids by the hand, the kids in leggings and flared English coats, if they were girls; flannel suits and beanie caps with phony coats-of-arms if they were boys.

"Jesus, what a shape!" we'd say.

"Look at that wiggle!"

"Have *you* got what *I* want!"

"Lady, have *I* got what *you* want!"

If a bowlegged woman passed the corner, you heard the Wop say: "Pleasure bent!"

If she was knock-kneed, Murph would say: "There goes Miss X!"

It was something a smarter Marine had taught him and for him it was always funny.

WE HUNG AROUND.

It was something to do.

A woman came by, knocked up. Higher than a kite, maybe seven months gone, so big she met herself coming around corners.

"Look at Moitle," Murph said, "carrying last year's fun around."

The woman turned, weight balanced on her spread feet, and slapped Murph so hard that his eyes began to tear.

"You miserable loafer!" she said.

I thought that Murph would hang one on her but all he did was to give her a push: "For Christ's sake, lady, can't you take a joke?"

The next evening the woman came by, holding her husband's arm. You saw the woman looking at us, pointing and talking as fast as a salesman, and the little husband nodding his head, trying to squeeze half an inch more out of his five feet seven.

Murph yelled when the pair came past: "LITTLE MAN! I didn't know you had it in you!"

The husband turned and walked back.

There were five of us on the corner, Murph in the middle with his head above the others, a grin on his flat red Irish face.

Murph looked down and laughed; the husband tried to hit him. Murph caught his arm on the upswing, turned it and slapped the husband's face. With the man's own hand. He put his hand on the husband's chest and pushed so the guy went ass-over-biscuit, right into the gutter. The wife came back to help him up and we heard her talking as they walked away, talking and brushing off his coat: "I'm sorry, Herbert. I'm sorry, Herbert, honey."

Murph laughed, watching them go.

"What a winner that Herbert is. What a winner!"

WE HUNG AROUND.

"Hey, Gertie! Your slip's showing!"

The woman would turn and lift up the mink, look and laugh and walk on. We made up names for them: Moitle and Sadie and Goitie and Riffke. We got to know them, and they must have known us. They came from the houses toward the River, on Eighty-sixth between York and East End, and East End, toward Doctors' Hospital. Murph said they were kept broads, but most of them were just married to men who made fifteen or twenty thousand a year, men too busy making the money to know or care what the dames did. We saw them at eleven o'clock in the morning, on their way to a cab or the liquor store, dressed up, always in mink. In that section, east of York, in the houses made of rough dark brick, with canopies and doormen and signal lights to call your car, there must be two thousand mink coats. Mink is the uniform of the day.

The kids from those houses went to private schools in various parts of the City and bright-painted buses called for them early in the morning. Doormen handed them into the buses, touched their caps and winked at the drivers. Some of them wore soldier suits, grey and brass with ostrich-plumed hats and swords which hung from scarlet sashes. Some of them had money in their pockets, three, four, even five dollars: little kids, eleven, twelve, thirteen years old.

We caught one, from the Knickerbocker Greys, and took him in the hallway to mobilize him: get him on the ground, take out his wee-wee and spit on it.

"You hoodlums!" he screamed at us. *"Leave me alone. I'm an officer and a gentleman."*

We took his sword and his money and his hat, kicked his backside and let him go.

WE HUNG AROUND.

Murph caught one of the girl kids and dragged her into the hallway of a house on Eighty-fourth Street. He backed her up against the wall, opened his pants and laughed at her.

"How would you like a piece of this, girlie?"

She screamed and broke away from him, running home to East End Avenue.

"I wouldn't have touched her," said Murph. "A little kid, twelve, like that. I was only trying to scare her."

"Heh-heh-heh," laughed the Wop, with his nasty Shadow-knows chuckle. "Heh-heh-heh!"

AND WE HUNG AROUND.

Vince Rhattigen stopped on the corner, wearing his new Legion uniform, blue like a cop's, with POST COMMANDER embroidered in gold on the cap, his good grey hair cut by hand by a two-dollar barber in Wall Street.

"When are you fellows joining up?" Vince wanted to know. "We want you all in the Legion."

"When it gets cold," Murph said. "Too cold to hang around the corner."

"Sure," I said. "When it gets cold, Vince."

Vince laughed, a big man's laugh, and took a Hamilton watch from his pocket. He started as a sandhog, risking his life to build a North River tunnel, but a smart tip from a clubhouse boy told him all he needed to know to get a contract for twenty blocks of subway. That morning he had five thousand bucks; by the time it was dark on the same day he had over a hundred grand.

"It's cold enough to be thirsty now," Vince Rhattigen said and winked.

We followed him through the door into Greene's and drank his bonded bourbon twice, the three of us watching the crisp new money he put on the bar to pay the bill.

"Short, fellows?" Vince asked, holding the money the way a pro dealer holds a deck of new cards. He paid no attention when we didn't answer, but dealt the money to us on the bar, two thin smooth dollars apiece, so new and sharp they would cut your finger.

"So long, fellows," he said, nodding at Greene for a third drink to be served to us after he was gone. He waved his hand as he went out and closed the door softly behind him. We saw him through the window, walking away with his head up, waving his hand to greet someone passing him on the street. He wanted the votes in the neighborhood, for himself as district leader. He wanted the votes in the Legion post, for himself as post commander.

"Good man," said Greene, wiping the bar with his damp towel. "A smart man, Rhattigen."

"Yeah," said Murph, taking one of his dollars from the bar and shoving it into his watch pocket, pushing the other one toward Greene. "Smart. Smart man. Three beers, Greene, huh?"

The Wop turned and looked at Murph.

"Are you sick, Murphy?" he asked, touching Murph's forehead with his fingers.

"Huh?" said Murph. "Whaddya mean?"

"How come you're springing for beer?"

"Leave him alone," I said, putting a hand on Murph's shoulder. "He's my friend. My buddy. You leave him alone."

"You girls," the Wop said. "Heh-heh-heh."

WE HUNG AROUND THE CORNER.

"Yeah, there's good ones," Murph said, "but they're dead."

"That's right, Murph," I said. "There *are* good ones, but I never saw one."

The Wop laughed: "Heh-heh-heh," and hid a fake hooked nose with his hand.

"Let's go on a mockie hunt."

"Yeah," said the Wop. "Something to do."

It was cold, three in the morning, over there on the East Side, with a damp wind coming in off the River. We took the bus to the subway station and rode downtown to a local stop, sitting on the bench near the men's can, watching for some Jewboy.

After a while a Hebe came down the stairs that led from the street, fed two nickels into the slot and pushed the turnstile for his girl. They stood near the edge of the station platform, looking downtown through the tunnel, trying to see the lights of a train. It was quiet and a little damp, the way it gets in the subway early in the morning, with a stagnant smell coming from the tunnel and the smell of steel and electricity coming from the tracks and the third rail. There was no one else on the platform except for an old Bowery drunk, asleep on a bench at the other end, thinking he was safe in a local station where no subway cops came.

"Hey, look at the Hebe," said Murph, loud enough so the guy could hear him. The guy pretended not to notice and turned away from the three of us.

"Look at Ikey, out with Riffke," said the Wop.

"Yeah," I said. "Look at the Jewboy, risking a nickel to ride on the subway like anyone else."

The Jewboy turned but the girl caught his coatsleeve.

"Don't pay any attention, Melvin," we heard her say.

Then Murph said, "Melvin! Do what Riffke tells you to do, or you won't get none of that Jew meat."

And the Wop said: "Oh, RIFF-kee! SAY-dee!"

The guy walked over and said, "Shut up." He was trembling as if he was cold.

"Screw, Jew," Murph said.

"Hike, kike," said the Wop.

"Take a walk, mock," I said.

And Melvin stood there, shaking, his fists closing and unclosing.

"Where were you when I was at Tarawa?" Murph wanted to know from the guy.

"Yeah, mock," said the Wop. "If you want to fight, join the Army."

"I was in the Army," Melvin said, still shaking.

"In what?" said Murph. "The Qvattermesster Corps?"

Murph stood up, laughing at the guy, and Melvin, the sucker, swung at Murph. Murph hit him, a clout on the head, and down went Melvin to the concrete platform, pitted with spit and chewing gum. The Wop stood for a second, watching, then kicked the Jewboy right in the crotch and the Jewboy screamed so you heard the echo through the long quiet subway tunnel. The girl ran over and grabbed Murph's arm and the old drunk woke up with the noise, folded his coat and walked away, into the men's toilet.

"Leave him alone," the girl said.

Murph slapped her across the face.

"He hit me, didn't he, bitch?"

He pushed the girl to the bench and said, "See if Melvin has got any money."

He bent down and hit the Jew right on the head so he went to sleep, then opened his pants and took it out, looked at it, and spat on it.

"Whaddya want him for, sister?" he said to the scared girl. "Melvin's only half there."

The Wop laughed and reached into the guy's coat for his wallet.

"Five lousy bucks," said the Wop. "And all these mockies are supposed to be rich."

"Yeah," said Murph. "He keeps it in the bank."

And he kicked the Jew again, in the stomach. We went up, onto the street, leaving Melvin lying on the platform, with his face bleeding and his fly open. There was a taxi standing on the corner, so we rode it back to Greene's bar and spent the mockie's money for whiskey.

WE HUNG AROUND THE NEIGHBORHOOD.

The dog came by with the paper in his mouth, prancing, too good to live.

"I am going to ruin that dog," Murph decided one day.

A rich old man on East End Avenue owned a trick police dog, trained to walk from the old man's house to the candy store in the morning, carrying back the New York *Times,* held between his teeth. The dog went through Eighty-sixth and cut down York to the store, lifting his knees, with his head in the air, knowing that people were watching him, giving you the impression that he said: *Watch me go! Watch me go!*—waltzing along with his head up, acting as if he was better than we were: *Whaddeeyasay! Whaddeeyasay! Watch me go! Watch me go!*" with an arrogant look on his dumb dog face.

"I'm going to ruin him," Murph said. "That snotty bastard dog."

Murph went into the butcher shop and bought a frankfurter, then waited for the dog on the corner. When the dog came past with the paper in his mouth Murph held out the frankfurter and called:

"Hey, dawg!"

The dog stopped, noticing the meat.

"Hey, dawg! Come here!"

The dog trotted over as though he was pleased by the chance to show that he understood English. He looked up at Murph, being good-natured, then dropped the paper on the sidewalk. Murph gave him the frank to eat; we picked up the paper and read it.

"Go home, dawg! Go on home!"

The dog looked at the paper in our hands, tilted his head, trying to figure it, then trotted away toward home, light on his feet, still proud of himself.

The next morning when the dog came by with the *Times* in his teeth, Murph called:

"Hey, dawg!"

And over trotted Fido, just as if Murph was boss. He dropped the paper at Murph's feet and looked up with his long tongue out, panting and grinning a stupid dog grin. But instead of a frankfurter he got a kick, right in the slats, which made him yelp.

"Go home, dawg!"

Murph laughed at him. Off he went, bewildered, going home without the paper.

After that the dog never knew what to do with the *Times*, whether to drop it at Murph's feet or carry it home to his master. The old man stopped sending him after a while, and we would see him, in a square-cut derby and a mink-lined overcoat, leading the dog on a costly leash, walking down to the store in the morning to buy the *Times* for himself.

HANGING AROUND, NOTHING TO DO.

Father Fliegel, the priest from St. Michael's, caught me horsing on the corner with Murph, bouncing a ball against the brick wall.

"When are you coming around, Matt, and have that talk with me?"

He was a big young priest who had played guard for Holy Cross.

"Sometime, Father," I said. "Sometime soon."

"Come along with me now, Matt. We can talk for an hour or so."

"I'm pretty busy," I said. "I have to meet a fellow."

"Come along, lad," he said, taking me by the arm.

We walked away and I heard Murph give us a big Bronx cheer. The priest turned and Murph got red, touching his cap as he mumbled, "I'm sorry, Father, honest. I didn't mean a thing."

Fliegel grinned and poked Murph, in a friendly way, but hard, in the stomach.

"I know that, Francis," he said. "I know you didn't mean a thing."

We sat in the study of the parish house next door to the church, an oak room with an oriental rug and Irish lace at the old-fashioned windows.

"Here, Mattie," Fliegel said. "You might be interested in this, being a ballplayer yourself."

He handed me a leather book, with a purple cross on the outside.

"A sin of Vanity, keeping that, but I couldn't bear to part with it," he said. "Excuse me for a minute, Mattie."

He went out and I looked through the book, a scrapbook of the kind most football players keep, photographs and news stories, pasted on the heavy black pages with the names of the papers and the dates lettered under the items in white. He looked different in the photographs, wearing a jersey, with his knuckles taped, a big tough lineman who must have known all the tricks. I knew that he had asked me to look at the book so I would think he was a regular guy, and be that much more willing to listen to him.

After a while he came back, wearing a skirt over his pants, holding a lighted pipe in his hands.

"Do you believe in God, Mattie?" He spoke in a straight, matter-of-fact voice, as if he had asked me the right time, looking at me over his pipe.

It is an unfair question.

"Why, sure. Sure I do," I said.

He began to talk and I sat and listened. It was hot in the study and the old-fashioned steam radiator sputtered and hissed as the priest talked.

"First God created the Angels..."

He talked and I listened, sweating in the too-hot room, hearing the sound of the clock in the hall, going *tick-tock* in its wooden case, driving you crazy as a metronome, with no break in its even beat. An old woman dressed in black carried in coffee and cups on a tray, and the priest poured for himself and me, going on talking, handing me a cup. After a while he sat back, spilling ashes from his pipe on his front.

"Well, that's enough for today."

I nodded.

"You go around with one of our girls? Little what's-her-name...from Eighty-fourth Street?"

"Me?" I said. "You mean Gina. Gina Tragorna."

"That's the girl. Dark little thing. Pretty."

"I don't exactly go around with her. I went out with her a couple of times. She's a little wild, Father. She goes out with all kinds of fellows. Men too."

He looked at me, wondering whether to believe me or not.

"You don't say?"

"Sure," I said. "She's a little wild."

"Ah, I'm sorry to hear that."

He stood up and took two paper-bound pamphlets from his desk.

"Read these, Matt, when you have the time."

"Thanks, Father."

"Come back next week. Same time?"

"Sure, if I can. Sure."

We shook hands and I went out, holding the paper books in my hand. When I got to the corner I threw them in the sewer. Back at the corner Murph stood with the Wop, holding his hands in his pockets.

"What are you doing?" he wanted to know. "Horning in on a good religion?"

"He only talked to me," I said.

"About what?"

"Nothing," I said. "God."

"Heh-heh-heh," laughed the Wop, holding up the ten fingers of his hands. "Listen, if you marry that Tragorna kid the bet don't count for you. You owe me the ten."

HANGING AROUND, NOTHING TO DO, LOOKING FOR A FREE MEAL.

Old man Tragorna was sick, pillows piled up behind his back on the feather mattress in his bedroom. Hanging on the wall over his head was a crucifix with the Body of Christ, just hanging there, waiting for the time the old man would be ready to kiss it, and kissing it, kiss the world good-by. He was thirty-eight years old, but on that bed, waiting to die, he looked no age under a hundred. His face looked rubbed with wood ashes and I saw that he had lost weight, thirty or forty pounds.

"You like Gina, Mattie?" he asked, putting his hand on top of mine.

"Sure," I told him. "Sure I do."

"She's good girl, Mattie," he said. "Not too smart, but good girl."

He leaned forward, glancing at the door, and whispered, smelling of sickness and a little sour, the way Hunkies do.

"Her mother a little too hard with her. Too strict."

"Yeah, she is strict," I said.

"Mattie," he said. "I die soon. You try to keep Gina happy, eh? Little bit?"

"Aw, you aren't going to die, Pop."

He nodded.

"I die." He tapped his chest. "Weak chest. No good."

He patted my hand again.

"You hungry, Mattie," he said. "Go and get dinner. Help yourself to slivovitz after."

I ate in the kitchen with the old lady and Gina, another of those Hunky roasts, sweet and sour, and pretty good.

"Gina made it," the old lady said.

"Yeah?" I tasted it. "Pretty good. Pretty good."

I smiled at Gina.

"I only helped," she said.

"You get a job yet, Mattie?" the old lady asked.

"Not exactly. But I'm looking. I'm registered with the government for a job."

"He went to see the priest, Ma."

"That's good," the old lady said. "But a job is much better."

"Aw, Ma—"

"Shut up," said the old lady. "Eat. Eat."

We finished dinner with no more talking. I drank a little of the old man's brandy and looked into his room before I left. He was asleep, breathing hard, as if he had barbed wire in his chest.

"Good night, kid. Thanks for the meal."

We stood in the doorway; I was leaving early so that she would have time to do her homework. The old lady was in the kitchen, washing the dishes.

"Good night, darling," Gina said. "Don't mind Ma. She's just strict."

"Skip it," I said. "What do I care what she thinks."

"She don't want me to see you no more. Much."

"Do you *have* to tell her what you do?"

"Well-no."

"So okay."

I kissed her good night and went downstairs, looking at the stars in the winter's sky, fed up, feeling like a fool, wondering why I was wasting my time, getting sick of hanging around.

BUT I HUNG AROUND.

In Greene's, sitting in a booth, Murph was stripping a Luger pistol, with all the parts spread out on the table, gleaming with oil in the yellow light.

"You horse's ass, Murphy," I said. "Put that thing away."

He took the stock in his hands, pointing the barrel frame at me.

"Boom, boom!" he said. "A slug from this will knock you down even if it only hits you in the hand."

"Put it away, you dumb donkey. Put it away."

He assembled the weapon and put it in his pocket.

"I got shells for it," he said.

"We could knock off a joint," said the Wop. "Pick up a few grand."

"Sure," said Murph. "Easy."

"Yeah, something to do," said the Wop.

"Listen," I said. "You know the something you'd get to do? Two and a half to five years, sitting on your backsides, up the river."

"Would they stop me from getting my pension?" asked Murph.

"They'll stop you from living if you're not smart."

"Aw, Mattie, don't be a chump," said Murph, with a dumb grin. "Suppose we get caught? What do we get? Veterans and all. Suspended sentence. What the hell."

"Yeahyeahyeah. Wise guy."

"Spring for a beer, huh, Mattie?"

I threw three dimes on the table.

"Heh-heh-heh," laughed the Wop, going to the bar to get the beer. "Good old Mattie, spring for a beer."

"You bastards," I said. "I hate you."

I got up and walked out, leaving my beer on the table.

WINDY ON THE CORNER, FOUR IN THE MORNING.

The saloons were closed and nothing was open except the Sandwich Shop behind us.

"Jesus, I'm hungry," Murph said. "I'm so hungry I could eat a horsebun."

"Yeah, me too."

The Wop took a penny out of his pocket and scaled it into the dark street. We waited and heard it tinkle.

"That is the last of the Mohicans," he said.

"I think I'll go home and get warm," I said, shivering from the cold.

"I got an idea," Murph said. "Wait a minute."

"What?" I said.

"What?" said the Wop.

"Wait a minute. Wait a minute."

We waited, standing in front of the White Cat, pretending it was warmer in the light from the window. After a while a man came through Eighty-sixth and stopped at York, with his wife hanging onto his arm. He was middle-aged, about forty, happy-drunk and humming a tune. He and his wife stopped under the street light, then turned back and went into the White Cat.

"Come on, let's eat," Murph said.

"What's the gag?"

"You'll see."

We went into the White Cat, sitting on stools at the enameled counter, enjoying the blast of warm air that came from the oven and grill behind it. We ordered the meal and ate it, Murph watching the middle-aged drunk, who was slopping his scrambled eggs on his plate. After we had drunk our coffee, Murph leaned over and pushed the drunk, so that he slipped and fell from the stool. We gave him the leather, on the tile floor. His wife screamed and the counterman stood beside the coffee urn, with his mouth open and a turner in his hand, the food in his frying pan sputtering away.

"Come on, fellows," Murph said. "Let's get out of here. It ain't safe."

Through the window we saw the wife and the counterman help the drunk get to his feet.

"What did you do that for?" I said.

"For confusion," Murph explained. "So we didn't have to pay."

"Where did you get hit?" I asked.

"In the leg," he said. "I'll show you."

"Yeahyeahyeah," I said. "I was just sure that the bullet must have gone through your head first."

JUST SHAKING THE PENNIES IN OUR PANTS, USING UP AIR.

Two precinct detectives wearing plain clothes, flanking the drunk from the White Cat, got out of a black car pulled up at the curb. One of the cops was small, a Jew. The other was beefy and flannel-faced, low-class Irish from Hell's Kitchen. The drunk we had slugged was wearing a bandage and looked nervous, afraid of us.

"Okay, line up," the little cop said. "Over here, facing the wall."

We lined up with our hands in the air and he patted our pockets and the legs of our pants. Luckily for Murph, the Luger was home.

"All right, turn around."

We stood with our backs against the stone wall.

"Are these the guys?"

The fellow we had clouted looked us over. I stared right into his eyes, trying to tell him to keep quiet. After a little he scratched his head.

"I can't be sure," he said.

"Come on," said the beefy Irish cop. "Are these the guys that hit you?"

"I can't be sure. I don't think so."

He had changed his mind about trying to have us locked up. He was afraid we would get him later, at night, on one of the side streets.

The Irish cop, as big as Murph, stood with his hands on his hips and said, "Boy, Goldberg, would I like to give these monkeys a going-over."

The Jewboy nodded and moved his shoulders, snugging the fit of his velvet-collared coat. He looked more like a bookmaker's runner than a cop.

"We used to be allowed to handle them," he explained to the civilian. "What we did was to line them up, wherever we found them—ginmill, cathouse, poolroom, right out on the street corner. We went down the line and slapped them around, made them miserable and made them move. After a while they caught wise that the percentage was lousy, all against them. They quit the corner and got jobs. A few of them turned into real crooks, but at least we didn't get complaints the way we get them now. All day long at the House we get nothing but calls about these hoodlums."

"Listen, cop, I'm a war veteran," Murph said. "I got the Navy Cross. Don't you call me a hoodlum."

The big Irish cop laughed.

"You'll get a right cross to the head if you don't shut your big mouth."

"Yeah, you bum," said Murph. "Lay a hand on me and you'll lose that badge so fast you'll think somebody picked your pocket."

The cop said, "You see what I mean?"

He moved toward Murph with his fist cocked. When Murph flinched he laughed.

"I wouldn't dirty my mitts."

They climbed back into the car and drove through a light with the siren going. Murph stood with his hands in his pockets, watching the car turn east.

"That bum. That Irish bum," he said. "I should have hit him right in the puss."

"Heh-heh-heh," laughed the Wop. "You and your Navy Cross. Why didn't you show him your gimpy leg?"

Murph turned and slapped the Wop, so that his pasty skin turned red.

"Shut up, Guinea," he said. "Shut your Guinea mouth."

"Jeez, Murph!" The Wop backed away with his hand on his cheek. "Jeez, can't you take a joke?"

Murph grinned his dumb red grin, to show that he wasn't a bad guy at heart.

"Sure, Wop. I was only kidding."

He put his arms around the Wop's waist and squeezed, in fun, but hard enough to hurt.

"ooooOOOOH!" said the Wop. "You gorilla."

"My pal, huh, Wop? My buddy."

WE STOOD IN FRONT OF THE LEGION HALL...

Six of us, broke, bored and looking for something to do, standing in the cold, waiting, where Vincie Rhattigen told us to wait.

A Cadillac cabrolet pulled up, brought to a gentle, bumpless stop by the deadpan chauffeur who sat out in the cold under an oilcloth awning. The old arthritic woman got out. She was fifty, wearing sables and a hat made for a movie star, carrying a straight black gold-headed cane, her face thin and evil as a hawk's, with the skin stretched tight across the bridge of her nose, showing a hundred small burst veins.

"I am Mrs. Gordon Mellquiest," she said, addressing me. "Are you gentlemen from Mr. Rhattigen?"

"That's right, lady. Vince told us to wait here."

She gave me her hand and through the suede glove I felt a diamond big as an olive.

"Shall we be off? I have my car."

She nodded toward the Cadillac; the chauffeur sat, under his tent, with his eyes focused on the radiator emblem, used to his job, seeing nothing.

"Vincie said you'd take care of us," I said.

"A sawskie each, Vincie said."

That was Murph, sounding off.

"He means ten dollars," I said. "Mr. Rhattigen told the fellows you would make it worth their while."

"Of course."

She gave us each a ten-dollar bill. We climbed into the warm car, which smelt of perfume and clean upholstery, and the chauffeur started, shifting gears as carefully as you would set the hands of a thousand-dollar watch. Murph was on a jump seat, with his big body squeezed into the corner.

"Where is the place, lady?" he asked.

"Washington Heights," the old woman said. "Uptown."

"You mean Kike's Peak," someone said.

"Yeah, the Kosher Alps," said Murph.

"Heh-heh-heh!" laughed the Wop, making his trick hooked nose.

"Kike's Peak," she laughed. "I must remember that."

We crossed the Park and turned uptown; the driver was expert, soft as silk.

"How about a drink?" asked Murph. "I can get madder if I have a drink."

The old woman picked up the tube and spoke to the chauffeur. She had some kind of English accent. The driver nodded and touched his cap. He pulled up at a bright neon sign, got out of the car and came back with a bottle. We drank it, rolling uptown, past the Jew delicatessens and the kosher restaurants, filled with men eating dinner with their hats on ... past the dark cemetery and the stone buildings of the Indian Museum, into the bright lights again above One Hundred and Sixty-eighth Street ... handing the bottle back and forth. Somebody cursed as he chipped his teeth when the car went over a bump in the street.

"Excuse *me*, lady!" he said, and offered the bottle to old lady Mellquiest.

"No. No, thank you. It's for you boys."

We stopped at a big stone building with an oilcloth sign across the facade:

WASHINGTON HEIGHTS
COMMUNITY CENTER

The chauffeur parked an inch from the curb, handling the car like a baby carriage. He hurried to hold the door for us. We followed the old lady. In the lobby a dark-haired girl was selling tickets from a long roll, tearing them off as they were sold. It was a damp, tiled lobby.

"Seven, please."

Mrs. Mellquiest put five dollars on the table in front of the girl, who looked at the money and then looked up.

"You can't come in here," she said. "You just want to make trouble."

"Young woman!" Mellquiest tapped the five-dollar bill with the sidewalk end of her cane. "You have advertised a public meeting. I am a member of the public. So are these young gentlemen. If you refuse to sell me the tickets I shall call the police and have you arrested."

She was a duchess all right; born knowing how to bluff. The girl tore seven tickets from the roll and counted out the change.

The hall looked like a small movie theater, sloping toward a stage that was decorated with American flags on staffs. A sign stretched across the stage said: CITIZENS FOR DEMOCRATIC ACTION. There was a speakers' rostrum, with a pitcher of water and two glasses, and behind the rostrum in a row sat half a dozen uncomfortablelooking people. About a hundred cash customers sat facing the platform. The seven of us took seats in a row.

"What do we do?" asked Murph, redder than usual from the straight whiskey, blinking his eyes in the hard yellow light.

"Just wait," said Mellquiest. "You'll see."

After a while the chairman, an old fellow who might have been a tailor, looked at his pocket watch, then at the hall, and decided that no one else was coming. He rapped on the rostrum with a gavel and everyone quieted down.

"Uhhhnh, ladies and gentlemen."

He rapped again, and got quiet.

"Before we go into the regular meeting," he said, referring to a paper, "we are going to hear from a representative of the American Veterans' Committee. The AVC. A young man who has something important to say to all of us here in the Heights."

He looked at the paper again and said:

"Ladies and gentlemen, Mr. John Dolan."

It was Rusty; I took a second look.

There was a lot of applause. Rusty walked up to the rostrum and I saw that he was nervous. He opened his mouth to speak his piece and Mrs. Mellquiest climbed up on her chair. She took a small American flag from her purse and waved it over her head.

"How dare you call yourself a veteran?" she yelled. "You dirty Red!"

The audience turned around in their seats and someone yelled: "Shut up! Throw her out!" Rusty stood with his speech in his hands, nervous, wondering what to do.

"That man is a dirty Red!" Mellquiest yelled, waving her flag. "He should be in jail!"

I started to tell her that Rusty was a veteran, even if he was a jerk, then I figured: *what the hell?* it was his hard luck if he wanted to travel with a communist crowd like this. Mellquiest was still on her chair, yelling, screaming and waving the flag. Murph and the rest of our fellows banged the floor with the heels of their shoes, as the crowd will do at a football game when something exciting happens. It is a sound like a jungle drum that gets you excited in spite of yourself. All over the small hall people were on their feet, yelling. Rusty stood, stupid on the platform, looking bewildered and wondering why the old girl was screaming at him.

A thin guy in the row in front of us stood up and Murph grinned, chopping the guy with the side of his hand, a mean half rabbit punch that sent the guy tumbling into the aisle. Then someone swung at Murph and the fight was on.

I had a fellow backed against the wall, giving him his lumps for the hell of it, when a girl with hair like a Hottentot pulled at my sleeve and yelled: "You fool, you damned fool. We're not communists. We're anti-communists. We're Roosevelt Democrats."

"Listen, lady, Roosevelt's dead," I told her. "And this is Bank Night."

When the cops came they just cleared the hall, instead of arresting anyone.

"Come on, folks, break it up."
"Come on, folks, let's go home."

"Break it up, folks! Break it up!"

"Let's go, now, let's go."

Talking it up, moving along, the cops kept the crowd walking in the direction of the door, being nice to everyone, using their nightsticks very gently, getting hard with their voices once in a while when someone gave them an argument.

"Officer! We paid for this hall and we have a right to hold our meeting."

"You didn't hire it for a prizefight, lady. That's another kind of a license. Come on now, let's go home."

Rusty, coming down the aisle, held a bloody rag to his nose. Someone helped him, holding his arm. He saw me and stopped short, taking the rag from his smashed-up nose. I think he would have hit me, but the cop gave him a friendly push.

"Come on now, break it up. Break it up."

"That son-of-a-bitch is my brother. My own goddamned brother."

"Yahhhhhhhh!" I yelled. "Mockie-lover."

A cop noticed my Legion button and gave me a grin.

"Come on, soldier," he said. *"Let's go home. Break it up. Break it up."*

"Sure, officer, I'm just going."

On the sidewalk in front of the Hall, talking to the sergeant who stood with his foot on the running board of the radio car, Mrs. Mellquiest opened her bag. I saw the bill in the street light, a hundred dollars as new and clean as the tens she had handed to the six of us.

"Thank you," the sergeant said, touching the peak of his cap like a doorman. *"Thank you, Mrs. M."*

She walked to the door of the Cadillac and stood with her hand on the knob.

"Come along, boys," she called. "Come along."

She tapped on the sidewalk with her cane and we all got into the car. We went to her house on East Sixty-third, a couple of doors from Park Avenue. In the high-ceilinged dining room, under the glitter of a crystal chandelier, was a buffet supper on a long table, with knives and forks in rows like soldiers, and little plates with gold around the edges.

"Help yourselves, gentlemen. Help yourselves."

There was a turkey, twenty-five pounds, a crisscrossed roast Virginia ham, steaming and studded with sticks of clove, a big shrimp aspic affair molded in the shape of a swan, a crown roast of red beef, with a white-coated nigger with a knife to serve it. There was whiskey, all you could drink, scotch and soda in tall, rich glasses. The old lady had a martini, a pale, straw-colored martini with no olive at the bottom of it; she was the type, you guessed, who lived on dry martinis and rye-crisp.

Murph followed me into the toilet, after the colored boy told me where it was.

"Let's rob the joint, Mattie. The old dame is too screwy to know if anything should be missing."

"Don't be a sucker, Murph," I said. "That old dame is a friend of the cops. She and the cops are like that."

I made a gesture with my thumb and forefinger.

"Just like that. Like brothers."

I GOT HOME LATE, HALF DRUNK AND LOADED WITH FOOD.

Rusty was in our room, sitting at the window, looking out.

"Hello, sucker," I said.

He got to his feet, tensed up, then decided not to bother.

"Don't talk to me, Mattie. Just don't speak to me at all. You make me sick at my stomach."

I turned and threw back the covers of the double bed I shared with him.

"Have it your way," I said. "It's no loss to me at all. No loss at all."

CHAPTER FOUR

The boys' gym was decorated with red and green streamers and in one corner was a Christmas tree twelve feet high, covered with bright-colored balls and strands of tiny electric lights. Cut-out cardboard Santa Claus faces had been tacked along the walls, and the place was full of Christmas spirit. But nothing could really take the curse off the gym, because you saw the horses and parallel bars pushed to one side, and the basketball posts, with streamers curled around them, still looked like basketball posts. And underneath the Christmas smell, from the fir tree and the crepe-paper decorations, and underneath the perfume smell from all the girls in their formal dresses, you caught the armpit whiff of the gym, left by the thousands and thousands of guys who had worked out on the floor.

I stood at the door with Gina. She wore a pink cheesecloth formal, made by her mother from a pattern. It was the kind of first evening dress all poor girls have.

"Come on, kid, let's dance."

We danced out into the stream, Gina's cheek against mine, her big breasts pressed against my chest, the smell of her hair and skin strong because she was so close.

"Did you have any trouble getting out?"

"Gee, Mattie, I told her it was a Newman Club party. I told her I was going with some kids from school."

"Did she bitch?"

"Well—you know."

"Yeah," I said. "I know."

We danced clear, toward the center of the floor; I did a few tricks.

"Do you like the band?"

"It stinks."

The band was a dozen high school kids dressed in mouse-grey tuxedo coats, wearing maroon ties and cummerbunds…playing hard, trying hard, and also trying to look as bored as they thought a real band would look, playing for a school dance. There was a colored horn player, black and shiny and pretty good. He gave out:

"Wah-wah-wah—WaaaaAAAAAAAHHHH!"

He got to me.

"Come on, baby, let's show them how."

I danced, cutting loose, throwing it around and enjoying myself. Then a white-faced kid in a rented tuxedo tapped my shoulder and wanted to cut.

"Beat it, bum."

I danced around, full circle again. When we passed him, he tried again. I handed Gina to him.

"Take care of it, son. It's not insured."

"Heh-heh," laughed the kid, dancing away with Gina.

I walked to the sidelines, looking at the girls, my knees still lively with the rhythm of the music. I almost bumped into old lady Webber.

"Excuse me," I said, then recognized her.

Even here at the dance she wore the horseblanket suit and her heavy brogue shoes.

"Hello, Dolan."

"*Mister* Dolan," I said. "*Mister* Dolan," and grinned to show that I was making a joke. We shook hands.

"Would you like to dance, Mr. Dolan?"

"Gee, somebody borrowed my girl. I'll catch the next one."

"I mean with me," Webber said.

"Oh. Why, sure. Sure. Why not?"

She wasn't a bad dancer for her age, but she could have used an all-day session at the beauty parlor. Her face looked scrubbed with a brush, and she smelt of laundry soap, more like a dog that's just been washed than a woman.

"I see that you still go with Gina Tragorna."

"So?"

"Nothing," she said. "Just making talk."

We danced close to the band and the colored boy cut into a number of his own, leaving the band a mile behind. Webber smiled and bowed at him and he gave her a big African grin.

"Hay-lo, Miz Webber!"

He waved with his silver horn.

"Hello, Jackson," she called, taking her hand from my shoulder to wave.

"He's not bad, the nigger."

"Negro, Dolan," she said. "He's a Negro."

"Nigger, Negro, have it your way. For my money, *he's* the band."

"It's just a school band. What did you expect? Goodman?"

"No," I said. "Not Goodman."

I had the sense that we were engaged in a duel, flicking points at one another.

"Are you working?" she asked.

"Not right now. I'm going into business with my uncle, later. Right now I'm living on my income."

"Fifty-two Twenty Club?"

"For the time being."

The band was beginning to warm up and the kids were sweating as they beat it out. On the floor they were dancing close, girls singing low in the fellows' ears, fellows rubbing up the girls, trying to get what they could without making the chaperones sore. With the people dancing and the steam full up it was warm, too warm in the gym.

"If you get that girl into trouble," Webber said in a low, straight voice, "I'll see your throat cut from ear to ear."

I stopped, dead on the floor; a couple bumped us, hard, from behind. The guy lost the music and stumbled, glared at me and danced on.

"Listen, lady, up your back. I don't have to listen to you. You don't count."

I walked away, leaving her standing on the dance floor. I found Gina talking to the pale-faced kid in the pawnshop dinner coat.

"Come on, tramp. Let's get out of here."

"Listen, fellow, don't talk like that."

I pulled the end of his tie, so that the bow fell apart.

"Shut up, muzzler." I took Gina's arm. "Come on, kid. Let's go."

"Aw, Mattie, it's only started."

"Come on, or I'll go by myself."

"Aw, Mattie—"

We went to a place called Bresnahan's, a few blocks from the school, a clean, family-type bar with holly wreaths along the walls and a Christmas scene painted on the mirror with soap and some kind of crystal chips that gleamed like silver in the light: Santa Claus, driving a sleigh, with a house behind him and real-looking smoke coming out of the chimney. Worked in soap on the mirror were the words: MERRY CHRISTMAS-HAPPY NEW YEAR—1947.

"Whiskey. Two whiskeys," I said.

"I'll only have beer."

"One ball and one beer."

We sat in the back of the bar in a booth, too close to the juke box, which was playing a hopped-up arrangement of "Jingle Bells."

"I told you I didn't want to go to that Four F school dance. I told you."

"What's the matter you're sore, Mattie?"

"That bitch Webber," I said. "Sticking her nose in my business. What do you tell her, anyway?"

"She knows me from the Newman Club, that's all."

"I know her kind."

"Don't be sore, Mattie. Don't be sore at me."

"I told you I didn't want to go."

"Yeah. I didn't like it either, I guess."

I got up and put Crosby on the juke box, putting a quarter into the slot to prevent the lush at the bar from playing "Jingle Bells" again.

"Who was that chump in the hock-shop tux?"

"Oh, just a kid in school. He likes me."

"Yeah? I bet he don't like me."

She giggled.

"Gee, Mattie, the way you pulled his tie, I thought I'd scream, he looked so funny."

A big cop came into the bar, his face as red as a fire-truck, clumsy looking in his heavy overcoat. There were tears in his eyes from the cold outside and flakes of snow on his blue shoulders. He blew his nose with a blast that seemed to shake the bar.

"Ah, Mick, me bye," he said, putting his nightstick on the bar. "Let me have a taste of rye."

"Aye, Sully," Bresnahan said. "A cold night."

"Bitter," the cop said. "Bitter."

Instead of a shot glass Bresnahan used a tumbler, pouring out half a pint of whiskey. The cop drank it without a breather, then wiped his mouth on his sleeve.

"Good night, Mick, me bye," he said, going back into the cold, waving good night with his stick.

"A taste of rye," I said. "What does he do when he wants a *drink*? Use a pitcher?"

"Oh, Mattie—!" She giggled, then laughed. "!—you're a scream."

"Yeah, I'm a card," I said. "I can just keep you in stitches."

She drank four beers and began to feel high. I took her home in a cab. It was snowing, coming down hard, and I decided not to bother with having a wrestle with her in the hallway.

"Gee, Mattie, thanks a lot. I had a wonderful time, no kidding."

Her face was flushed from the beer and the cold. She looked pretty, like a pretty kid. I kissed her. Her lips were cold. It was like kissing a cold lamb chop.

"Good night, kid."

"Good night, Mattie. Good night, darling."

I rode to Greene's in the cab. *Good night, darling,* I said to myself. Sucker Dolan. *Good night, darling.*

The next day she had a black eye, blue and purple, with green streaks in it.

"Who the hell hit you?"

"Aw, she smelled the beer on my breath and hit me right in the face with a stick. Honest, Mattie, she's strict."

"Did you tell her you were with me?"

She looked frightened at that.

"Gee, no, Mattie. I told her a kid from school."

Then she began to cry.

"Listen, kid," I said. "The next time she hits you, you clout her right back."

CHAPTER FIVE

Noontime, but we were eating dinner, because the old man was working nights and wanted time to digest his meal. The old lady was on the wagon, making her second attempt to quit, since the day the truck knocked her down. The first one had lasted five days. This drought was three days old. She put the meal on the table and called to the old man: "Matt!"

He sat down at the dinner table just the way he got up from his nap, black grease in his knuckles and nails, dressed in his faded navy shirt and the black work pants he wore in the cab. He sat down and picked up his fork, started to eat, then got up and went back to the bedroom. When he returned he was wearing his cap, with the union buttons pinned along the band.

"There's a draft in here," he said, touching the back of his neck.

It was as stuffy as a Protestant church; not a breath of air moving. He simply liked to wear his cap at the table, the way he did in the coffeepot.

"I had a fare to Brooklyn," he said. "The god-damn cab broke down right in the middle of Park Avenue. Two hours waiting for the service car."

"You don't work it right," I said, "looking for fares to Brooklyn and Queens. That's old stuff, long hauls. Behind the times."

He put down his knife and fork and looked at me with his hands on the table.

"What is your idea?"

"Why don't you get a couple of girls on the string? When a guy is cruising, who does he ask? A hack driver, right? And there are lots of chippies who'd rather toss a dollar to an honest cabbie than to give it to some Guinea who just beats them up for their trouble."

"What am I, a pimp?" he wanted to know.

"Don't ask me. Other drivers do it."

"Yeah." He went back to his dinner. "Other drivers."

"Hundred and a half a week," I said. "I talk to the fellows."

"You and your hundred and a half a week. What do you think I made last week?"

"How should I know?"

"Sixty-seven dollars and forty-four cents. We'll be riding the ghost again next."

Before the war, when things were tough, cab drivers had a quota to make. If they missed the quota, they lost the cab, so on bad days they rode the ghost, driving around with the meter running and the cab empty, paying the bill with their own money.

"You're riding the ghost right now," I said.

"Leave your father alone, Mattie," the old lady said.

The old man spoke with his mouth full.

"Who the hell asked you to put your two cents in?"

"Eat your dinner," she said.

He finished the food on his plate, then picked his teeth with a paper match, split in half with his dirty thumbnail.

"You ought to have more respect for your parents," he said.

"For what?"

"For bringing you up."

I looked at him and had to laugh.

"How do you figure it, Pop?" I asked. "Before the war you were on relief, or the WP and A. During the war I was in the service, or making good money at Langley. You never gave me a thing. How do you figure you brought me up?"

"You son-of-a-bitch," he said.

I laughed at him.

"I figure that Roosevelt is my old man. He's the guy who gave me the handout."

"I ought to give you a good beating."

"Don't be a fool, Pop," I said. "Those days are over with. You couldn't punch your way out of a paper bag with your fists on fire."

"No?"

"No-o-o."

He would beat us, in the old days, with a piece of trunk strap that came from a cab, beat us for nothing and curse at us, because we were smaller than he was.

"Who paid for the food on your plate?"

"That's different," I said. "I'm entitled to some rights. I'm a veteran."

"Veteran!" he said. "You ought to be ashamed of yourself. You ought to be ashamed to take the money. When I think of what we went through in the Argonne. The old Sixty-ninth."

He wore a last-war Victory ribbon in the lapel of his coat.

"Argonne," I said. "Was that in the Spanish-American War?"

He reached across the table and slapped my face. I caught his wrist and twisted, not quite hard enough to break it. You could see in his face that it hurt him.

"Let go, Mattie," he said. "For Christ's sake, let go."

I let go.

"Don't fool around with me, Pop. I'm bigger than you, and I don't like it."

He sat, holding his wrist, looking at me as though he hated me more than the despatcher down at the cab garage.

"Get out of here, Mattie, will you? Get the hell out of here."

"All right."

I got up and put on my hat.

'Sometime I'll go out and not come back."

"Get out," he said. "Get out of the house."

He was holding his wrist, rubbing it a little.

"Go on, Mattie," the old lady said. "You'd better go."

"Okay, I'm going."

I walked across town to Third Avenue and down Third to the movie house, shaking the small change in my pocket. I stood on the corner for ten minutes, until the girl came into the box office, holding her trays of tickets and change. I stood in front of the shined brass grille, watching her feed nickels and dimes into the change-making machine. Then I pushed half a dollar across the counter.

"One, sister. The best in the house."

She pressed a button and down came a dime, pressed another and up came a ticket, through a slot in the brass plate.

"Don't you get sick of going to the show?"

She smiled through the brass bars.

"No," I said. "Something to do."

The theater was empty, half dark, smelling of vacuum-cleaned plush and the perfume that ushers squirted from flit guns to kill the germs and the smell of the people. I climbed to the balcony and sat on the aisle, halfway up, looking down on a thousand seats bolted to the floor in curved rows, with red light from the EXIT signs gleaming on the chromium number plates screwed into the plush seat backs. It was so quiet that you heard an echo when an usher moved across the back of the house. An old man walked down the orchestra aisle, leaning on a cane and the usher's arm, and sat down with his hat on, getting settled before he took it off, making a lot of noise with his cane as he stowed it under the seat. The organist climbed into the pit and a violet spot was thrown on his head from the projection booth behind me. He played, working the stops, and on the screen the words of the tunes were spelled out in white letters, with a white ball bouncing to beat out the time, the organ playing, full blast, to no one but me and the lame old man in the orchestra—and the god-damned ball bouncing up and down like a toy in the hands of a feebleminded child. A dozen, two dozen people came in, women and old, old men, with a few young fellows like myself, with nothing to do in the afternoon, going to the show, looking for women. The lights went dim and the sound apparatus crackled, then roared as the newsreel began to run.

I usually sat through the show before I began to prospect, because you can't watch the movie on the screen and love up a woman at the same time. But today I was restless because of the fight I'd had with the old man. After the feature picture started and the house was a third full, I saw a woman a few rows down, sitting one seat off the aisle. I got up and moved down.

"Is this seat taken?"

She looked up with bright shrewd eyes; I saw that she was blonde, thirty, not bad looking. She decided she liked my looks.

"No. It's empty."

I sat down and offered her a cigarette, held the match and permitted it to burn after the cigarette was lit, so that she got a good look at my face. After a while I put my arm on the back of her seat and let my hand fall to her shoulder. Sometimes, in a neighborhood movie, you can love them up, do almost everything, only to have them get up at the end, whisper: *"Don't follow me!"* and hurry off, down the aisle, home to cook supper for their husband and kids. Sometimes you can take them home, to their apartments in the bright afternoon. You meet some strange women in the show, and a lot goes on, there in the dark, warm, perfumed air, besides the pictures that are played on the screen.

"Not in here," said the blonde, taking my hand away from her shoulder. "Let's watch the picture and fornicate later."

I left my arm on the back of the chair, just to show other fellows I was with her, but I didn't try anything more. When we had both seen all of the picture she put her lips near my ear and whispered, her hot breath strange in my ear, her voice, in a whisper, husky and exciting: "Follow me when I go out and give me a minute to get into the house. Then come on up. Act as though you were a delivery man. It's Apartment 5C."

I followed her out of the movie and east to First Avenue, then stood on the street corner, watching her go into the house. She lived in one of those flat-faced houses made of expensive-looking brick, showing a wallside of casement windows, with a canopy in front and a patrolling doorman wearing a long military overcoat. I waited for a minute then walked into the amber-lighted Tudor lobby as though I lived in the place.

"Where to, sir?" said the elevator man.

"5C, please."

He took me up, looking me over in a way that made me wonder what was on his mind. I pressed the bell marked 5C and she opened the brass peekhole in the door to be certain it was me before she let me in. She had changed to a terrycloth robe, white and clean, and her long yellow hair was loose on her shoulders. Her face showed a lot of strain, as if she'd been questioned by the cops for hours.

"Come on," she said, "we haven't got much time."

It was four in the afternoon, with the late winter sunlight coming almost flat through the lead-framed casement windows. The apartment consisted of one room, with a pair of couches along two of the walls covered with striped material, a table with a lamp in the corner between them. Near the window, in a shaft of sunlight, stood an English carriage with a baby in it, a kid about eighteen months old.

"What is the gag?" I said.

"No gag. Get undressed."

"How about Junior?"

"He's used to it," she said. "He knows his mother is a whore."

I looked at her, ready to get mad.

"You mean you want dough for this?"

"No," she said. "That's not what I mean."

She took off her terrycloth robe and dropped it on one of the beds. All she wore was a satin brassiere and a pair of pants with lace on the edges. She let the pants drop to the floor and bent to pick them up. Then she took off the brassiere. The sun lit her pale skin, showing the fine blonde down on her body.

I took off my clothes. She threw back the covers on one of the beds, cold-blooded as a doctor's nurse getting ready for an operation, or as a hangman, springing the trap for practice. In bed she was like a maniac, screaming and babbling dirty words. In the middle of it the kid cried and she jiggled his carriage to make him stop, then, when he kept on crying, she swore: "Shut up, you little test-tube bastard," and looked at the baby as if she wanted to kill it.

"Hurry up," she said. "Get dressed and get out of here."

I had been in the place for fifteen minutes, twenty at most.

"What's the big rush?"

I looked at the bottles on the liquor table, hoping she would offer me a drink. I stood naked in the center of the room, then walked over and looked at the kid, chucking him under his fat chin.

"Hello, Junior," I said. "How you doin', fat stuff?"

She turned, wearing her robe, looking savage enough to murder me.

"Get out of here!"

I dressed and put on my hat.

"Good-by," I said.

"Good-by."

She closed the door behind me and I heard the lock snap into place. A moment later, standing in the quiet hallway, I heard the water running in the shower bath. I pressed the bell for the elevator.

"How was it?" said the elevator man.

"Fair."

"Yeah," he said. "Only fair."

He was a thin, Greek-looking guy in a uniform that didn't quite fit; not the type the girls would go for.

"Did *you* knock it off?"

"Once. Only once," he said.

Two days later, on a day like spring, I had nothing to do with my time. When she answered the doorbell she was wearing a housewife's apron and had a towel wrapped around her hair. You could hear the motor of the vacuum cleaner buzzing away inside the apartment. In those houses you rent them from the super: one dollar and a half a day.

"Hello, sister. How's about it?"

She looked at me as if she thought I was selling Fuller Brushes or magazine subscriptions.

"How's about what?"

"A little you-know-what," I said.

"Look." The same savage streak showed that I'd touched when I fooled with the kid the other day. "I don't know you. I don't want to know you. If you don't get out of this building I'll call the hallboys and have them put you out."

I put my foot in the door.

"Come on, what's the gag? If it's money, I have some."

"What do you think I am? A whore? Get out of here!"

I took my foot out of the door and she slammed the door in my face. I stood in the hall, trying to figure it, looking at the polished brass peephole countersunk in the steel door.

"You tramp!" I said out loud. "You no good tramp. A fine mother you are."

The elevator man explained.

"She has a husband that got both legs blown off in the war. He stepped on a mine. He can't get to first base. He can't hit a sacrifice fly. He can't even bunt."

"How about the kid?"

"The kid they got out of a test-tube. His idea."

"So?"

"So for about a year she stood it, a hotpants dame like that, just laying up there at night, with the no-legged bastard in the next bed, and the kid howling in the corner, and her tossing around on the mattress, arching her back and going crazy. Then one afternoon she came back here drunk, slopped and swaying, and just went off her nut, laying everything in sight. Even the West Indian fireman from the boiler room got his. Once. No repeats. No refills."

"How does the husband like this?"

The elevator guy shrugged his shoulders.

"What can he do? She's like a nut. A psychiatric case like you see in the movies."

What *could* the chump do?

I walked back to the neighborhood, feeling gypped because all the way down to the blonde's apartment I had been thinking of what it would be like, remembering, more than anything else, more than what had happened in the apartment, the way she had whispered into my ear in the movies, with her voice husky and full of excitement.

I found Gina, sitting on her stoop, holding her schoolbooks on her lap.

"You want to go to the show?"

"Sure, Mattie."

In the movie, sitting in back, I kissed her and put my hand under her dress.

"Don't, Mattie. Please don't."

I had scared her, scared her too much.

"Oh, for Christ's sake," I said. "Anyone would think you had the only one in the world, the way you take care of it."

She started to cry in the dark; I was fed up with her.

"There's lots of other places to get it," I said. "I can get it just like that. From a married dame I know, a blonde, with a crippled husband from the war."

"Honest?"

"Sure, any time I want. It's doing her a favor. Her husband too. I told you he's a cripple."

"Is she good looking?"

"Good looking? I told you she's a *blonde*."

Gina smoothed her dark hair.

"Aw, Mattie, don't talk like that."

We sat and watched the show. In the hallway of Gina's house, making love to her the way she liked it, kissing her and holding the kisses the way she saw them do it in the movies, I knew that I had started her thinking about the blonde with the crippled husband, because she hung on to me and whispered: "Do you love me, Mattie? Honest?"

"Sure, sure I do, kid."

"Don't go with that married woman no more, will you? The blonde one?"

"Okay, kid, if that's the way you want it. But you have to be good to me."

She kissed me and went upstairs. I stood in the pee-smelling hallway, wondering why I hung around.

CHAPTER SIX

In his satin-lined coffin, laid out, old man Tragorna looked less than life-size. His little hands with their broken knuckles were crossed on his chest and the undertaker had freshened his cheeks with rouge, light pink, wrong for his skin, so that the grey face looked greyer. The coffin rested on a pair of horses covered with black velvet, and a pair of tall wax candles burned near the old man's head, casting lights and shadows which moved on his face. There were flowers piled high around the coffin; most important was a large wreath with a gold-lettered purple and black ribbon which read:

FROM THE INTERNATIONAL LONGSHORE-
MEN'S ASSOCIATION

Hunky relatives sat and cried, quietly drinking the old man's brandy, the slivovitz he thought was so good; once in a while a wrinkled old woman got up and kissed the corpse on the cheek.

"I'm sorry, Gina. Honest to Christ I'm sorry."

"Sure, Mattie. I know you are."

The old lady, black and efficient, tried to keep the relatives moving. She had let me come as a friend of Pete's, but I don't think she liked my being there. After a while the undertaker's men came and carried the coffin to the street. Then the pallbearers took it, and carried it through the streets to the church: six Hungarian workingmen, dressed in black broadcloth suits hired from the undertaker, bearing the heavy box on their shoulders, careful of their footing on the sidewalks, where there were scabs of ice and snow, left from the last storm.

In the church, Fliegel's voice, singsong Latin, started Gina crying. But the old lady, kneeling in front, didn't have a tear in her eyes. You got the impression, there in the church, that the old lady was tough and hard all the way through to her bones, tough in a Hunky, European fashion, like a resigned and beaten mule, but tough as steel on top of that with her new American ideas. The priest turned—*"Pater Noster…"*: and the mumble of the Latin continued, people striking their breasts: *"Lamb of God— have mercy on us…"* and the priest on the altar, making the sign of the cross and saying: *"Dona eis requiem."*

When it was over, the six longshoremen carried the coffin down the concrete steps and loaded it into the varnished hearse.

"In Europe," the old lady said, "they go on foot all the way to the grave, a mile, more, maybe, sometimes."

We stood in the cold at the cemetery, watching Tragorna go into his grave. It wasn't snowing but the ground was hard and there were traces of snow on the fresh yellow earth and powdery patches on the grass. The sky was grey and so low you could touch it. It was a hell of a day to be buried. The wind blew at the peoples' clothing, standing at the graveside, crossing themselves, and, at the fringe of the crowd, you heard someone crying loud enough to call attention to herself.

The black undertaker's limousine carried us back to the neighborhood. The old lady sat up straight, with her black veil tucked away from her face.

"What do you want to do, Ma?"

"You know I go working. It's Thursday. I go to Gottlieb's."

"Jesus, Mrs. Tragorna," I said, "wouldn't those kikes understand, at a time like this?"

"They pay me."

She got out of the car and went upstairs to change from her black to her working clothes. I stood beside the car, wondering whether it would be all right to offer the driver a tip. I took out two one-dollar bills and handed them to him.

"Thanks, Mac."

"Mac," I said, "For Christ's sake! Haven't you got any respect?"

He shifted gears and drove away.

"What would you like to do, kid? Anything you say."

She stood with a cold nose, shivering in the winter wind, a black felt heart badly sewn to the sleeve of her cheap plum-colored coat. She thought about it.

"You know what I'd like to do?"

"Just name it."

"I'd like to go over to the West Side. To the docks where the old man works."

"Used to work, you mean."

"Yeah," she said. "That's what I mean."

"What for?"

"I just feel like it."

"Anything you say."

We walked downtown along the West Side waterfront. It was about as friendly as the outside of the moon. A strong wind blew off the River and out in the stream there were chunks of ice that had floated all the way from Albany. The broad-shouldered dray-horses, wrapped in heavy blankets, snorted and blew steam from their noses, scuffing their hooves to keep warm, making sparks fly from the cobbles. There was the funny smell of the docks: of horsepiss and cinnamon, canvas and rope, raw sugar and sassa-fras, of paint from the ships and of fuel oil smoke, and the cold, salt smell of the River, carried on the wind across the ice. A cop wearing black velvet earmuffs, carrying a nightstick in the day-time, because of the waterfront communists, looked us over and said, "Hi, kids."

"I bet he knew we are in love," said Gina, hanging on to my arm.

"Sure. Sure he did," I said.

We walked down to Fifty-eighth Street. There was a big Swedish tramp tied up, with a tow-headed kid on the fo'c's'le head, wearing a white steward's coat, and looking across the water at the City, wishing he was ashore. A longshore gang was unloading the ship, swinging cases out of the holds with big net bags on cranes, bags like the ones women take shopping to the supermarket, except that these were a hundred times larger. The stuff coming out of the ship was cheese, Swedish cheese that smelled through the green planking of the cases, making you a little hungry.

I stood with Gina behind a wire fence, watching them work, Polacks and Wops, with a few Irish and one big colored boy, husky, sweating in the cold, laughing every once in a while in that high-pitched way that scares you. An Irishman was bossing the job, watching the Wops and Bohunks work, a ten-cent cigar in his mouth and a mean look on his pig-eyed face, feeling big because he wore a suit, straw-bossing the other guys.

"Isn't that a lousy way for a man to make a living?"

The way she said that made her sound a hundred years old. I felt sorry for her.

"It sure is."

"Pneumonia," she said.

"What?"

"Pneumonia. It sure works fast. He was getting better and he got pneumonia."

"Didn't they give him penicillin?"

"Yeah. But it didn't work."

"I'm sorry, kid, no kidding."

She nodded, watching the Bohunks, making sure the old man was dead because he wasn't out there on the windy pier, breaking his back with the rest of them.

"How about you and me having a glass of beer and a sandwich, then, maybe, taking in a show? Something to do. Take your mind off it."

"All right, Mattie."

We went into an oystery waterfront place with sawdust on the tiled floor. There was a lot of marble and brass and dark oiled walnut, old-fashioned fixtures that had cost money: decorative polished brass hinges in a fleur-de-lis design, stained glass in the little windows that worked on swivels, high up. An urn of clam broth stood on the bar, steaming and smelling good, and beside the broth was a keg of still ale, tilted to make it run free through the heavy wooden spigot. We sat in a booth with half-doors. Out on the river a liner whistled, a long, low blast, then a short one, pointing her nose downstream, heading for Europe or South America.

"A ball of whiskey and two still ales."

"I'll have whiskey too," she said.

"Two balls and two still ales. And a couple of hams on rye."

When the whiskey came Gina looked at it for a long time before she took a sip. It was her first glass of whiskey. She drank a little and gagged.

"Chase it with the ale," I said.

The ale was sweet, light as wine, served in thin glass goblets. Gina tasted it, then took a good mouthful.

"Watch out, kid, you'll become a lush."

She giggled; warm and happy.

"Like my old lady," I said.

"Oh, Mattie—!"

She giggled again.

"Come on, eat your sandwich."

The ham on rye with lots of mustard killed the taste of the rank straight whiskey. We finished and I paid, then we went back out into the cold.

In the movie, sitting in back, I held her hand, trying to be nice. After a while I saw that she was crying, looking at the screen, tears running down her flat face.

"Don't be like that, kid. We all have to go."

"It's not Pop. He's better off in a way. He was sick. It's my old lady."

"What about her?"

"She'll be worse than ever now. Strict. She got worse with me after Peter was killed."

"You're old enough to know your own mind."

"Yeah. I'm going to be sixteen. Next week."

"I'll take you out New Year's, huh, kid? Celebrate."

"Okay, Mattie."

"That is a date."

After the movie it was dark outside and the streets were wet, sludgy from all the millions of feet that cross Forty-second Street every day. We stopped at Nedick's, on the corner, and ate frankfurters, red hot. I took her home in a taxi. Standing on the stoop she said, "Gee, Mattie, honest you're swell."

Then she kissed me on the mouth and ran inside. I walked up to the corner to see if any of the fellows were there. It was a hell of a way to waste an afternoon, but I figured that it was the least I could do.

Murph sat in a booth in Greene's with a cheap-looking girl who looked familiar.

"Hello, Mattie," he said. "You know Loretta?"

"Hi, Mattie."

I sat and had a beer with them.

"I thought you were married," I said.

She was a scrawny, made-up girl with a large loose mouth.

"I am, but the guy run out on me. I got a kid too."

"So I heard."

"So I'm back in the old neighborhood."

Murph, pleased to have a girl at all, treated her like a movie star.

"She looks good, huh, Matt? Old Loretta looks good."

I nodded.

"She looks fine. Just fine."

I guessed she was looking for another sucker, to replace the one who had had enough. Murph might have been a candidate, but I certainly wasn't, not even for a one-night stand. I paid for the beer and said good-by.

"I'll see you around, Mattie."

She gave me a smile and a long look that was supposed to tell me something.

"Yeah. Sure."

I took the Eighty-sixth Street bus across town and walked up Central Park West to Fred's. I rang the bell but no one answered, so I opened the door and walked in. I heard voices in the living room. I stood in the living-room door for a minute, watching Fred. There were two men with him. Then I coughed and one of the men came to his feet with a gun in his hand.

"Who the hell is that!"

Fred stood up, with a hand in his pocket. Then he recognized me and laughed.

"Hello, kid."

The fellow with the gun said, "Get him out of here." Fred made a motion with his hand: *everything under control.*

"Take it easy, Borntz. Take it easy."

He took me by the arm and we walked down the hall.

"Listen, kid, I have some business with these hoodlums. Do you mind taking a walk?"

"No. But if you need any help I can take that wise guy with the gun."

Fred laughed. "Don't fool yourself. Those are bad boys."

"I could take him, no hands."

"So forget it. Do you need any money?"

"Well, I'm broke. But that's not what I came up to see you about."

"Why not?"

He took out his wallet and gave me some money.

"How is your little girl friend? The Hunky?"

"She's not my girl friend. Just a tramp from the neighborhood."

He laughed, patting his stomach.

"Are you getting it yet?"

"I could, I guess. Any time."

"What is she saving it for?"

I laughed.

"Well, enjoy yourself. And keep your nose clean. I'll be seeing you soon, partner."

"You mean that?"

"What?"

"About being partners."

"Sure. Sure, why not?"

"Because I'm getting sick of hanging around with chumps like Murph and the Wop. And sick of living with the old man. And sick of Rusty, the communist bastard. And sick of Gina, the Hunk tramp. If I hang around like this I'll turn into a small-time slob."

"Take it easy. Take it easy. You got a whole life to live." He put a hand on my shoulder. "I tell you what. Let me finish up what's on the fire. Another week or so, maybe. Then we'll take a little trip. Just the two of us, eh?"

Someone called from the living room: "Come on, Fred, for Christ's sake. We haven't got all night to waste on you."

"Let me poke that bastard."

He pushed me through the door.

"Go on, go on. Have a good time. Get drunk. Get laid. Enjoy life."

"So long, Fred."

"So long, kid."

CHAPTER SEVEN

All that winter Rusty stacked books in the college library after his classes were over. He studied at night, at the round table in the front room if the old man was hacking and the old lady was out, in our bedroom if they were home. I think his studies came hard to him, because at night, when I'd get home, at three or four o'clock in the morning, he would still be at it, trying to burn the eyes from his head, beating the thick books.

He didn't speak to me.

He hadn't said a word to me since the night we broke up the meeting, except, once when I made a remark, to say: *"You're a Jew-baiting fascist bastard."* We shared the room, slept in the same bed, but we didn't speak. Not a word. Not good morning, or good night or hello or good-by.

So I was surprised that night, when I got home after seeing Fred, to have Rusty say: "Hello, Mattie," just as though nothing had happened.

I thought: *why bear a grudge?*

"Hello, Rusty. What's the matter? Do you want to borrow a deuce?"

I pretended to reach for my wallet; he laughed.

"No, it's not that."

He stood up. When Rusty has something earnest to say he stands on his feet. You get the impression that he holds the words in his hand before he lets them go, feeling them, the way a drunk holds coins in his hand before he puts them on the bar.

"We haven't been getting along so well," he said. "It's partly my fault."

"Oh, entirely mine," I said, using a phony accent.

"Anyway, let's call it off."

"Sure," I said. "I never was sore anyway."

We shook hands.

"I'm getting married," he said. He took off his glasses and put them into his pocket. "I want to have her here to dinner."

"Are you crazy?"

"Why?"

"The old lady—"

"She'll be all right. She promised."

"Oh?"

We shook hands again. I went into the kitchen. The old lady sat at the table, sober and reading the paper. I offered her a cigarette.

"No, Mattie. It's a drug. Nicotine's a poison."

"Jesus! Cigarettes too?"

"Yes, Mattie. They're poison."

This was her third trip to the wagon since the accident. After the first attempt Rusty brought her books to read, books that tried to explain drinking. I don't think the old lady, in all her life, ever read anything but the *Daily Mirror* and, occasionally, the *Journal-American,* though the *Journal,* for her, was pretty deep stuff. But she read the books Rusty brought her, a page at a time. Then she showed off to me, quoting the page she had memorized.

"It's a compulsion, Mattie. A compulsion."

All the books were based on the same idea: that drunks don't really like to drink, but do it because they have to. You don't have to read a book to come to that conclusion. All you have to do is glance into a neighborhood ginmill at ten after eight in the morning, and see the drunks along the bar, with the shakes so bad they can't hold a glass, making the barkeep pour an ounce and a half into an eight-ounce beer glass so they can drink it without spilling, coughing and gagging the way they do in order to get the first one down, then coughing more, red in the face, until you think they're going to strangle, finally getting two or three drinks into themselves before they're halfway normal and able to look at the world. Anyone who has seen that doesn't need a book to tell him that drunks do not drink for pleasure. They drink because they can't stand the sight of themselves sober.

I sat down at a kitchen chair, across the table from the old lady.

"I hear Rusty's engaged."

"Yes. And she's a fine girl. My future daughter-in-law."

Sober, on the wagon, she was apt to put on a mother act, based on something she had seen in the movies.

"Have you met her?"

"No. But she's a fine girl. I know that your brother would only pick a fine girl."

I stood up.

"Oh, for God's sake, Ma, get drunk. Sober you make me sick at my stomach."

"That's no way to talk."

"Talk-talk-talk-talk! I'm getting out of here."

I slammed the door going out. In Greene's, sitting by myself, I looked at my clean-shaven face in the mirror and tried to figure out what it was that had made me so mad.

A fine girl, I said to myself, *your brother would only pick a fine girl.*

For a Jew she wasn't a bad-looking girl: dark hair, dark eyes, creamy skin like smooth old marble with deep color showing through it. She was a better-looking girl than I thought Rusty would ever get. But Jew was written all over her.

"And what do you do, Miss Feinberg?" the old lady asked.

She was wearing a silk dress and her hair had just been done. The old man wore a collar and tie; as a special concession to Rusty's girl he left his cap in the bedroom.

"I'm a nurse," said Rusty's girl. "At Bellevue."

"She was in the Army," Rusty said, as if that was something to be proud of.

"Yeah, so was I."

The old man glared at me.

"Argonne," I said, and grinned.

The old lady said, "Was that where you two met? In the Army."

"Oh, no," Feinberg said.

"At the AVC," said Rusty.

"American Veterans Committee," said Feinberg.

We'd promised Rusty, the three of us, to be nice and try to give the impression of a happy family. But it was so long since the family had done anything but fight with one another that, when they couldn't be nasty, no one could think of anything to say.

"She's going to stay on at Bellevue," Rusty said. "Until I make enough from Law."

That was about like saying that she was going to stay until Bellevue retired her on a pension, but I didn't mention it.

"But what if you have some kids? Children?" the old lady asked.

"Oh, we don't plan to have any for a while."

"No," said Rusty. "Not for a while."

The old man pointed at me with his fork.

"If it wasn't for these two bastards, I might amount to something, instead of driving a hack."

"Why, Mr. Dolan," Feinberg said. "What's wrong with driving a taxi?"

"Better off dead."

Rusty saw that it was no use; when dinner was over he said, "Esther and I are going to the show. Would you like to come, Mother?"

She started to say yes, then looked at the old man.

"Oh, no. You two go."

"Matt?"

"No, thanks."

After they were gone the old man took off his coat and sat down in his regular chair, with his thumbs hooked through his heavy suspenders. Then he walked into the bedroom and came back wearing his greasy cap.

"There's a draft in here."

He sat down, looking at me.

"Well, Mattie," he said, "you're no bargain. You're no bargain. But at least you haven't sunk so low that you would stoop to marry a kike."

"Some chance," I said. "I hate the bastards."

"You're a good boy, Mattie," the old lady said.

"He is not a good boy. He's not a Jew-lover, that's all," the old man said.

He stood up, with his thumbs in his galuses, rocking back and forth on his heels, looking at me and the old lady, pleased with himself for some reason.

"Come on, the pair of you," he said. "Let's go out and drink some beer. Us Christians got to stick together."

He took us to Mallin's on Third Avenue, his regular hangout. The juke box has Irish songs: "Kevin Barry," "The Rose of Tralee," "The Soldiers' Song," "Fair Sligo"—all the Old Country crap. The old man ordered beer for us, then went to the juke box and put in a quarter, pressing all the old songs. We sat at a table in the back and listened. There is a backroom at Mallin's, with red-checked tablecloths. The walls are covered with photographs of old Irish heroes and there are two mosaics, red and gold: *Made Entirely from the Cigar Bands of Wealthy Men*. High above your eye level, on top of the women's water closet, stands the stuffed figure of a fox terrier bitch who for years was mascot in Mallin's. There is a copy of the proclamation that established the Provisional Irish Republic, illuminated, full color—IRISHMEN AND IRISHWOMEN.... !!! There is a picture of a very young man, wearing black judicial robes, looking like a Fordham honor graduate: TERENCE McSWINEY, LORD MAYOR OF CORK. And there is a map, the inevitable map, showing the six and the twenty-six counties, with the Border marked in black. Pasted under the map is a notice, lettered by hand with India ink: *Smash the Border!* It is a place to which the diehards come, to drink thick black stout and cry over the Lost Irish Republic and the deviltry of De Valera, to listen to their thirty-year-old songs and to argue, to get sentimental and praise one another, pretending here under the El that they are in Dublin or Cork or Kerry—rebel boyos on the run, ready with a pistol concealed in a trench-coat, ready to die for the dear Old Cause.

The tin-thin voice of an imitator of the late John McCormack came from the lighted, glistening juke box:

> *'Twas not her beau-tee-e-e*
> *Alone that t'won me-e-eeee.*
> *Ah, no, 'twas the TRU-U-th*
> *In her eyes ever dawning…*
> *That made me love Ma-a-reeeee*
> *The Rose of Tra-leeeee*

In the back room there were three or four Irish working-men with their wives, solemnly sitting over glasses of Guinness, taking their time about drinking it. And there was a party of young people, from the swanky houses on First Avenue, women in mink with thin gauge stockings, men with expensive shirts and neckties, young, babbling and being clever. When "The Rose of Tralee" finished and the juke-box mechanism ground down another Irish record, one of the girls in the swanky party said in an accent that cost money: "Freddie, for Christ's sake see if you can't get something else on that bloody machine." My old man and the old Irishmen, jarred by the arrogant high-pitched voice, all turned and glared at the women. Freddie, a faggot, put his hands to his lips: "Brenda, darling! I do declare, you've said the most unfortunate thing. We shall all be discovered dead in an alley."

After that they were quiet and the old man played his songs. Mallin, the proprietor, came over, wearing a starched grey store coat, looking more like a priest than a saloonkeeper.

"Matthew D*oo*-lin! Matthew D*oo*-lin!" He spoke in a rippling Leitrim brogue.

"Hello, P.J."

"Matthew D*oo*-lin," Mallin repeated, "you black Protestant Far Down."

They shook hands.

"An' is *this* the Missis?"

"It't'is."

"A pleasure," said Mallin, rubbing his hands. "An' is *this* young Matthew?"—looking at me.

"It't'is. Say hello to P.J., Matt."

I shook hands with Mallin.

"A fine-looking lad," he said. "Have you noticed at'all, Matthew," he said, "that the lad's a bit like Michael Collins, that you can see on the wall in his officer's uniform?"

He pointed to a picture which showed a young, good-looking fellow, black Irish and self-satisfied, wearing a high-collared soldier's uniform. He was the type that lands here broke, fights to the top and winds up mayor, or maybe the head of a big trade union.

"Michael Collins," said the old man, crossing himself like a Catholic. "God rest his soul."

"A great man," said Mallin.

"The best."

Mallin sent a round of whiskey to the table and the old man bought a second round. Then we drank beer until two o'clock, with the old man feeding nickels into the slide of the juke box, listening, again and again, to "The Soldiers' Song," the Free State national anthem.

Soldiers are we
Whose lives *are pledged to* Ire-*land.*

Over and over and over again, until the rhythm of your blood seemed to have altered to suit the rhythm of the god-damned song.

Soldiers are we
Whose lives *are pledged to* Ire-*land.*

Someone standing at the bar cursed and turned to spit at the juke box. Mallin said, in his little bird voice: "Leave him alone now, Mister, or get out of the place altogether."

That pleased the old man; he pulled at the visor of his cap and looked defiant. He was beginning to get drunk.

On the way home, walking up Third Avenue under the steel pattern of the El, with long, cold shadows on the sidewalk when the street lights were behind us, the old man suddenly squared his shoulders, lifted his head, and started to sing, in a quivery, beer-laden voice that he intended to sound like the voices he had been listening to, on the juke box, back in Mallin's:

Old Mount Joy, one Monday mor-r-nin,
High upon the gallows tre-e-eeee
Kevin Bah-ree, gave his young life
For the CAWSE of liberteeeee-e-e!

And up went his hand, clenched to a fist, as he shouted at the silent El that crouched like an iron caterpillar across the wide dark street:

"UP THE REBELS!!!"

An old cop keeping warm in a doorway lifted his club to his cap and answered: "I-vvvvery toime!"

The old man laughed and kept on singing, songs I'd never heard. The old lady tried to guide him, taking his arm and saying, "Now, Matt," but he pushed her away, and went on singing, singing to himself as if we weren't there.

> *Right proudly high in Dublin Town they flung out the flag of war,*
> *'Twas better to die 'neath an Irish sky than at Suvla or Sud El Bar—*
>
> *'Twas England bade our Wild Geese go that Small Nations might be free*
> *But their lonely graves are by Suvla's waves or the fringe of the Great North Sea.*
>
> *O' had they died by Pearse's side, or had fought with Cathal Brugha,*
> *Their names we'd keep where the Fenians sleep, 'neath the shroud of the Foggy Dew.*

Weird songs, the ones he sang, songs that scared you, repeated in that high keening voice, thin as wire and somehow recalling the voice of a choirboy soprano. There was no stopping his singing and he marched along with his shoulders back, marching along like the bold soldier boy that he mentioned in one of his songs.

Then he tired of singing, stopped on a corner clinging to a lamppost, took off his hat and tried to recite:

> *In Dublin Town they murdered them*
> *Like dogs they shot them down,*
> *God's curse be on you, England!*
> *God strike your London Town!*

And cursed be every Irishman
Alive, and yet to live,
Who'll dare forget the death they died,
Who'll ever dare forgive!
In Kilmainham Jail they murdered them
Who fought for you and me—

He gave it up and stood swaying in the street-lamp light, drunk and fanatic, feeling the gallons of beer he had poured on top of the two whiskeys at Mallin's. He turned sullen, walking home, and I thought that he was finished, but when we got to the house he wouldn't go upstairs to bed, but sat in the hallway on the dirty steps, crying and wiping his face with his cap, streaking his cheeks with the grease from it.

"Think uv it, Mary Grace Dolan," he said, with his old brogue becoming pronounced, "think uv it: ME! A man that was out in Nineteen Six*teen*, out with the boyos and Michael Collins, even if I am an outsider—a black heathen Protestant Far Down, still I fought with the best of the Papist boys, fought right beside the best of them. You don't believe me!" He wiped his face with his cap again. "Ask Mallin! He'll tell you. Ask Finneran! He'll tell you. I was there. They'll tell you. A man that was out in Six*teen*, doin' his bit for the counthry, shedding his heart's blood for Ireland, adjutant of a company that held a sthrong point near the GPO for six hours and forty-three minutes, by the commandant's watch and with foive men killed, God rest their souls. A man loike that, that was a soldier, come to this: droivin' a cab loike a nigger, with his woife gone drunk and his kids gone bad, with wan of 'em nawthin' but a strate-corner loafer and the ither wan marryin' a dirty sheeny. Oi tell you, it's a sin and a shame."

The old lady pulled at the sleeve of his coat.

"Come on, now, Matt. They'll all be hearin' you."

"What if they do?" he said. "What if they do? Who cares what they hear? Papish bastards! Mackerel snatchers! Who cares what they're hearin'?"

But he started up the stairs, walking on all fours like a dog, with the old lady following him. I stood in the hallway, watching.

"Jesus," I called after him, "Jesus, I hate you, you old slob."

PART IV

CHAPTER ONE

NEW YEAR'S EVE, at seven-thirty, Murph and I sat in Greene's, having a few but taking it easy because we knew that something would develop later on. I wore my good grey suit and Murph, for a change, had put on a tie.

"What are you gonna do?"

"I have a date with Gina."

"So let's knock off a heap."

He was suggesting that we borrow a car, without telling the owner about it.

"All right," I said. "But let's get one on the West Side. The last one was too close to the neighborhood."

We rode downtown on the Eighth Avenue subway, to the Village, and waited beside a parking lot near the Sheridan Theater. It was a bad night, chilly, and beginning to rain. Pretty soon a couple drove up in a new-looking Forty-two Buick.

"He has the look," said Murph.

"Yeah."

The woman was wearing a mink coat worth seven thousand dollars. The man was a large, prosperous-looking character wearing an emblem on his watch chain, smoking a rich-smelling cigar. We got a good look at them as he stopped, then made his turn and drove into the parking lot. We followed them across the street and I heard him ask for two loge seats.

"How long does the show last?"

"Five hours, tonight, sir. It's a special. For New Year's Eve."

Murph and I walked back to the lot. A colored boy was sitting on a stool in front of the shanty which housed the cash register. Murph winked and drifted away; I walked up to the dinge.

"Hey, Mac. I lost my ticket. I wonder if I can get my car? Red convertible. Ford."

"Can't get nuthin' without a ticket, mister."

"Yeah, but I left the ticket in the car. By mistake."

He tilted forward on his stool.

"Okay. If it's in the car."

He walked through the lot with me, a full block south, looking for a red Ford convertible. I saw a maroon that looked like a Ford.

"There it is."

I opened the glove compartment and pulled out the seats, pretending to look for the ticket. After a while I said, "Jesus, am I dumb!" I snapped my fingers. "I know where I left it now. It's at the hotel."

"Yeah, boss," said the colored boy. He had to laugh at me for being so stupid.

"Here." I handed him a dollar bill. "Give it a wipe and sweep it out, will you? I'll be back for it later. After midnight."

"Okay, boss. You got to be taken care of."

I walked north two blocks and there sat Murph, at the wheel of the Buick, looking like an automobile ad.

"What a load," he said, patting the wheel, "what a load."

He stepped on the gas and we drove east, across Fourteenth Street to Second Avenue, then uptown.

"Do you think the eightball tumbled?"

"No," I said. "Too dumb. I left him working on a red Ford."

Murph laughed.

"Let's get Gina," I said. "Go through Eighty-fourth."

"What about me?"

"What's the matter with Loretta?"

"Okay."

"But I guess she needs a little lushing up."

"So let's get a bottle."

Murph stopped at a liquor store and I bought two bottles of blend. One I put in the back seat. The other I stashed in the glove compartment.

"One apiece," I said. "Big night."

Murph nodded, letting go of the wheel, then slapped his armpit with his hand, making his fist come up the way Guineas do. His hands were back on the wheel in a second.

"Push-push!"

"Sure."

"Man, can I stand some."

Driving the car made him happy and excited; I think that combat, and being in the islands, had affected Murph's brain. He was childish most of the time.

"Happy Nooooooo Year!" he yelled.

"For Christ's sake, Murph, shut up."

"Frig you."

"You too."

He laughed and squeezed the back of my neck.

"Pals, huh? You and me?"

I got my neck away from him.

"Let's pick up the dames, for God's sake."

Gina was waiting on the stoop. I whistled, leaning out of the car, and she hurried down the steps. We drove through the block and turned uptown, three blocks north, to get Loretta. She and Murph sat in front; Gina and I took the back. It was like riding in a hearse, coasting along in that big car, with the coil springs under the body taking up the shock.

"Where did you get the car?" asked Gina.

"We borried it," said Murph.

"Heh-heh," laughed Loretta. "But does the guy you borried it from know about it? Heh-heh!"

Murph pretended he was going to clout her.

"Yeah, smart stuff. Shut up!"

Loretta laughed, "Heh-heh," and put her arm through Murph's, shifting closer to him in the seat.

"Happy New Year, Mattie."

"You're a little early, kid. Couple of hours yet. Lots of time to celebrate."

I put my arm around her and kissed her. Up in front, Murph was driving with one hand and holding Loretta with the other.

Murph, if he understood nothing else, knew how to drive a car. In City traffic he could outsmart any taxi-driver on the streets, and on the open road he was expert. We climbed the cobbled ramp to the West Side Highway and he moved the speed to fifty, keeping it there, so that the speedometer needle didn't waver, but pointed steady as a rock at the big illuminated 50. He would approach a car that was doing thirty-five, and never break his speed. You would swear that Murph was going to drive right through the guy, but he always found a hole. He knew exactly where the right-hand fender was, and he didn't really take chances; he just seemed to be reckless. Driving fifty or sixty with Murph was safer than driving thirty with the average chump at the wheel. Behind the wheel of a heavy car he looked like a different guy and you would have trusted him to take you anywhere. I guess that he should have been a pilot in the war, but he didn't have the brains to pass the tests.

We crossed the City Line and drove north into Westchester on the Parkway, hitting sixty and seventy, snug and safe in the fast lane, with the southbound cars going into the City bumper to bumper, crawling along, filled with people coming in from the country to hit the hot spots on New Year's Eve. Some of them had started early, and they were half-slopped, blowing horns and ringing cowbells. A girl leaned from the window of a car with her hair streaking back in the breeze, and screamed in a way that might have meant anything. We caught the noise going by, just for an instant, the way you get a high note when you twist the radio dial through the stations.

It was cold outside and drizzling but Murph had the heater on and the powerful wipers clicked away: *Sweep*, SWEEP, *sweep*, SWEEP, so that the piecuts on the windshield were clear. The radio was playing low: Bing Crosby, on a record, singing "The Bells of St. Mary's."

I held Gina close in the darkness and she whispered, "Mattie, this is fun, no kidding."

It was fun, driving through the night. Beyond the shoulders of the four-lane roadway there was nothing but wet darkness, with the occasional lights of a town, dancing in the misty air, far away like the lights of a plane in the sky. Doing sixty and seventy per, passing the peasants as if they were dirt, with all that power under the hood and Murph driving as if he hadn't been born to do anything else, you felt like a king; as if you owned the world.

We swung left across the Parkway and stopped at Reiber's for a drink. I told the waiter to fix Gina's with ginger ale.

"I'll have a beer, Mattie."

"Oh, no, kid." I winked at her. "You're a whiskey drinker. Remember."

"Come awn," said Murph. "This is New Year's."

"Come on, honey," said Loretta. "Have a little fire water."

Loretta had two and Gina had one. The place was beginning to fill up with Westchester people too smart to hit New York on a holiday night. Murph was eager to move, eager to be back at the wheel of the car.

"Let's go."

Back on the road, rolling along, Loretta started to sing.

Without taking his eyes from the road, Murph said, "No singin'."

Loretta giggled and kept it up.

Murph caught her on the cheek with his fingertips and she yipped: "Jeeeee-sus, Murph!"

"No singin'."

Gina whispered to me, "What'd he wanta hit her for? He didn't ought to hit a girl."

"She didn't ought to sing," I said, imitating her voice.

I put my hand on her breast; she didn't move away.

We drove for an hour, then turned off the Parkway and stopped at a place way out in the country, a wooden shack the size of a warehouse, with a neon sign that said:

COME ON INN
BEER—WHISKEY—WINE
!DANCING!

There was a bar and a floor for dancing in a room as big as a barn. No band, but a big juke box. I liked that better. Why have a third-rate band, three or four guys grinding away, sick of the songs and sick of themselves, when, for a nickel, you can take your choice and listen to the best music in the world? And when your girl friend has a request, you don't have to brown-nose a horn player and give him a dollar before he will play the "Anniversary Song." You just walk up, drop in your nickel, press a button, and you're in.

I danced with Gina and once or twice, when we passed the juke box, I held her close, warming her up. When we danced down into the dark I saw her face get scared, then excited, with the colored lights from the juke box on it, her eyes brighter than usual, and that red mouth turned up, with her lips full of blood, bursting almost, wet and shiny where she rubbed her tongue over them. She was sixteen, I remembered, sixteen, and not really jailbait any more. *Maybe this is it, Dolan,* I said to myself, *maybe this is the big night, Bank Night on New Year's Eve.*

I held her tight while we danced, so that her breasts were close against my chest and her legs and thighs, when we moved slowly, couldn't help rubbing against mine. She hung on to me as if she was drowning. She backed away, with that scared look on her face, her eyes half closed, her mouth opened just a little, showing her white teeth, with the lights from the juke, purple and red and yellow and green and violet and orange, playing on her face, and she dancing, dancing really for the first time in her life, with her whole body, her breath and her blood, keeping time to the rhythm of the music.

"Oh, Mattie, I love you. Honest."

The music stopped. We went back to the table and Gina drank another whiskey and ginger ale. It tasted so sweet that the dumb kid hardly knew she was drinking liquor, but from the brightness of her eyes I saw that she felt the two drinks she'd had.

I danced with Loretta, who was getting tight. She socked it, trying to get me excited. She had her eye on me.

"Why do you fool around with Gina? She's a virgin, you know that."

"Maybe I'm in love with the kid."

"Yeah-h-h."

"Why not?"

"You're a boy-lover, Dolan. You're in love with yourself. You queer."

She laughed in a way that made me want to hit her. I marched her back to the table.

"For Christ's sake, Murphy, can't you keep this tramp happy?"

"Sit down, bum," said Murph. He grabbed her arm and twisted it; he had a mean way with women, as if he had something against them, just because they were women.

"Jeeeee-sus, Murph!"

Then his hand crept under the table and into Loretta's lap. She sat there, drinking whiskey while his hand moved, and for all the expression that showed on her face she might as well have been sitting in church.

It was dark in the place, the way people wanted it, with a few colored sidelights and the lights from the juke box, and overhead a chandelier made out of squares of colored glass, turning around and around, so that the colors were splashed on the walls and on the people's faces as they danced. There was a sign over the bar in letters cut out of crepe paper:

HAPPY NEW YEAR
1946-1947

"Happy New Year," Murph read. Then he turned to the rest of us. "What's new about it? What's so happy about it, huh? What's good about it?"

Murph was a beer-drinker; when he drank whiskey he might get moody.

"Take it easy, Murph."

"Frig you."

"Come on, Murph, be nice."

"I'm not nice."

He stood up, knocking over a glass.

"Let's get out of here."

I paid the bill and we went out into the drizzle. Murph drove back to the Parkway. In front of us you could see the fog, through the rain, hugging the concrete pavement, thick as a cloud. But Murph didn't mind. Other cars were inching along, drivers afraid because they couldn't see. Murph switched the foglights on and the amber beams showed up, low, then he stepped on the button and the high beams lit up the fog close to the car, so that the fog curled in the lights like smoke. He stepped on the gas and took it up—sixty—seventy—eighty—ninety, Gina and I in the back seat, leaning forward, watching the clock, with the car swaying on the curves and the tires, once when he touched the brake, complaining like a cat whose tail has been stepped on. When he hit one hundred the needle wavered, hesitated and dropped back: ninety—eighty—seventy-sixty—fifty. We all felt better when Murph had proved it, and decided to relax. He kept it at fifty for ten minutes, then slowed for a ramp and turned off, driving over a back road toward the Hudson River. The road ran along the ridge, through the woods, so that you saw the River through the trees, with boat lights reflected on the water. Murph cut into the woods, driving off the road, into the rough, so that the car staggered in first gear. He drove until he thought he was out of sight from the back road, then stopped and switched off the engine, turned off the lights and tuned in the radio, low.

"Now we'll have some singin'," he said. "And a drink."

He took his bottle from the glove compartment. I opened mine and took a short drink, then passed the bottle to Gina.

"Here, kid. Happy New Year."

"Honest, Mattie, I don't want no more."

"Come on."

She tipped up the bottle and faked. I could see that she was faking, holding her tongue against the mouth of the bottle. I tipped the bottle back and the glass made a noise as it hit her teeth.

"Like that. Take a good belt."

She coughed and the whiskey spilled.

"All right, Mattie. I'll try."

This time I helped her nicely, holding the bottle while she drank. I got about three drinks into her, four or five ounces, before she started to fight. I took the bottle away and she gagged.

"All right, bitch. I'll show you how to drink."

I tipped the bottle up and pretended to take a large drink. After that she took a little more. I saw that she was beginning to get loaded, because her voice thickened and she started to giggle.

"Happy New Year, Mattie. Happy New Year."

She giggled again, like a kid who is proud of having done something wrong.

"Do you love me, Mattie?"

"Sure I do. What do you think?"

Murph and Loretta were moving around. You heard Loretta's high, dirty laugh. I put the bottle on the floor of the car and pulled Gina toward me. I kissed her and unbuttoned the top of her dress. It was a dress that buttoned all the way down the front, and I undid the top buttons and pulled up her brassiere so that her breasts were out, with the light from the radio dial showing them up. The booze had made her reckless and hot; she kissed me back and held me and after a while she wriggled around and unbuttoned the rest of her dress and stripped off her bloomers so that there she was, under me on the seat, stark naked.

"Go ahead, Mattie." Her voice was fuzzy and choked up. "Go ahead and do it to me. I love you, Mattie. Honest I do."

I kept on loving her up, running my hands up and down her body. She drew in her breath through her teeth, making a hissing sound, and in the dim light I could see her face, strained and eager, with her eyes closed.

"Aw, no, kid," I said. "You don't want to."

"Yes I do, Mattie," she said. "Honest I do."

"Okay, but remember—you asked me."

She cried and bled and cried some more. She prayed:

"O Mother of God, protect me. Holy protect and save me. Mother of God, forgive me. Mother of God, forgive and save me."

Afterward, she sat there crying, then she crossed herself. In a little while she got sick and had to get out of the car. She was drunk and when she got out her dress came off, so that she stood there without any clothes, with the rain drizzling down on her, so that her body was wet and the curves showed up the way they do on a wet statue, she bending over naked, being sick. After a while she was through being sick; she put on her dress and got back in the car, turning on the sidelight to fix her face.

"Remember, you asked me," I said.

She didn't say anything.

After a while she said, "Do you still love me, Mattie?"

She looked right at me, scared and still sick, hurting, I guess, from what had been done to her.

What could I say?

"Sure I do," I said. "Naturally."

Murph backed the car out, over the rough ground, swung in an arc and drove ahead until we could see the lights of the avenue. Then he pulled up at the curb and switched off. We got out of the car and stood under a street light while Murph looked at the keys. He locked the doors of the car, then tossed the keys in his hand, looked at them again, and threw them as far away as he could, into the bushes on the other side of the street.

"There, ya mockie bum. Try and find 'em!"

We walked to the avenue and caught a cab, riding as far as the Interborough Subway. We were miles from the neighborhood, somewhere in the wastes of the Bronx, and the streets stretched away into the darkness, block after block of twenty-year-old, jerry-built five-storey apartment houses. The subway is an elevated railway up there and we stood on the cold wooden platform; when a train went past on the other side, going uptown, loaded with drunks, you felt the boards of the platform shudder.

"Why didn't we take the auto back to the fella that owns it?" asked Gina.

Murph looked at her, then slapped her face, not hard, but sharply enough to make her cry.

"Oooooh, you thief!" said Loretta.

He slapped her, harder than he had slapped Gina.

On the subway train, riding down, Gina sat on the wicker seat, staring at the floor of the car.

"What'd'ja let him hit me for, Mattie? Whyn't'ja do something?"

"Aw, you had it coming to you, asking a dumb question like that."

We rode the subway as far down as One Hundred and Twenty-fifth, then got off and took another cab. That way it would be impossible to trace us even if the hack uptown had noticed us especially.

A drunken group on the neighborhood corner, five or six men and women, stood with their arms around one another, singing: "Happy Noo Year to YOU, Happy Noo Year to US." On the other side of York Avenue a young blonde wearing a negligee under a tightly wrapped fur coat, her satin slippers splashed with mud, rang a cowbell and yelled at the street: "Happy *NoooooooOOOOO-OOOOO* Year! Happy *NooooooooOOOOOO* Year!" She must have crawled into bed drunk, slept some of it off, then decided to go out again. She wandered down the short hill, ringing her bell, wishing everyone well, and turned into the ginmill. I wondered, watching her weave, whether the barkeep would serve her.

"You wanta go to Greene's? It's open all night."

"Sure," said Loretta.

"Sure," I said.

But Gina wanted to go home.

"I'll see you later," I said to Murph, and Gina and I walked home, up the hill to Eighty-fourth.

"How do you feel, kid?"

She didn't look at me, just kept on walking, eyes down.

"All right, Mattie."

"Did I hurt you?"

I looked at her, in the yellow light from the street lamp, seeing the panic in her face and understanding that she was ashamed. For some reason I felt good, having hurt her and made her commit what she thought was a mortal sin. *So, bitch,* I thought, glancing at her, walking beside her, *you thought you were going to save it up!*

We stopped, in front of the house, and she looked up into my face.

"Gee, Mattie, I love you. Honest."

Old lady Tragorna leaned out of the window and I pulled back into the shadows, so that she wouldn't see me.

"Come upstairs, you dirty little tramp. Your father just under the ground and you out all night. Come upstairs, before I come and get you."

"Good night, kid."

"Good night, Mattie."

She turned and ran up the stoop, stopped at the top and came back.

"If she lays a hand on me tonight I'm going to hit her back," she said.

Then she went in.

I walked up York, whistling a tune, going into Greene's to finish the night with Murph and Loretta.

CHAPTER TWO

I found the Wop, in Greene's, alone, sitting at the bar with his chin in his hand. It was New Year's Day.

"Let me have the ten you owe me."

He turned, looking green, hungover.

"Are you crazy?"

"No. Give me the sawskie you owe me."

"For what?"

I told him.

"I don't believe you. I always heard she was a good kid."

"She is a good kid. Because she gets laid, does that make her bad?"

"I don't believe you."

"Listen, you Guinea muzzler. Ask Murph."

"I ain't got ten. I got five."

"Give me the fin. You'll owe me the rest."

"Ooh! You Irish shylock!"

But he gave me the five dollars; I put it in my wallet, then bought him a beer.

"You'd better watch out," he said. "Old lady Tragorna is tough."

"I was doing the kid a favor. Now she'll be able to sleep nights."

Murph arrived. He had shaved, to make himself feel better, and his skin looked tender under the layer of dead-white face powder.

"Ooh, that Loretta," he said. "Ooh, that bitch Loretta."

"Shut up, Murphy, and drink a beer."

We sat in a booth. From inside his pants leg, where it was held by the garter, Murph took a long kitchen knife, sharpened away so that the blade was less than half an inch wide, keen as a razor, with a vicious-looking point.

"Look at the shiv!"

"Put it away, Murph."

"Ahhhh-h-h!"

He stuck the point into the table top and left the knife there with the heavy handle quivering.

"Put it away."

I pulled it from the wood and handed it to him. He pretended to lunge at me.

"Yeah-h-h!" he said, when I moved away from the knife, "yella. Mattie Dolan's yella."

"Yella-belly says I owe him a sawskie," said the Wop.

Murph frowned, picking his nails with the knife.

"Yep," he decided. "You do."

I looked at the Wop.

"See, Guinea? Why don't you trust me?"

The Wop put his feet on the booth bench.

"That's all the money I had," he said. "The pound I gave you. I'm sick of being broke all the time, waiting for the lousy twenty bucks. We ought to knock off a place."

"You're crazy," I said.

"Crazy nothing," said Murph. "I know a place we can knock off easy. Like that."

He snapped his fingers.

"Where?" asked the Wop.

"The ginmill, down on Fifty-fourth," said Murph. "In and out, before they know it. And the big thing, there's an incinerator chute on the corner."

"So?"

"So you stash the money in the chute, throw the gun in the sewer. Then, even if they pick you up, what have they got? The guy's word against yours."

"You're crazy, Murph," I said.

"So who asked you? I was talking to the Wop. We know you're yellow."

"You're not kidding," I said. I turned around and pointed to my back. "See it? A yard wide."

"I'd just as soon be in jail as hanging around," said the Wop.

Murph became enthusiastic, proud because it was his idea. He behaved like a movie mobster, glancing at the bar and the whiskey-sour drinkers before he said, one hand raised like a cop's holding traffic, "We'll do it on Saturday. A Saturday night. About three in the morning, just before they close. The till should be loaded. Three grand, maybe four."

I slid out of the booth.

"You guys are crazy. I'll send you cigarettes. Maybe I'll send you a file and a gun, baked into a seven-layer cake."

They were just simple-minded enough to think they could get away with it ... Murph with his silly kitchen-knife shiv, the Wop with his *sick being broke allatime*. I was fed up with them, both of them, tired of hearing them talk, talk, talk, tired of clowning around with them.

I walked out of Greene's and stood on the corner. I took a quarter from my pocket and juggled it in my hand. A little kid in a mackinaw, carrying firewood home to his mother, passed and gave me the Bronx cheer.

"Yeah, bum," he said. "Fifty-two Twenty Club bum."

I reached down and slapped his head. He ran up the block and stood on the sidewalk, jumping up and down and yelling.

"Bum, bum, bum, bum. No-good dirty bum. Dolan is a dirty bum. Dolan is a dirty bum."

I pretended to run after him and he dashed downstairs into a cellar. Kids that age understand the cellars the way a rat understands the walls.

I went back to the corner and tossed the quarter into the air, trying to catch it every time so that the head came up on my palm, doing mental arithmetic to see if it followed the law of averages. Behind me, in the White Cat, a couple of whores were having breakfast and one of them smiled through the window at me. I watched them while I was tossing the coin, and watching them made me think of Gina. What came into my mind was the picture of Gina naked in the rain, being sick from all the whiskey and ginger ale she'd had to drink. *Ah, frig her,* I said to myself, turning away from the smile of the whore; *I was doing the bitch a favor.* Then I saw Fred's Cadillac coming through Eighty-sixth Street, seven thousand dollars' worth of beautiful automobile. Fred leaned across the seat and called.

"What are you doing, kid? Matching yourself?"

I put the quarter away.

"Just hanging around," I said.

The whores in the White Cat brightened up when they saw Fred's car. I turned and thumbed my nose.

"How would you like to see a little sunshine?"

It was a slate-grey day, with streaks of cold yellow in the sky; your thin shadow on the sidewalk was cold and hardly a shadow at all.

"Are you kidding?"

"Would I kid you, Mattie? I'm going to Florida for a week. Miami. How about it?"

"Twist my arm."

He pretended to twist.

"That's enough."

"Okay, hop in."

"I have to get some clothes," I said, wondering what I owned that I could wear in Miami.

"Get in the car," said Fred. "We'll get you some clothes on the road."

The next day in Richmond, Virginia, I tried on a tweed sports jacket, then tried on another.

"I can't make up my mind," I said, studying one of them in the mirror.

"Take 'em both," said Fred.

I picked out some slacks, some shirts and ties and two pairs of shoes.

"How much?" Fred asked.

"Two hundred and thirty dollars, sir." The clerk stood with the jackets and slacks draped over his arm. "Shall I charge it?"

Fred laughed. He took three hundred-dollar bills from his wallet and handed them to the clerk.

"Make one package," he said, "we're taking it all with us."

I got a look at Fred's roll while he paid the clerk. The wallet was filled with C-notes and thousand-dollar bills. On that trip I don't think Fred bought anything more important than a package of cigarettes without breaking a hundred-dollar bill. He had a great belief in the idea that people are impressed with them.

We made it to Florida fast. Driving with Fred in that big car made you feel that you owned the road. In New York State, of course, Fred had a courtesy card and never got a ticket. In the southern states he enjoyed making chumps of the police. We would be rolling along, hitting it up, sixty or seventy miles an hour, going through the roadside villages making dust and scaring chickens, when, a long way behind us we'd hear the rising sound of a motorcycle siren, growing, growing, getting closer. Fred would look into the rear-view mirror, grin and feed the car more gas. Sometimes, at the state line, the cop came to a slow stop, pulled off his cap and slapped his breeches, disgusted. Sometimes he overtook us, came alongside and jerked his glove: *pull over!* When the Law walked slowly up, taking off his goggles and reaching for his book, Fred had a C-note ready in his hand.

"I'm sorry, officer, I lost my head. My boy here has infanteel and I'm trying to get him to Warm Springs before he croaks."

Fred was right in his idea that a C-note encourages people to see things your way. I suppose it is the number printed on the bill: 100.

And Florida, Miami Beach, was still the land of the hundred-dollar bill, a place you could spend any kind of money, hot, cold, or luke-warm. In the sitting room of our suite, Fred passed the bellboy a C-note from his roll.

"We are going to want service. Lots of service," he said.

"Yes, sir."

The bellboy tucked the hundred into the pocket of his tight pants. He was a shrewd, insolent kid who gave you the impression he had heard it all. He pulled the curtains, opened the windows, gave the bowl in the bathroom a wipe and flushed the john just to see if it was working. When he had gone, Fred looked around, rubbing his hands together. Then he took one of his rich cigars out of its glass case and lit it.

"One hundred a day," he said, tossing the burnt match in the basket. "One century a day."

"What's the big idea?"

"Of what?"

"Of tossing the dough around?"

He looked at me, irritated.

"Whose is it? Yours or mine?"

"Gee, yours," I said. "I didn't mean anything."

"So shut up."

Then he grinned and put a hand on my shoulder.

"Forget it, Mattie. Forget it. I was just kidding. Enjoy yourself. Have a good time. There'll be enough left to stake you."

"Aw, that wasn't what I meant."

"Sure it was. Is that wrong? You should look out for yourself. But don't try to kid me. You and I, we kid the peasants. Not one another."

I laughed. He was in a good mood again.

"Now let's get some booze up here. And some women."

He sat down and picked up the phone, an old-fashioned hand-set. He held both pieces in one hand in a way I tried to figure out.

"Room service."

While he was waiting he smiled at me and said, "Did you knock it off? The little Polack?"

"Huh?"

"The Polack kid. The cherry. Did you knock it off?"

"Oh. Gina. She's a Hunky."

"Since when has a Hunky got a different kind? Did you knock it off?"

I looked through the wide open windows at the sand and the blue ocean, reaching all the way to Spain. There were people on the beach, men and women, stretched out, taking the shade from striped umbrellas. I guessed there was a billion dollars, on the hoof, resting on that little stretch of clean sand I could see from the window.

"Sure," I said. "Sure I did. What do you think I am? A chump?"

He licked his cigar in a way that made you know what he meant.

"Was it any good?"

I turned away.

"It was all right."

I could hardly remember what had happened in the car. What I remembered was the damned kid, standing in the rain without any clothes, bending over and being sick, and with that picture, like a double exposure, I kept seeing the face of the whore who had smiled at me through the White Cat window, and, cutting across that, the face of the mean bitch old lady, screaming at the street from the fifth-floor window: "Come on up, you tramp, come up!"

"Sure," I said. "It was all right. I was doing the kid a favor."

He laughed.

"Hot pants, no conscience."

"That's right, Fred," I said.

He finished with room service, hung up, and called another number.

"Fred, honey. Your old pal Fred from the Big Town."

I heard him laugh into the phone.

"And a friend," he said. "I have a pal with me."

He put the phone away, then rubbed his hands together.

"Cheer up, kid," he said. "Whiskey coming. Women coming. Champagne coming. Cheer up. You're not the only guy that ever copped a cherry."

"Aw, I wasn't even thinking of that. What do I care about that?"

"Don't get sore. I was just clowning."

I looked out at the ocean, over the top of a palm tree that was one of a double file planted along the hotel drive. The sun was bright, warm as summer; I remembered the cold corner in front of the White Cat, the cold, damp floor in Greene's, the chill winter drizzle on New Year's Eve, the onionskin shadow your body made on the ice-pocked New York winter sidewalk.

"Sure, Fred," I said. "Anything you say. Whatever you say."

The next morning, in the high, paneled dining room, I sat opposite Fred, wearing one of my new sports coats, looking over the rich crowd while a pair of waiters served our breakfast. The way they served two fried eggs made the eggs as impressive as solid gold. The dining room was filling up with two kinds of people. There were thin, hawk-faced men who looked like bankers, with their half-starved, pop-eyed women, scrawny and tanned and peevish because they breakfasted on melba toast and black coffee while they watched young, good-looking girls eating eggs and toast and jam. That was real, semi-permanent money. Then there were heavier, better-natured guys, dressed in clothes that were sharper than those worn by the banker-type people, having breakfast with women who might have been their wives but who, nevertheless, had been bought and paid for—the way Fred paid for the girls last night. They were the hundred-dollar-bill boys, from the black, the white and the grey markets, boys who had started with a little stake, used their brains, and run it up. They looked different from the bankers and brokers, and the bankers and brokers didn't want them around, but here they were, in the same hotel, using the same kind of money.

"See that guy?" asked Fred. "The one wearing the green coat?"

"You mean the one with the loose-mouthed blonde?"

Fred nodded.

"He started the war with a hamburger stand. You couldn't buy him today for less than three million bucks."

"Meat?"

"Meat, gas, cigarettes, scotch. He's dealing in cars now. He's an operator. A middleman."

"Smart."

"You bet he's smart. All legal. All clean. No Atlanta for a boy like that."

He pointed with his fork.

"That guy, the thin one, with the schoolteacher wife, was running a two-bit factory making timers for automobiles. Today you couldn't touch him under ten million dollars."

"What was his angle?"

"He bought a general. A two-star general."

I laughed.

Fred pointed them out to me, dozens of them, in every business, clothing, liquor, cars, machinery—men who had seen the opportunity and hit the jackpot during the war. when money was free, rolling down the gutters of towns where the war industries mushroomed.

"All legitimate businessmen," Fred said. "And that should be a lesson to you."

"What do you mean?"

"Be a petty crook and what does it get you? Nothing. A long time to think it over, a long, long time to wear out your fingernails, picking jute in the jute mill, in the Old Homestead, up the River. Be a mugg like me, half on the level, and you're better off. You don't have to worry about the cops unless you were born unlucky. It's your friends you worry about in my kind of business. But the best thing to he is a businessman—steal legal, steal like a gentleman, and who can touch you? Even if they catch you, in that class, what does it cost you? Look at Lustig. He steals a million from Mr. Whiskers. If you did it you'd get thirty years. If I did it, I'd get the same. But Lustig? A couple of years, maybe less, and he's out. Look at Whitney. Look at all of them. Steal big, steal legal. That's the secret of legitimate business—knowing how to steal without breaking any laws."

I nodded, staring at the man who had run a hamburger stand into three million dollars. He was ten, twelve years older than I: twenty-nine, thirty, thirty-one at most, a heavy man with tight-stretched skin and lots of muscles that showed when he moved, under the fabric of his gabardine coat. You knew that he was the kind who always won in the crap games, won without loading the dice, because he had bluff and enough money to ride him past the breaking point. I wondered how he had avoided the draft, then noticed that three of his fingers were missing. I laughed because it occurred to me that the son-of-a-bitch might have done it himself, just to avoid the Army. I thought of Rusty, going to law school, then going out into the world to try to compete with a guy like that, who had more law in his tight-stretched fists than Rusty could learn in a lifetime.

Fred poured more coffee and tipped a dot of rich cream into it.

"These guys, the ones you see, could have done it without a war. The war just made it that much easier. But they would have done it anyway. They're wise boys, smart boys, boys that always have an angle."

He took a sip of his coffee and said, as if he had just remembered it, "Of course they are also tough boys. They would probably kill you just as soon as look at you, if they were sure of not being caught. They never do things that people get caught at."

We got up from the breakfast table, with waiters pulling back our chairs, and walked out into the sun, under the palms, walking over the palm-pattern the sun made on the flagstoned walk, full of food, full of ideas, glad to be here, away from the City.

Miami was the place for spenders and we did everything right: beach, racetrack, whiskey, women.

At the track, watching them run, Fred used money as if he wanted to get rid of it. He was like the man in the movie who had to spend a million in a month. He bet five hundred on a race, tearing the tickets into confetti and letting the pieces fall to the boards at his feet, watching the winded horses rein up and walk slowly away from the race, bright colored jockeys talking to them, patting and stroking their long necks.

"You know, Mattie, I've dropped a couple of hundred grand on the gee-gees in the course of a lifetime, but I've hardly ever seen them run. Not more than a dozen times."

"You're watching them now," I said.

"Yeah. I'm watching them now all right."

There was something on his mind, something bothering him. He focused the glasses on the horse he was backing, waiting for the barrier to come up. They got away and he followed them around, then let the glasses rest on his chest, took out the ticket and tore it up.

"Come on, kid. This bores me."

We walked through the alley at the foot of the stands and passed out through the masonry gate. A thin Italian with patent-leather eyes, wearing a white gabardine suit, touched Fred's arm. Fred brushed off the arm.

"Hello, Rico."

"Getting some sun?"

"That's right."

"Get a lot of it," said Rico. "Get enough to last you for a long time."

"Get away from me," said Fred. "Get away from me, smalltimer."

We heard Rico laugh as we walked away from him.

"Come on, kid. Let's go to the room. Get some booze. Booze and dames. All you want. Anything you want."

Late that night after everyone had gone I woke up hearing Fred's voice in the sitting room, talking over the phone. I walked to the door and stood watching him, sitting in his bathrobe, with the shambles of the party around him—glasses and bottles, champagne bottles, an ice bucket and someone's handkerchief, stained with bright red lipstick.

"I'm too old to change for a cheap Guinea muzzler."

There was a long, dead silence, with no sound except the buzz of the receiver in Fred's hand, the *tick*-tock of the marble clock, and the *swish, swish, swish* of the ocean kissing the sands of the beach outside.

"If it comes, it comes. Am I kicking?"

I heard the other end hang up, but Fred sat with the phone in his hands. After a moment the operator's voice came through the diaphragm, thin as a file working on brass: *"Hello, sir, hello, sir."*

"Is anything wrong, Fred?" I asked, standing in the doorway in my pajamas.

He looked up then, looked at the phone and put it back on the hook.

"Wrong?"

"Yes." I asked, "Is anything wrong?"

"Nah-h. Hell no. What's wrong with you?"

He pretended to hang one on my chin.

"Go to bed, kid. Go to bed."

A day or two later, on the beach, watching the girls in their midriff suits, I thought of Gina, standing in the rain, drunk and sick with nothing on.

"What's so good about a virgin?"

Fred laughed.

"It's supposed to make you feel big. The way Guinea hunters feel big when they go out and kill a deer. Just, you know, something to do to show you can do it."

I understood what he meant.

"You have to remember this, though."

"What?" I said.

"They're only virgins the first time. After that it's just push, push."

I nodded.

"But, they say, if you want the dame you've got her for life. They never forget the first guy."

"Jesus, I don't want this tramp," I said.

For a second, resting on the beach, I was afraid, thinking that Gina might have told her mother or the priest from St. Michael's. I stood up, rubbing my chest.

"I'm going in. You coming?"

"No, kid, I'll stay here. Snooze in the sun."

I swam out, fighting the surf. The water felt crisp and good on my skin. When I came back Fred was asleep and I stood watching him, then let water drip on his back from my fingers. He jumped and woke up; I saw that he was scared.

"Jesus Christ, kid! Jesus Christ! What did you want to do that for?"

"Jesus, I'm sorry."

Back in the suite he drank scotch, standing at the window, looking at the ocean.

"Let's get out of here," he said. "Let's get out of here tonight."

"Whatever you say."

Driving the smooth, powerful car seemed to be good for his nerves. We loafed along, at forty and fifty. One day away from Miami he was laughing again, cracking jokes and kidding me.

"How much did the girls cost?" I asked. "The ones we had in Miami?"

"A hundred a platter," he said, not taking his eyes from the road.

"What!"

"That's right."

We rode along through Georgia, red clay banks on the sides of the concrete highway, scruffy towns with sagging porches, niggers, niggers, niggers, and coca-cola signs. I knew this country, or country just like it.

"I never paid for it," I said.

"That's where you're wrong. You always paid, except that you didn't know it."

"How do you figure?"

"You'll see. You'll see."

I watched the white line in the center of the slab, reaching ahead of us, a thousand miles north. The car still smelt new and the hood gleamed in the sun; it had been polished in Miami. Fred liked a clean-looking car.

"Fred?"

"Yeah."

"If I get a stake, a saloon, say, fifteen or twenty grand, do you think I've got enough on the ball to run it up? All the way up?"

He looked at me, then looked away, at the white stripe in the center of the road.

"You've got your mind set on that ginmill, haven't you, kid?"

"Sure. It would be a good start for me."

He nodded.

"Why not? Why not?"

"I want to be a success," I said. "All I need is a break."

He nodded again.

"That's right."

Outside of Baltimore Fred said, "I'm tired of driving this jalopy. How would you like to fly to New York?"

"Gee, Fred, I'll drive."

"No. I'm sick of the car."

"You must be crazy."

"It's my car, isn't it?"

"Well, sure, but—"

"Then shut up."

We drove into Baltimore, down those streets with thousands of houses, one just like the other, and thousands of white marble stoops, scrubbed as clean as a kitchen table. We rolled up the ramp into a big garage. When the colored boy handed Fred the check, Fred said, "How much for a month, black boy?"

"Foh'ty-two dollah."

Fred handed him fifty.

"Keep the change, black boy."

"Yes, sah!"

Outside the garage Fred held the ticket in his hand, looking at it. Then he handed it to me.

"Hang onto this for me, kid. Just stick it in your wallet and forget it."

At LaGuardia Field we got into a cab and drove through Queens, across the Triborough Bridge, into the City. Fred didn't say anything until we dropped off the Bridge, down the ramp to the East River Drive.

"Listen, kid." He spoke slowly, looking out the window, at the River passing on our left side. "I may be going out of town for a while. Suppose I want to get in touch with you. By mail. Where's the best place?"

"The house?"

"No. Somewhere else."

"How about Greene's? On the corner."

"Do they know you well?"

"Sure."

He wrote the name on a piece of paper: Greene's Bar and Grill, with the address on York Avenue.

"You may hear from me, kid, before I see you again."

"Okay."

He touched my chin with his fist.

"Don't let the little Hunky hook you. You'll wind up wearing a ball and chain, like any sucker."

"Don't worry. I'm too smart to be hooked."

At the corner I got out and shook hands through the cab window. He gave me a hundred the way he always did.

"So long, Fred."

"Good-by, kid."

I went into Greene's with the. hundred-dollar bill in my hand. Murph and the Wop were at the bar, sitting in front, near the window. A bunch of neighborhood kids were in the back, playing the juke box and making noise. Greene would throw them out soon.

"Look at HIM!" said Murph, arms around me, halfshot. "Look at the sunburn on Mattie."

"Florida," I said. "Florida. Two weeks in Florida."

"Yeah, Florida," said the Wop. "He's been hidin' in the barber, under a sunlamp."

"Shut up," said Murph. "He's been to Florida. He says."

I put the money on the bar.

"Three glasses of scotch whiskey. And one for yourself makes four."

The bartender looked at me and the money, winked and reached for the bottle. He made change from the strong box they kept in the safe under the bar.

"A little luck on the races, sah?" He snapped the bills as he counted them out. "Did you hit them at Hialeah?"

"A little. Just a little," I said.

"How about a touch?" said the Wop.

"Yeah, we're your buddies," said Murph.

I gave them each ten dollars.

"I expected to find you both rich. You and your stickup. You two phonies."

Murph looked around; he made it a secret when he told you the time.

"We're gonna do it tomorrow. No kidding."

"Yeah," said the Wop.

The Wop put his ten dollars away; Murph rapped on the bar for a drink.

"Your girl friend was in here looking for you," he said.

"I haven't got any girl friend."

"Your twist then. Your tramp. Gina, you dope."

"Was she *here*? In the ginmill?"

"Couple of times. Looking for you."

"Well whaddyaknow? Some of them just can't get enough."

"Heh-heh-heh!" laughed the Wop.

I walked down York to Eighty-fourth, turned the corner and saw Gina, playing potsie with a half-dozen kids, hopping the chalk-drawn squares on the sidewalk, in the light of the yellow street lamp.

"What's this? Your second childhood?"

"Mattie!"

"Who do you think? The Little Lord Jesus?"

"Mattie, you scared me."

"Come on."

She took my arm. The kids stood over the potsie box, watching us as we walked away. When we were halfway down the block we heard them, chanting: *"Gina's got a fellah! Gina's got a fellah!"*

"What's the matter with you? Playing potsie in the street."

"Aw, there wasn't anybody around."

"Playing potsie!"

"I see you play stickball."

"That's different."

We sat on the seawall, looking at the River.

"What did your old lady do?" I asked. "The other night? New Year's?"

"She locked me up in the room four days."

"Did she see me?"

She shook her head.

"I told her one of the kids from school. She thinks I go mostly with a kid from school."

I gave her a cigarette. We sat smoking, in the dark, listening to the noise of a bell-buoy at the edge of the deepwater channel. I hadn't lost the sense of movement, of traveling, of being away.

"Gee, Mattie, I missed you."

"Yeah. Yeah, I missed you."

I was waiting for her to say something about what had happened to her in the car. I hoped she would say something, blame me, so I could blast her and get rid of her. But she didn't say anything. She turned her head so that her face showed softly in the light; I couldn't help thinking of the girls in Miami, the hundred-dollar whore, and of how different this kid looked, of how I could get to her, own her, run her, be the boss, in a way I could never get to them.

"Were you really in Miami?"

"That's right."

"What was it like?"

"Warm. Warm as summer is here."

"You got a tan."

"Yeah. From the sun."

"What were the girls like?"

"All kinds."

"Pretty?"

"*What's the matter with you!* I told you I was on business. With my uncle."

"No, you didn't."

"I did so."

You couldn't talk to Gina; the only way we could communicate was by making love. I kissed her.

"Gee, Mattie, I missed you. After what happened, you know. I missed you."

"Are you sore?"

"No. No, Mattie, I'm not sore."

There is a row of remodeled tenements near the river on Eighty-sixth.

"Come on. Let's go in the hallway."

"No. I don't want to."

"Come on!"

There was a baby carriage parked behind the stairway. I rolled it out and we moved into the dark, slant place under the stairs. You could smell the dust from the hall carpet.

I kissed her.

"Come on, Gina, come on."

"Aw, Mattie."

"Come on. How about the other night, in the car?"

"I'm scared, Mattie. You'll hurt me."

"I won't hurt you. Come on."

"Somebody coming!"

"Shhhhhhh! For Christ's sake, keep quiet!"

I heard a door open and close, then a guy said. "What the hell are you doing here?" and he kicked me, hard, in the backside.

"You god-damned kids," he said, "making a whorehouse out of the hallway. Every night I have to chase you."

I got to my feet and looked at him. He had expected a kid, fourteen or fifteen. I moved toward him and he stepped back. Then I hit him, hard enough to hurt.

"Come on, let's go!"

I grabbed Gina's wrist and pulled her to her feet. We went through the doorway fast, down the stoop and west along the street, running until we reached the corner at York. The man stood on the landing of the stoop, looking up and down the street. After a while he turned and went back into the house. I took Gina's arm; I didn't care about making love to her any more.

"Come on, bitch. I'll take you home."

When I got to the apartment the old man snarled at me: "Where the hell have you been?"

"To Florida, Miami. Can't you see the sunburn?"

"Florida, is it? You no-good bum."

"Aw, lay off it, Pop. Don't you think a person gets sick of listening to it?"

"I get sick of the sight of you. Don't think you were missed."

"So what are you bitching?"

He got up, with his galuses trailing, and walked to the kitchen. When he came back he held a letter in his hands, in a long, franked government envelope. A brown ring showed on the paper where a coffeecup had rested.

"The United States is interested in your whereabouts," he said, taking the letter out of the envelope.

"Is that letter addressed to me?"

I took a step toward him.

"It's addressed to Matthew Dolan."

"That's me."

"Well it's me too."

I took the letter out of his hands and read it.

He laughed.

"So they want you to go to work, Mr. Florida, instead of living off the taxpayers in the Fifty-two Twenty Club."

The letter was from the government employment service, a form:—*please call in reference to—*. I tore it up and dropped the pieces on the floor.

"If they want me bad enough they can come and get me. I'm not taking any crummy job for thirty-five a week."

"Maybe this one pays forty."

"Oh, go to hell!" I said. "Go straight to hell."

The big-shot feeling of Florida was gone, lost in the stink of the lousy apartment and the evil grin on the old man's face. The optimism I had felt with Fred, riding home in the heavy car, turned sour, sour as piss. I felt like another neighborhood slob, good for nothing but hanging around.

"GO TO HELL, YOU OLD BASTARD!" I yelled. "Go straight to bloody hell."

CHAPTER THREE

Saturday night—Sunday morning, rather, because it was half-past two, they sat in a booth, talking it over, Murph's red face redder than ever, the Wop looking nervous and probably scared. I saw them put their heads together, scheming, Murph drawing a diagram with his fingertip in the spilled beer on the table. They checked the time with the clock on the wall, then got up and drank a whiskey at the bar. Murph winked and touched me as they went out. I made a circle with my thumb and forefinger: *Good luck!*

From my barstool near the window I watched them board the big red bus. When the bus began to drag uphill I went into the street and flagged the cab that stood in the feed line, down the block. He flashed his toplights on and pulled up beside me.

"Casey's on Third."

"O-kay."

At the first red light I watched him write the call on his card. At Casey's I gave him a fifty-cent tip, pretending to be comfortably lushed. Then I looked at my watch and said, "Not much time to drink."

"What time you got?"

"Two-thirty."

He fixed his watch and drove away. I was five minutes up. I wrote his name on a piece of paper. Gresham, a neighborhood hack. He would remember me because of the half-dollar tip and he would have the time on his card. I saw an empty cab cut between the El pillars and flagged him down.

"First and Fifty-fourth," I said.

I stood in a deep store doorway across the street from the bar and grill they intended to stick up. It was a warm winter night, part of a three-day thaw. There were winter stars in the sky, brilliant and winking even through the City haze. There were no cars moving on the street, but lots of them parked beside the curbstones up and down First Avenue. The saloon was still pretty busy, serving the drunks who hated to go home; there were a dozen men and women sitting on chromium stools at the bar, and behind the bar worked a busy Dutchman wearing a white monkey jacket.

Murph and the Wop got off the bus, the Wop holding a black bag under his arm in the folds of his coat. They stopped and seemed to hesitate; I guessed that the Wop was turning yellow. Then Murph. grabbed his arm and they went into the place.

Murph had his gun out, backing the people against the wall. The Wop leaped across the bar and I saw him filling his black bag. Then Murph waved his gun and drove the people through the trapdoor, down the cellar stairs. A moment later they were in the street. I saw the Wop put the money bag into the incinerator chute. He joined Murph on the corner just as the radio car came through the block, with a cop on the running board holding a gun. Murph started to throw his gun into the sewer as they had planned, changed his mind and shot at the cop. He and the Wop ran west, with the cops shooting at them. They ducked into a cellar stairway and the cops went after them. I crossed the street fast, got the bag from the incinerator chute, and kept on walking to Sutton Place. Behind me, on First Avenue, I heard the chatter of the crowd that gathered in front of the bar, drawn by the shooting. A cab stood on the corner of Sutton and Fifty-fourth.

"Casey's, on Third."

"Okay, Mac."

At Casey's I ordered Johnnie Walker Black Label and paid with a twenty-dollar bill. It was a quarter to three and I stayed until the bar closed, knowing that the bartender would remember the twenty and the Black Label, and probably back up the fact that I had been in. Casey's from half-past two until they closed.

In the toilet, at home, I counted the money. Three hundred and twenty-three dollars. I was so mad that I held the bills in my hand and spat at them, sitting on the bowl. That damn fool Murph and his *three grand, may be four.* I flattened the money and put it into an envelope. The checks I tore into little pieces and burned in the bowl. It took about an hour. In the morning I got up early and carried the bag to the River, weighting it with stones before I threw it in. Then I had coffee at the White Cat and went home to hide the money. There wasn't enough to put in the bank.

"What did you say, Mattie?"

It was the old lady, calling from the kitchen.

"Nothing, Ma. Nothing at all."

I hid the money under the floor of the closet, then went into the kitchen. I took ten dollars from my wallet and dropped them on the table in front of her.

"Don't say I never gave you anything, Ma."

"Thanks, Mattie," she said. "Thanks."

At least I had taught her to say thanks and not to act as if it came from heaven.

CHAPTER FOUR

Miss Webber came up the block, swinging her arms like an English sergeant. It was a bright winter day, cold in the shade of the sidestreets but warm in the sun on the avenue. I leaned against the glass front of the White Cat Sandwich Shop. It was a few days after the boys had been caught for sticking up the bar and grill.

"Dolan, I want to see you!"

She talked just the way she walked: *Take that soldier's name!*

"You're looking at me, lady."

"I want to talk to you."

"Talk," I said. "It's free."

She looked up and down the street.

"Isn't there some place we can sit?"

I nodded at the ginmill.

"How about Greene's, up the block?"

In the booth she took off her gloves and put them on top of her saddle-leather bag. The bag was worn to a high polish at the bottom where her hand held it. All of her clothes were British looking; they reminded me of military equipment—leather and brass and long-wearing cloth. The bartender came to the booth, wiping his hands on his apron.

"Bourbon," she said. "What do you have?"

"Kentucky Tavern, Old Forester—most anything you want, lady."

"I. W. Harper?"

"Sure."

She did know something about whiskey.

"A double of Harper," she said. "Give this young man a beer."

"You want a beer, Mattie?"

"I'll have what she's having."

We sat in the booth, squared off. There was tension of the kind you feel waiting for the bell to start the fight.

"Are you laying Gina Tragorna?"

The whiskey stopped, on the way to my mouth.

"What's that to you?"

"Are you?"

"No."

I tasted the whiskey, then said, "I don't see much of her any more. I used to go with her, when I was in school, love her up a little, but that's all. She goes with some kid, now, some kid from school. I hear she goes with men, too."

Webber looked at me, not believing me.

"She quit coming to the Newman Club. Her mother came to school to see me. It's hard for the mother, working the way she does."

"She's too strict."

"She wants the child to amount to something. And Gina's not too bright. She's a year behind in school."

"She's a moron. She ought to be somebody's housemaid."

"She's not a moron. She's just slow. And her mother wants her to be someone."

"By going to school?"

I finished the whiskey and rapped on the table with the glass. The bartender brought more.

"You make me sick, you and your school. All your life you've been going to school. And what have you got? Nothing. A lousy one-room apartment in one of those flossie houses made out of trick brick. All front. All brass. Nothing, really, but four walls and a pair of doormen. All day you go to school and wrestle with the kids. At night you come home, smelling of chalk, and make a meal in your little kitchen, so small you burn your ass if you turn around. You eat dinner all by yourself, then wash the dishes, taking your time, shining them up, just so you'll have something to do. Then you turn on the radio, and then you turn it off, because you don't like radio except for concerts and commentators. Then you try, maybe, to read a book, but you've read all the books there are, all the books that have ever been printed. You've read so many books that the sight of the print on the page makes you want to be sick in the john. So you sit there, by yourself, looking at those four walls and the clean dishes piled in the sink. Everything neat, everything clean, because who is around to get anything dirty? You sit there, all alone. Outside, in the streets, the City is going on around you: people drinking and making love, sitting in bars and riding cabs, fighting, stealing, enjoying themselves. You sit there, all by yourself, until you decide that if you sit there much longer you'll walk to the window and take a dive—ten stories down to the concrete courtyard. Just so you won't have to look at the same color paint any more. You go to the window and pull back the curtain and look out across the courtyard, into other people's windows, maybe a husband kissing his wife, or a woman playing with one of her kids. After a while you can't stand it. You put on your hat and coat and take a taxi to some saloon where you aren't known. You sit at the bar on a high stool, drinking the same bonded bourbon you have in front of you now, sitting there till the place closes, hoping one of the middle-aged lushes will drink himself blind enough to make a pass, but even if he did you wouldn't have the nerve to take him home to bed with you. Because you are scared—scared stiff, hiding out in school all day, wetnursing a bunch of kids, looking for a place to hide at night."

I stopped and took a breath; I had made all this up, guessing from what I saw before me, but I knew, from the look on her face, that I wasn't wrong about much.

"—and that's the way you go along, year after year after year after year, getting older, getting greyer, drying up like a puddle of water left in the bright summer sun, until at the end there's nothing but mud, dried up, dried up mud, bone dry soon, because you are going to be finished up, done with and swept away. And nobody, no one at all, except maybe one of the Sisters you go to visit on Sunday afternoons, will know or care, give a god damn, whether you live, die or evaporate."

"That's enough, Dolan," she said. "That's enough."

"Sure. That's enough. But it's true, all of it. And that's the reason you're sticking your nose into my business. Because you have nothing else to do. You people—all alike: schoolteachers, Army officers, slobs like my old man, Navy guys, strawbosses working for fifty a week, trying to make *you* sweat for forty—all alike, all with the same idea: to make everybody else as miserable as you are yourselves. You just want company."

She stood up, sliding from the booth, and stood in the aisle, buttoning her coat at the neck. Then she opened her purse and took out money.

"I'll take care of the bill," I said. "This is my treat. From me to you."

"I'll pay for mine."

She went to the bar and paid for her drinks. I got up and leaned against the bar, watching her through the winter-steamed window, standing on the corner blown by the wind, scanning the long, grey, empty street, looking for a cab that would carry her home.

"Friend of yours?" the bartender asked.

I watched her get into the cab without looking back at Greene's.

"A schoolteacher. From John Jay, where I used to play football."

He glanced through the window.

"She looks like a lady cop."

Then he poured a drink from the green-labeled bottle of I. W. Harper.

"Have one on the house, Mattie. You must be lonesome without your pals."

"I get along," I said. "They were chumps, the pair of them, sure losers."

"Yeah." He tapped his forehead. "That Murphy's a little off in the top storey."

"Murph's all right."

"Sure, sure." Eager to agree. "They're both good kids. Neighborhood kids. They just made a mistake, that's all. Vincie Rhattigen was in this morning. He's gonna try to get them out on bail."

"Yeah?"

"Sure. He woulda got it, but they didn't find the money yet. They think the kids hid it. So they're gonna make 'em sit for a while, down in the Tombs until they loosen up."

I finished the bourbon and said good-by.

At the White Cat I ate two hamburgers, little ones on soft rolls, looking through the window, watching the snow begin to come down in big flakes like feathers that melted when they hit the pavement. After a while it began to stick and pretty soon the street and sidewalk were covered with thin white fur, except at the manholes and cellar holes where the heat melted the snow. It was a long, dull afternoon, lonely, looking at the snow, keeping warm in the sandwich shop.

At half-past three I walked down to Eighty-fourth and stood leaning against the stoop in the snow, waiting for Gina to come home from school. When she came I caught her wrist and twisted hard enough to hurt her.

"What did you tell that bastard Webber?"

"Gee, Mattie, you hurt!"

"What did you say to that old bag? Come on, tell me, or I'll hurt you worse."

She looked up, crying, with flakes of snow dropping on her cheeks and sticking to her hair, then melting, so that the drops looked like glass beads against her black hair.

"Honest, Mattie, nothin'. I didn't say nothin'."

She was telling the truth; I let go of her wrist and she rubbed the red ring my hand had left on her skin.

"Okay, kid. Forget it. Let's go upstairs."

"To the *house?*"

"Sure, why not? Your old lady won't be home till eight. What she don't know won't hurt her."

"Suppose she finds out?"

"Don't be a chump. She won't find out."

"Aw, Mattie—"

"Come on!"

I followed her up the steep stairway, built around an open well. The Tragorna apartment was on the top floor. I stood on the landing and looked down, five storeys to the tiled landing, the slant of the railings repeating itself like a master sergeant's chevrons.

"I'd hate to come down these stairs drunk," I said. "One slip and you could take a dive."

I leaned out and spat, head and shoulders into the stairwell. Gina pulled at my sleeve.

"Gee, Mattie, be careful. You might fall."

"Yeah, yeah."

Inside the apartment she said, "Wait till I pull down the blinds."

"Okay, okay."

The apartment was overheated; those old houses are always freezing or so hot you could keep all the windows open. It was dark in the bedroom, with winter light coming through the space between the cracked green blinds and the window frame. There was the big European bed, with its feather mattress, that old man

Tragorna had died in and, for all I knew, that Gina had been made in. There was the cross with the figure of Christ, hanging on the wall behind the bed, dead center between the high bedposts.

"Come on, Gina. Take off your clothes."

She turned around, her hand on the window blind. Being alone in the room with her made me excited.

"Aw, Mattie, I don't want to."

"Why?"

"I don't know. I'm embarrassed."

"Come on!"

She took off her sweater and stood in her skirt and brassiere.

"Come on, I want to see you."

She unhooked the skirt and it fell to the floor. She stepped out of it, then pulled off her stockings and brassiere and stood in front of me, wearing nothing but her bloomers, outlined sharply in the cold grey light. It was the first time I had really seen her.

"Come here, kid."

She crossed the room, in a trance, acting as if I had hypnotized her.

"Come on!"

I pushed her back on the feather bed and made love to her, kissing her, being nice, trying not to get her scared. She whispered in the hot, dark room: "Oh, Mattie, don't hurt me. Please don't hurt me."

"Who's going to hurt you?" I whispered. "I wouldn't hurt you, kid. I love you."

When it was over we lay in the bed, looking at the water stains on the ceiling.

"See, what were you scared of? It's a good thing your old lady works. Otherwise where could we go, in the wintertime, when it's like this out?"

She rolled closer to me, pushing the hair away from my forehead, then tracing my eyes and nose, running her fingers across my lips.

"Gee, Mattie, you know what?"

"What?"

"You know who you look like?"

"Who?"

She mentioned the name of a movie actor.

"Yeah? Why?"

"You know, like him. Manly."

I met her, most afternoons. It was something to do, some-place to go. And it was nice to make love in the old lady's feather bed, instead of in a hallway, or in the back of a lifted car.

"You know, Mattie," she said one afternoon, "I have to tell Father Fliegel."

"You what!" sitting up in the bed.

"I have to go to confession. Two weeks now I didn't go."

"You mention my name, I'll break your neck."

"I won't tell him who did it to me. I'll just tell him one of the fellows."

I sat up in the bed, being reasonable, trying not to lose my temper.

"Listen, Gina, tell him some other sin. Stealing, maybe. Lying. Something else. It's just as good, isn't it? As long as it's a sin."

"I got to tell him the truth."

"For Christ's sake, why?"

"Because it's confession. I have to confess."

"Tell him some other sin," I said.

If she told Fliegel the truth he would get her to tell him my name. He was too smart for her, too sharp.

After a while I said, "Why don't you quit school? You can type already. You can do shorthand. Why don't you get a job, fifty a week. Then you could have your own joint."

"She wants me to graduate school."

"Is she God?"

"I'm sixteen, so she says she still has control over what I do."
I laughed.

"She hasn't got much control right now. What would she do if she caught you here, in bed with me?"

"She'd kill me, Mattie. Honest she would."

In the hallway going out, I said, "Listen, Gina, promise me something. Promise you won't tell Fliegel."

"Aw, Mattie, I can't."

I put on my hat.

"Okay. That's the end of you and me."

"What do you mean?"

"I mean we're through. Finished. Busted up. Who wants a dame that's going to get him in trouble all the time? You tell the priest and he'll be on my tail."

She stood in her bathrobe, thinking it over. Then she put her hand on my arm.

"All right, Mattie," she decided. "I'll tell him I stole something. Some money from the old lady."

"That's better. But don't forget, because I'll find out."

"I won't, Mattie. Honest."

I went down the smelly stairs, through the dogpee-smelling hall, out into the smelly street. A little kid in a ragged coat was scribbling on the wall with a stump of chalk:

GINA LOVES MATTIE DOLAN

I poked the kid with the toe of my shoe.

"Get out of here, you little bastard."

She went into the house, squealing, giggling, chanting: *"Gina loves Mattie Dolan, Gina loves Mattie Dolan."* I rubbed the chalk from the wall with my foot. I was sick of Gina already, so that sometimes I was disgusted in the middle of making love to her. I was sick of her kid ways, and sick of her "Aw, Mattie." I had knocked it off, as I promised I would, and that was all there was to it. I walked up the street, scuffing the sidewalk, wishing I knew a livelier dame, some dame my own age, nineteen, maybe, or twenty, some dame with lots of clothes and a line of patter, someone you could take out.

I was sick of Gina all right, but there was nothing else to do, with Fred away and the fellows in jail, and the streets clogged with slush and snow. So I waited, most afternoons, all through the rest of the month and into the middle of February, until it got to be a habit, waited for her to get home from school, then took her upstairs to bed. After a while I hated the room, with the frayed blinds down so people couldn't see, and I hated the big feather bed, and hated the sad-looking figure of Christ, hanging there, over my head.

It was almost a relief when the government wrote to me again and made me go downtown to talk about a job.

PART V

CHAPTER ONE

RENTZAU HAD A salesman's hand-shake, *man to man,* not hard enough to hurt your hand, but hard enough to let you know that he thought you were a regular fellow. His clothes were designed to flatter his figure.

"Glad to see you, Dolan. Sit down."

I sat on the honey-colored chair, glad to have my hand back. He held a gold case out toward me, reaching across five feet of polished honey-colored desk.

"Cigarette?"

He got up to light it for me.

"What were you with? What outfit?"

"Eighty-second Airborne," I said.

That had impressed Kieran.

"Oh, a paratrooper."

"Just for the money," I said. "I'm not a hero."

He laughed.

"We're all heroes. Were you at Arnhem?"

"Sure. Five days in the line."

He shook his head.

"Mag-nificent operation. Mag-nificent. Too bad the British didn't come through."

"Never trust a Limey."

"On the other hand," he said, "they are very good at holding positions. Not taking territory, mind you, Dolan, but holding it.

Put an Englishman on the spot and tell him to stay there and he'll stay. Until hell freezes over."

Like all important people, Rentzau had a simple-minded act that he used to fool you, throw you off guard. The craftiest, meanest bastards in the world develop a dumb front that makes you think you're smarter. Then, while you're congratulating yourself, in goes the knife. Rentzau used this veteran act. His Bronze Star and colonel's leaf were mounted under a crystal paperweight, kept in sight on his desk. His officer's Certificate of Service had been framed and hung on the wall. Hanging next to it was a reproduction of the SHAEF Service Forces patch, lightning breaking a length of chain, helped by the ASF star.

I was not fooled.

A man who was paid two thousand a week could not have been taken in by the Army. It was an act.

"Well," he said, "get two old sweats together and all they talk is Army. That's not why you're here, is it, Dolan?"

"No. No, sir."

He leaned back in his swivel chair and made a gesture that included all of Fifth Avenue, Saks', Bonwit-Teller's, Bergdorf-Goodman's, Radio City and St. Patrick's Cathedral.

"Big opportunity here, Dolan. Chance to learn the one business that makes the rest of them go."

He waited for me to say: "*What?*"

"Merchandising."

We looked at one another; I think he understood the fact that I understood him. He changed his tone a little.

"You'll like it, Dolan. Big opportunity."

"What kind of money do I get?"

"Thirty-five a week to start. But there's no limit. The sky's the limit. If one of you youngsters can push me out-after a few years, of course—so much the better."

Who do you think you're kidding, mister?

We stood up and shook hands. He told me where to go to have my name put on the payroll.

The store was Bramwell's, on Fifth Avenue, and what they sold was style. It was a place where money didn't matter...a squat, flat-faced smoothstone building displaying a lot of brass and glass...everything underplayed, the way it is in a quiet, smart bar, one of those places in the Fifties, near Park, where scotch is a dollar and a quarter. Two old doormen with rhubarb faces held umbrellas over the women, between the curb and the brassglass doors. Inside there were heavy rugs, white plaster, pictures on the walls and comfortable chairs. Everything was real.

It was a phony, a rich phony.

Behind all that plush, in the business-like employment office, I handed the form to the girl.

"Do I have to start today? I have some things to take care of."

"Tomorrow will do. Tomorrow morning. Nine-fifteen, employees' entrance. You'll find a card in the time-clock rack with your name on it."

Nine-fifteen until the placed closed, being a goddamned messenger boy, smelling nothing but women and clothes, hearing nothing but women, women, except the second-lieutenant's voices of the boys in dicky-bosomed shirts, section managers, junior executives, always hurrying, always busy, just being efficient.

Dolan! *Take this here—*

Dolan! *Take this there—*

Dolan! *Take this the other place—*

Three days, four days, I was afraid I'd get used to it.

For Christ's sakes, lady, keep your shirt on...

"Well, Dolan, if you don't want the job...!"

Lady, it wasn't my idea. Blame it all on Uncle Sam.

But there was something to learn in Bramwell's.

Just by being there you learned how much money there is in America.

A woman came into the fur department, one of those perfect, enameled women, somewhere between thirty and forty. If you included the sable coat, her clothes and jewels were worth about a hundred thousand dollars.

She tried on a mink coat, then tried on another. The third one was the one she took.

"How much is it?"

"Seventy-five hundred and twelve, with tax."

"I'll take it."

"Will I charge it, miss?"

"I'll take it."

She took eight thousand-dollar bills from her handbag and gave them to the girl. Then she nodded and a colored chauffeur, wearing a plum-colored uniform with breeches and putties, came forward and took the coat over his arm.

"May I have your name and address, miss?"

"Mary Smith. Fourteen hundred and nine Third Avenue."

I laughed. Fourteen hundred and nine is in the ginmill belt, under the El. The woman looked at me and winked. I winked back.

The salesgirl stood there, holding a pencil.

"Well, I paid for it, didn't I? Please get my change."

"Why, certainly, miss."

When she came back with the change the woman offered her ten dollars.

"No, thank you, miss."

"Go on, take it."

"No, thank you, miss."

The salesgirl was so angry that I thought she was going to cry.

"Have it your way."

The woman with the sables went out, followed by the colored chauffeur, holding the mink over his arm. The salesgirl stood with her sharp heels biting into the deep pile carpet, just looking at the elevator door, thinking of seven and a half grand—twice what she made in a year.

"Whyn't you take the ten?" I said. "You could have given it to me."

"Mary Smith. I wish I knew her real name."

"What would you do? Ask for a job as maid?"

"I'd report her. That money was hot."

"Is that nice? You take the woman's money, then you want to turn her in."

"It's against the law."

"So is breathing," I said, "if you do it in the wrong place."

"Go on, Mattie, go away. You're beginning to get me mad."

Upstairs, in the advertising office, another sucker sat at a desk, pasting clippings into a scrapbook.

"Christ," I said, "are we chumps, working for thirty-five a week."

"There's a big opportunity here."

"Listen, chump, how old are you?"

"I'm going to be twenty-one."

"So you'll be learning till you're thirty-five. Then, one morning, when you're all married up, you'll wake up middle-aged, still learning. Then it will be too late. You'll be just like the middle-aged jerks all over this store, making seventy-five a week, too old to make a change."

"You have to start somewhere."

"You want to be at the top, you have to start at the top."

"You're crazy, Dolan."

"Yes. Like a fox."

He looked at me, paste on his nose.

"Why don't you quit, if you don't like the job?"

"Why should I quit when it looks bad? The government might think I'm not trying. When I get good and sick of it, I'll get myself fired and go back into the Club."

"Excuse me."

I recognized the voice. It was Ambrose, the fellow who showed me the blue movies, last fall.

"George Murphy," he said. "Hello."

I straightened up, tougher than he was.

"Listen, my name's not Murphy. You've got the wrong guy."

He put his hand on my arm.

"George," he said, "I—"

"Lay off it, will you?"

He hesitated, then turned and walked away. The kid with the scrapbook said, "Don't you know who that is?"

I shook my head.

"That's Howard Ambrose, the artist."

"Who cares?"

He stood up and closed the book.

"Dolan, you have the wrong attitude."

"Were you in the Navy?"

"Yes, why?"

"I just knew it. That's all."

Afterward, in the copy department, I asked a hornrimmed writer about Ambrose.

"What is his take?"

"What?"

"How much does he knock off?"

"I wouldn't know," she said. "Plenty. All artists are overpaid."

"A thousand a week?"

"Oh, more than that. Much more."

"Two?"

"That would be more like it."

I went into the employees' toilet, where I could hide and smoke a cigarette. Downstairs, at six o'clock, punching my time card, I looked at the other people quitting for the day: salesgirls, stockgirls, colored maids, clerks and stenographers, shoemen and floormen, all tired, all wilted, all sick of being nice, nice, nice to the customers and the strawbosses. The day outside the swinging doors, beyond the time-clock, was dead too. I looked at the sand-colored card in my hand, with the blank days there as empty spaces, spaces for all the days that were left in this month, so that the store could gnaw them away, day by day, with a blurred stamp: 09:15 and a blurred stamp: 06:02, measuring out the amount of life you squeezed from yourself to give those bastards for their thirty-five a week. I held the card so that sweat from my hand stained the edges a darker tan, and wanted to tear it up, drop the pieces on the dark grey floor, and ring the clock on the empty platen, just for fun, to hear the bell. But I didn't. I punched it 06:04, giving the store four minutes of my life while I stood there, jostled, looking at the card.

At the drugstore on Madison Avenue I bought a carton of Camels. Then I raced for an empty cab, beating out a white-haired guy who thought that waving his cane would help.

"The Tombs."

The driver turned.

"You'll make it faster on the subway, buddy. Take me half an hour. Maybe more."

He wanted some short fast fares; it occurred to me that I should save the money, now that I had to work for it.

"I guess you're right."

I went down the steps to the subway, caught in the rush and banged around. A train came, loaded with people, all going home to Brooklyn. Another came and people fought to get close to the automatic doors, trying to close again and again. I climbed back up the stairs to the street and flagged a cruising cab.

"The Tombs."

He was cheerful, and didn't care. He reached across the car and threw the flag.

"Right! The Old Homestead."

Murph tried to grin through the wire grille. He was wearing a dirty shirt.

"Gee, Mattie, I'm sure glad to see you."

"I brought you some butts, Murph. A carton of Camels. They'll give them to you."

"My brand!"

"Sure. What do you think?"

They had worked over Murph. Even though he hadn't hit the cop, shooting at him had been a mistake. He looked thinner and less red; his confidence was gone and behind that grille he looked like another neighborhood bum who had caught up with himself. A sure, sure loser, Murph, too mean to do what he was told, too dumb to be mean and get away with it.

"Thanks, Mattie, for the cigarettes."

"For-get it. I'll bring you more."

It was an antiseptic room; a fly couldn't have found a meal on the floors or the walls of the visitors' room. You were conscious of the bars and the wire grille that ran down the center of the narrow table, with stools on either side.

"Are you going to get bail?"

"Vincie Rhattigen's trying, Mattie. He's getting a lawyer for us. It's just, they didn't find the dough. That's holding everything up. I can't figure it out."

"I can."

"Yeah?" he said. "How?"

"I'll bet some fat blue-coated cop is spending that money right now."

His dumb Irish face looked puzzled, then he understood what I meant.

"Yeah, that's right! Yeah. That could be it."

"Sure it is. What else? Could the money just evaporate?"

"Yeah," he said, rubbing his chin, "that's what happened, all right."

"Sure it is. The cops got it."

I stood up, buttoning my coat.

"So long, Murph."

"So long, pal. So long, Mattie."

I stopped.

"Murph."

"Yeah?"

"I'll leave some dough for you. Ten bucks. Maybe you'll want to send out for something. A sandwich. Something like that."

That pleased him.

"Gee, pal, that's swell! No kidding!"

He stood, admiring me through the grille.

"Murph."

"Yeah?"

"I'm working."

"Honest?"

"Yeah. In a store."

"For what?"

"Thirty-five per."

"How is it?"

"Lousy. Lousy. Worse than jail. Worse than being in here. In the Tombs."

"I'll trade."

The guard came and led him away. I went through the shiny bars, down a corridor, through more bars and out into the street. Murph would never suspect a fellow with money, any money, of going to work in a store. He would think it all over, then decide that the cops took the money. That was the way to deal with Murph; put the idea in his head and let it grow into one of his own.

I rode the Lexington Avenue subway uptown to Eighty-sixth Street, and walked east through Yorkville, passing the stubes and the bright drinking places: BIER ODER WEIN, EIN MUSS ES SEIN!—Original Bauhaus. ORIGINAL bauhaus. Original BAUHAUS. Friedl's, Maxl's, Original Maxi's. Through the doors, up the wooden gangway leading down to Original Maxl's, came the piping of a concertina and voices trailing the waiter's pointer: YAH! *Das ist ein Schnitzelbank!*

The Dutch bastards were starting early, forgetting there ever had been a war.

It was dark on Eighty-seventh Street, with snow in the gutters that had been there for weeks, scarred with garbage and the scabs of old fires, hardening into dark grey ice. At the garbage can in front of the house another alley cat was scratching, scratching away at the corrugated iron. I stopped and watched him scratch, with his pursed cat face and evil yellow eyes watching the bright scrapes left by his claws. Then I stepped toward him quickly and kicked him in the ribs that showed through his thinning, bastard fur. He rode through the arc of the street light, turned and twisted in the air, landed, screaming, and shook himself, then darted into a cellar. I went into the house.

CHAPTER TWO

A downtown cop in plain clothes, with his shield pinned to the lapel of his coat, sat across from the old man, writing in his notebook with a pen. The old lady had been crying and held a damp handkerchief by the corner, touching the edges of it to her eyes. I stood in the doorway with my hat on, holding my hands on my hips. They all looked up.

"What goes on?"

The old man smiled, trying to be crafty.

"Well, Mattie, your no-good uncle has finally got what was coming to him."

"What?"

"I said Fred has been bumped off."

He handed me the *Daily News*. There was a headline:

BLACK MARKETEER GUNNED OUT

The front page carried a picture of a man spread out in the gutter of the street, under the mudguard of a car. It was blurred and looked fake. It might have been a photograph of anyone, of a dummy or a sack of sand, dressed up in men's clothes. But there was an oval inset that held a picture of Fred, head and shoulders, asking for a number. *Story on page three ...* and on page three it said:

Fred Theobald, a beefy party who has been questioned about murders, was rubbed out late today on the sidewalk in front of his swanky apartment on Central Park West.

Theobald, it was learned, had been hiding out after a disagreement with members of the syndicate that controlled the sale of ration tickets in East Coast cities during the war.

Theobald had a long record of arrests but had never been convicted ....

I stood with the paper in my hand and felt the warm tears rise in my eyes and spill over, running down my cheeks.

"Jesus. Jesus Christ!"

I looked at the picture of Fred dead in the gutter with his face on the concrete, and recognized the coat he was wearing, a blue doublebreasted coat worth a hundred and fifty dollars. His good grey hat was near his head, with a streak of dirt from the street on the crown. As I looked at the photograph it seemed to me that the shape of Fred's big body grew into the lump on the pavement, so that the fake, painted picture became real, just for a moment. I took out my handkerchief and wiped my cheeks.

"Jesus. Jesus Christ!"

"Now, now, lad," said the cop, "this is no time to be swearing and taking the Lord's name in vain."

He was an old washerwoman of a cop, the kind who was always good for a touch when he was pounding the pavements in harness. A nickel or a dime touch, if you begged him for subway fare. I sat down and took off my hat.

"What's it to you?" I asked.

The old man laughed.

"He thinks he's tough. Mattie thinks he's tough."

"Leave him alone," said the old lady. "Leave Mattie alone."

"Yeah. Yeah," said the old man. "Leave him alone. Leave him alone. What's so good about him?"

The cop held up his hand: *keep quiet!* He turned to a clean page in his notebook, made some notes, and spoke to me.

"You went to Florida with him?"

"That's right. Miami, Florida, Miami Beach."

He wrote that down.

"Did you notice anything down there? Anybody threaten him?"

I remembered Rico, the Wop in the white gabardine suit, with his: *"Get a lot of it. Get enough to last a long time."* And the way Fred brushed him off: *"Get away from me, small-timer."*

"No," I said. "It was a pleasure trip. We just went to get some sun."

The old man grunted.

"Mr. Florida."

"Is that a crime?" I asked the cop. "To go on a trip with my own uncle?"

"No."

He asked questions that meant nothing and I offered the same kind of answers. He wrote it all in his book in a careful coppish eighth-grade hand. Then he closed the book and put it away. He unpinned the badge, took it from his lapel, and put it away in his wallet.

"We will want you later. Downtown," he said, standing up.

"What do you want me for? Why don't you catch the guys who did it? I don't know anything."

"We'll see about that."

He was the way they all are: mean underneath the boys' club manner. *Yes, lad. lad. Now, now, lad.* All honey. All friendly. Until he got you away from the public, down deep in the steel cell-blocks. Then he would take a rubber hose and beat you just because he liked it.

He shook hands with the old man.

"You hadn't seen him for some time, Mr. Dolan?"

"I wouldn't have the bum in the house. I wouldn't have him in the house."

"Let him be," said the old lady. "He's dead."

"Dead or alive he's a dirty bum. Wearing a discharge button when he wasn't in the war."

"War-war," I said. "For God's sake."

"And Mattie's going to be just like him. He'll wind up dead in the gutter."

"Shut up, will you?"

"Now, now, lad."

I was inclined to hit the cop, but what would have been the P.C.T.?

"For Christ's sake, mind your business."

"Have it your way," the cop said. "I was only trying to help you."

"I DON'T NEED ANY HELP."

"Tough Mattie," said the old man. "Tough Mattie."

After the cop had gone I sat down at the round table and put my head in my arms and cried. I couldn't help myself.

"Stop your bawling, Mattie," said the old man. "Good riddance. You'll be better off, not having Fred to influence you, now that you got a job."

That was his way of being nice.

I blew up.

I grabbed the row of buttons on his shirt and lifted him from the chair. My fist was back, ready to smash him. The old lady caught my sleeve.

"Don't, Mattie! Don't hit your father!"

I pushed him back into his chair.

"You should talk about good riddance. At least Fred made a buck. He got something out of his life, instead of sitting the way you do, looking at the wall in a fleabag apartment, eating out your yellow little heart."

He nodded, all the fight gone.

"Yeah, Mattie. Maybe you're right. Maybe you're right. Maybe you know it all. Maybe you were just born smart."

He got up and took off his cap, scratching the top of his grey head.

"Maybe you know it all," he said.

He went into the bedroom and closed the door behind him. We heard the bedsprings sing as he threw himself down.

"I know how you feel, Mattie," the old lady said. "I know just how you feel."

"What do you know?" I said. "You're just like him, the old man, except that you have sense enough to drink."

She went into the kitchen and sat at the window. From the front room I could see her, rocking back and forth in her chair, looking old, with the window and the tired kitchen curtains making a frame for her head and shoulders. After a while I heard her crying and I got up and closed the kitchen door.

I picked up the *News* and read the story, then looked at the pictures again. With Fred's face staring at me, out of the newsprint oval, it was hard to believe he was dead. Outside, in the City, the night was getting underway. I heard the grind of the big red bus, taking the long hill in low, and the toot of taxi horns, pulling in, pulling out of the canopied housefronts toward the River, bringing the well-to-do home, carrying them off to restaurants, to the shows and to night clubs. I sat in the old man's smelly front room, with the City busy all around me, looking at Fred's face in the paper, thinking to myself that if I had the choice, given by God, to be my old man and live to be a hundred, or to be Fred and live to be fifty, that it wouldn't be any choice at all. I'd be Fred.

At least Fred was alive. He had some fun.

The old man was deader than Fred, right now, with Fred downtown in the morgue and the old man, breathing for nothing, sulking in there on his bed. His whole damn life was a blank wall, deader than the bricks he watched, sitting in the chair with his cap on, after he finished the *Daily News:* looking, looking, looking at what? At the blank painted wall of the tenement house across the court. He's the one who's dead, I thought, deader than a dead cat in an alley, deader than the people he fought beside, in the Argonne, in the other war, or in his Nineteen Six*teen*, when he thought he was a hero, fighting for a cause that wasn't even his... thrown out, chased away, out of the country, by the people he admired.

I looked at the closed bedroom door and said, out loud: "You're just walking around dead. You might as well be buried."

But Fred?

Fred was dead, but when I thought of him he didn't seem dead at all, but just as alive as he'd always been. I could see his face, a little heavy, clean-shaven as he always was, clean-smelling of the stuff he used, smelling of that shaving stuff and of his good Havana cigars. And the suits he had, thirty of them, conservative but still lively, hand-sewn, hand-made, made for him, Fred Theobald, and not for anyone else. And the way he laughed, enjoying something. And the way he was tough when he wanted to be. And the way he would hand me a century note: one hundred dollars, and say, "Here, kid, buy a bag of peanuts."

What do you want out of living, anyway?

Dames?

Fred had all he wanted, and the best, the best you could buy.

Food?

Fred had a table whenever he wanted it, at the best places in the City.

Comfort?

You couldn't beat Fred's apartment.

Class?

He had thirty suits, each one of them perfect. When they showed wear, he gave them away.

Speed?

Very few cars could touch the Cadillac. And Fred knew how to drive.

Cash?

Fred always had a thousand or two, in his wallet, waiting to be spent.

Power?

People jumped when he spoke; people were afraid of him.

Respect?

He had respect, all right.

Freedom?

He did just what he wanted to do—right up until the last split second, when the bullets went into his chest.

He was alive, independent. Nobody owned him.

I got up from the round table and walked into the kitchen. She still sat there, in the window, looking out at the night.

"Ma?"

"Yeah?"

"Are you going to the funeral?"

She thought it over.

"Yeah," she decided. "Sure I'm going. I don't care what he says."

In the black hired car, a couple of days later, we drove into the City from Woodlawn, where they cremated Fred.

"Who was the fella took care of the funeral?"

"A guy named Tommy, Ma," I said. "I don't remember his last name."

She cried into her starchy handkerchief.

"My own dear brother."

We were alone in the black Packard; four cars had gone out.

"Take it easy, Ma."

She took the handkerchief away from her eyes.

"I wonder if he left anything?"

"What?"

"I wonder if Fred left like a will. Any money or anything."

"Don't be stupid, Ma. What Fred had, he spent. He didn't care about keeping money."

"He shoulda left something."

"Listen, Ma, I'm the one who should be crying. He was going to back me in a saloon, as soon as I was twenty-one."

"Honest, Mattie? Fred was gonna do that for you?"

"Sure," I said. "He promised."

She started to cry again. I don't know whether the tears were for Fred or for the saloon I wouldn't get.

"Take it easy, Ma. It's a bad break. That's all."

"You don't have to worry. You got a good job."

I made a Bronx cheer.

"That job? It stinks. It's just a gag, a come-on, to get you to work out your guts for nothing."

"I thought it was a good job."

She tried to be stubborn about it.

"Jobs are for suckers."

"You got a job."

"And I'm a sucker to keep it."

That was the end of the conversation. After we crossed the River she said, "Buy me a drink, will you, Mattie? I feel sad, seeing Fred go."

"Sure, Ma."

I had expected a touch.

I took her to a place on Third Avenue, full of the smell of beer and wet clothes.

"Two bourbons. I. W. Harper."

"Two Harper, coming up."

After a couple of bonded bourbons the old lady started to cry, building up to a long, sad drunk, her fuzzy, puddled brain taking command of the opportunity to get drunk in a cause anyone would have to respect.

"My own brother. My own dear brother."

She was dressed in faded black, a dress that once had pink lace sewn to the edge of the collar. You saw the needle-marks where the lace had been ripped off for the funeral.

"Lay off it, Ma. Lay off it."

I walked to the bar and took out my money, handing the barkeep ten dollars.

"Listen. See that old dame over there?"

"Yeah, Mac?"

"Give her what she wants to drink. When she gets slopped, put her in a cab and send her home."

"Sure, Mac." He was a middle-aged Harp, with a clean apron wrapped around his big middle. "Who is it? Your old lady?"

She sat with a glass in her hand, staring at the blistered booth partition, humming a tune to herself.

"No," I said. "Some relative. But see she gets home all right, eh?"

"I will that."

I wrote our address and the name DOLAN on a piece of paper and gave it to him. Then I went back to the booth.

"Ma?"

"Yes, Mattie?"

"I have to go. The bill is paid. So is your cabfare home. All you have to do is sit here and get your load on in peace."

"Thanks, Mattie. Thanks."

She was pleased, now that she knew she didn't have to worry about money, knowing she could order and drink as if she owned the bar or had credit. Money, to most people, means a lot: comfort and clothes and women and safety, good food and a place to stay, power, and what goes with it. To a lush it's not really money at all. It's just whiskey, dried out so that it can be carried around.

"So long, Ma."

She took my hand in both of hers and kissed it.

"For Christ's sake, Ma, what are you doing?"

I wiped the back of my hand on my coat and walked out into Third Avenue, standing in the cold sidewalk sludge, while an El train passed overhead making a noise like a landslide and shaking the heavy steel supports that pushed the tracks away from the street. I caught a cab, sliding in the slush, and told him to take me to Radio City. It is a little like a church, Radio City when the lights go down, and I sat on the balcony in a deep seat with a private ashtray, watching the stage show and the colored lights, hardly seeing the drilled girls dance, thinking about Fred and about how sorry I was that he was dead.

CHAPTER THREE

"You can go now, Dolan," the sergeant said.

"Thanks."

I put on my coat and hat; they had been talking at me for four hours and my eyes were burnt by the bright white lights.

"Watch your step, Dolan."

"For what? What did I do? Is it my fault somebody murdered my uncle? Why don't you catch the guys that did it, instead of taking up my time, making me lose time from my job?"

"Go on, get out of here."

I went out, glad to get away from the cop-smell and the mopped-board smell of police headquarters. In Center Street I looked down and saw the Tombs, where Murph and the Wop had been sitting for weeks waiting for a judge to let them out on bail. There were cops standing on the sidewalk, buttoned up in their overcoats, and people you knew were cops, wearing plain clothes. Along the street there were tailor shops with uniforms in the dusty windows. It is a cop neighborhood—cops and City and State and Federal marshals, all over the area. I was glad they were through with me. They had been mean, part of the time, but no one had hit me, as I thought they would when I told them I didn't know anything.

It was too late to go to work, so I went uptown to the neighborhood. When I walked into Greene's, Greene looked up from the *Racing Form*.

"Mattie! I been looking for you. I was going to send somebody up to your house."

"What did I do? Rob the fast mail?"

"There's a letter here for you. A package."

He bent down, behind the bar. I heard him moving the dial of the safe, then the hinges made a noise as he opened the door. He brought up a brown package with sealing wax pressed over the flap. It was addressed to me:

Matthew Dolan, Jr.
c/o Greene's Bar & Grill
York Avenue
New York City

There was no return address, but I knew who it was from. I felt the envelope; it was thick, substantial. I decided not to open it in Greene's.

"Let me have a rye, Greene. Beer chaser."

"Coming up." He reached for the glass and the bottle and said, "We haven't been seeing you lately, Matt. Don't tell me you've been working that hard."

"My uncle died."

"I heard about it. A sad thing."

"Yeah. It was too bad."

Greene mopped the bar, fishing for news that had not been printed in the papers. He liked to know what was going on.

"I seen him a couple of times. Big fella. Always laughin'. Big spender."

"That's right," I said. "That was Fred."

Greene leaned forward with his hands on the bar, his little eyes curious and bright.

"Did he leave yez anything at all, Matt?"

"No," I said. "He spent what he made. You know, here today, gone tomorrow. Those fellows don't save."

"Sure," he agreed, giving it up, "that's the way it is with fellas like that. Here today, gone tomorrow."

I buttoned my coat, leaving half the rye and all the beer standing on the bar.

"I'll be seeing you."

"Goodbye now, Matt."

I walked to the promenade over the River and stood in the wind, looking around. The flagstoned promenade was bare, blown with dust and old newspaper. I broke the seal on the envelope and saw the money inside. C-notes, lots of them, and a few thousand-dollar bills. There was a note.

Kid:

This is ten grand, the best I can do. It is clean. You get the car too. You ought to get 5 gees for it. I paid 8. But maybe not. I bought it from a thief.

Remember what I told you about learning to steal legal, like a gentleman. Put this ten, and what you can raise on the heap, in the bank, in a tin box. Then try to promote the rest.

Love

Fred.

I couldn't get over a guy like Fred writing "love" at the bottom of the note. It was not the way he would have talked. I read the note again, then tore it up and threw the pieces into the River. I counted the money. It was ten thousand dollars; more money than I had ever held in my hands before, and for several minutes I couldn't make myself believe that it was mine, the beginning of the stake I had been looking for, the break I told Fred I needed.

I tried three banks before I found one that had a safety deposit box free. An old man with yellowed white hair, wearing a gray uniform, took me into the vault and showed me how to unlock the box. They have a key and I have a key. No one else in the world can get into the box. I put the money away, then went home and found the chain that came with my Army dogtags. I put the key on the chain and put the chain around my neck. Then I took a cab to Penn Station and rode the train to Baltimore. They gave me the car without any trouble. I gave the colored boy two dollars.

I knew a man in Trenton who had bought and sold GI equipment, especially watches, during the war. He looked at the car as it stood in the street, not bothering to look under the hood, not bothering to drive it.

"Four thousand bucks," he said.

"I ought to get five. The car cost eight."

He held the registration in his hand.

"Are you Fred Theobald?"

"Sure."

"And I'm Franklin Delano Roosevelt. Don't be a sucker, kid. Take the four."

"Give it to me."

He counted the money into my hand, in twenties and hundreds, flat, new money. I took a last look at the Cadillac, wishing that I could afford to keep it, then walked downhill to the station and waited for the New York train. On the train, sitting by a window, looking at the scenery going by, I worked out a deal with myself. I decided that any money I promoted that came to a hundred dollars or more was going into the kitty: the tin box behind the lock in the bank. Anything less than a hundred was mine to spend.

On the corner of Eighty-sixth and York, Gina waited under the street light, wearing a scarf around her head, shivering and stamping her feet, because the cold of the concrete walk struck through the paper soles of her high-heeled shoes. I didn't want to see her. I cut toward Greene's with my face to the wall, but she saw me, recognized my walk.

"Mattie!"

I kept on walking.

"Mattie!"

I stopped. She ran across the street, slipping a little in the thin layer of snow.

"Mattie!"

"Yeah?"

She came up to me, out of breath.

"Mattie."

"Yeah?"

"Hello, Mattie."

"What do you want?"

"Gee, I don't know. Nothing, I guess. I was only waiting."

"So what are you hanging around for? Why don't you go home?"

"I only wanted to see you."

"I'm busy."

"Aw, Mattie—"

I gave her a push.

"GO HOME, WILL YOU, for Christ's sake?"

She turned and started toward Eighty-fourth Street, feeling her way on the slippery pavement.

"Gina!"

She stopped and turned around.

"Come here, will you?"

She walked back to me slowly, with her head down, watching her feet. The prints of her shoes showed up on the sidewalk, like black leaves against the white snow, as if they'd been painted on.

"Come on. I'll buy you a beer."

"Okay, Mattie."

We went to one of the German places in a half-cellar on Eighty-sixth Street, a rathskeller made of papier-mâché, with beer steins and long German pipes hanging on the fake stone walls. The beer came in Pilsener glasses tapered and thin and very tall, with the name of the brewery in Czechoslovakia etched into the glass. There was a three-piece band and you could dance.

There were a lot of sailors in the place and people who looked as if they had been sailors.

"Dance with me, Mattie."

"Okay."

We danced. I could feel the four thousand dollars in the breast pocket of my coat.

"Don't you love me no more, Mattie?"

"Why do you say a thing like that?"

"A week and a half I didn't see you."

"You're getting to be a regular tramp. Can't you do without it a week and a half?"

"Aw, Mattie, I don't mean that."

"Jesus Christ, don't you know my uncle died? I had things to do. Affairs."

"No kidding?"

She stopped dancing and I bumped her. Then she crossed herself.

"I'm sorry, Mattie."

Other people were smiling at her because she looked so earnest.

"Come on. Can't you see everybody's laughing at you? Come on."

We sat at the table, drinking beer, with the noise of the German horns in our ears so loud you could hardly talk.

"How is your job, Mattie?" she asked.

"That job."

"Don't you like it?"

"What good's a job like that? Thirty-five lousy dollars a week?"

"Yeah, but you could get ahead, they told you."

"Get ahead!"

I looked at her flat Hunkie face. If I worked at the store for ten years, got to make seventy, eighty a week, she would call me a big success.

"Sometimes you make me sick," I said. "Sick at my stomach so I want to puke."

She started to cry. I called the waiter and paid the bill. The band began one of those polkas and the Dutchmen were out on the floor with their women, stomping, making wild turns, spinning the women till it made you dizzy to watch them.

"Come on, come on home. You make me feel cheap, acting like a kid."

"Okay, Mattie."

I walked her home in the snow.

CHAPTER FOUR

I sewed a black armband to my sleeve before I went back to work at the store, one week absent without leave. They told me I should have telephoned, and I told them I was too distressed. They docked me a week's pay and sent me back to running errands.

The production manager, a worried man with heavy glasses, handed me a brown package, sealed with scotch tape.

"Dolan, take this up to Carla Adams' place. Get her okay and hurry back."

It was a flat package, four feet square.

"Can I take a cab?"

"The subway will do."

He was close with the store's money; he was the one who okayed petty cash. You couldn't steal. I paid for the cab with my own money, because I didn't want to look like a chump, riding the subway like an errand boy, holding that package under my arm.

The address turned out to belong to a private house in the Seventies, just east of Park Avenue, one of those red brick and stone houses with wrought-iron grille work to protect the glass doors and a pair of carriage lamps bolted to the outside wall. A colored maid in a wine-colored uniform opened the door.

"From the store?"

"That's right," I said.

I waited. The entrance hall had a black and white tile floor. There was a mahogany grandfather's clock, ticking away as if it liked itself, with the heavy brass pendulum swinging slowly, taking its time, reminding me of the errand-boy dog with his smug look: *Watch me go! Watch me go!* On either side of the double doors there was a statue of a coal-black colored boy, wearing red and gold pantaloons, holding a serving tray in his hands. The statues were identical twins and the colored boys stood there looking almost alive, with their black plaster arms reaching toward one another. There were two U-shaped chairs, enameled black and picked out with gold, and I sat in one of them. When the clock struck, after a whirrrr-rrrr-r, it frightened me and made me jump.

"Okay, white boy. Come on."

The maid led me up two flights of stairs to Carla Adams' bedroom. The bed was round, round as a plate, and stood dead center in the room under a tent made of pink satin. The room was larger than Greene's bar, with chocolate walls and a lot of French furniture, painted pink to match the tent. In the bed, with a tray on her lap, sat a woman with gold hair, wearing a pair of bright blue glasses, showing a lot of pink skin. The ends of the glasses turn up; harlequin style. On the little table beside the bed was a regiment of medicine bottles and a chromium-plated atomizer. You could smell the nose drops, vaguely, through the perfume.

"Come in, for Christ's sake! Come in and shut the god-damn door!"

I stepped in and closed the door behind me. The maid disappeared.

"Okay, lady, keep your drawers on."

She laughed and took the package, looking at me through her blue-framed glasses. She could have been thirty, she could have been forty. Whatever age she was, you knew, from her eyes and from the set of her made-up mouth, that she was smart, smart and tough.

"Would you like a cup of coffee?"

She didn't treat me like a messenger boy, the way the other buyers did; she saw, looking at me, that I wasn't just another slob.

"No," I said, "but I could do with a shot of whiskey."

This seemed very funny to her. At the store she was a big wheel, people always brown-nosing. She admired the direct approach. She laughed.

"Ada, you black bastard!" she yelled.

The maid poked her head through the door.

"Bring me a bottle of scotch and some glasses."

"Yes, *ma'am!* Right away!"

She returned with a painted tin tray that held a bottle of Black and White, three glasses, an ice bucket and a syphon laced into a solid silver basket. She mixed a drink for Carla Adams, one for me and one for herself. It was the first time I ever had a drink with a nigger.

We had a couple of drinks.

"Who are you?" asked Carla.

"I'm Mattie Dolan."

I made it a take-it-or-leave-it statement; I said it as if she should have known my name. We looked at one another and, the way it sometimes is, we knew one another, all about one another. We were the same kind of people: she a thirty-thousand-dollar buyer, me a fresh kid running errands. I knew, without asking why, that I would never make a pass at her; she knew, I would have made a bet, that something running through my blood also ran through hers.

"Mattie Dolan," she said. "You're one of Rentzau's veterans, aren't you?"

"That's right."

"You look too smart to fall for that."

I explained why I had the job. I told her that I hoped to get fired.

"What are you going to do with yourself? I mean with your future?"

"I'm going to open a place."

She nodded.

"Saloons?"

"One, to begin with. After that, who knows?"

"It's a good business. Saloons and call-houses. People will always want to get laid and a certain number of them will always drink."

I laughed.

"You sound like my uncle Fred."

She did remind me of Fred; it was something you sensed about her, the fact that she was independent, the fact that you knew that nobody owned her.

"Who was he?"

"A guy. He died."

I looked at her, propped up in bed with a bedjacket on, holding the highball glass in her hand. I guessed that she was bored sick of sitting in bed getting over a cold, and just wanted to talk. The envelope I had brought from the store lay on the bed. It hadn't been opened.

"What was he like?" she said.

"Something like you." I sat down on the edge of the round bed, feeling the coil springs give under my weight. "He knew how to live. All the way up."

"And how about you. The future Mister Dolan. Do you know how to live all the way up?"

"I'm going to find out," I said. "And not by working for Rentzau's thirty-five a week."

She laughed.

"Phil Rentzau doesn't think he's giving anyone a bad deal. Those people always believe their own propaganda. They convince themselves first."

"I'm smart enough to know that he didn't work up to a hundred thousand a year by saving up five-dollar raises."

She laughed, the way Fred used to laugh, no reservations, a real laugh.

"Dolan, you bastard, you're a relief. Honest to Christ, you're a relief."

She picked up the package and ripped away the tough manila wrapping. There were six fashion drawings, willowy women with long legs, wearing evening dresses. She looked at them, one by one, and let them fall to the floor. Then she reached down and picked them up, looking at them carefully again; I saw that she didn't like them. She put them on the floor and took off her glasses, sitting, looking at the chocolate wall, chewing the end of the glasses frame. I sat on the edge of the bed without saying anything.

"Do you really want to get fired?" she asked, as if the idea had just occurred to her.

"Sure."

"And you can't just quit, the way other people do?"

"If I quit the government will bitch. And I need the twenty a week for maneuvering dough."

"I'll get you fired."

"How?"

"When you leave here, take these drawings with you and throw them in the ashcan. You'll be doing me a favor. They stink, but if I turn them down they'll think I'm just being a bitch. So you throw them away. When they call up, I'll tell them you haven't even been here."

"Will they fire me for that?"

"Will they fire you! Do you know how much those drawings cost?"

"I'll bite."

"There is six hundred dollars' worth of so-called art there. Done by a pansy named Ambrose, who has hypnotized the fashion world. Those idiots have convinced themselves that beside Ambrose, Picasso is a bum."

"Who?"

"Ambrose. A pansy. A fruit."

"Yeah. I know him."

She laughed.

"You don't look like the type. Or maybe you do." She looked at me, over her glasses. "Mister Dolan. The fag's delight."

"Lay off it, will you?"

"Skip it. I was kidding."

I told her about the blue movies.

"Yes, I've seen them. I don't like dirty pictures."

"These are dirty, all right. Is he a friend of yours, Ambrose?"

"I know him. Sometimes I feel sorry for the poor bastard."

I picked up the drawings.

"He seems to do all right."

"Oh, he's hog rich. He's coining money. But he's such a sucker for the dead-end kids. The last little number he had, an Italian boy named Guido, who would have stabbed you just to see if you'd bleed, took Ambrose for five thousand dollars."

"No kidding?"

"Five thousand in cash. And God knows what in clothing and stuff. Howard was always buying him presents."

"What did he have to do? The Wop that clipped him for five grand?"

"Why? Are you looking for the job?"

"What do you think I am! I'm just curious."

"I suppose he just had to be nice. And pose for pictures. Howard likes pictures. Actually he's a very talented, very cultivated guy. He knows music, art. He's sick, that's all. And he can't find what he wants."

"What does he want?"

"Love."

I laughed.

"Give me that kind of money, the kind Ambrose makes, and I could buy all the love I wanted."

"You don't look as if you'd have to buy it."

"You always buy it," I said. "You always pay for it."

She laughed, then said, "Get out of here, Dolan. I am going to get up."

I picked up the drawings and wrapped the manila paper around them.

"I'll lose these."

"Come up and see me, at the office, after you get yourself fired."

"Why?"

"You appeal to me, Dolan. You're a kindred spirit."

When I got to the corner I tore the drawings in half, then in half again, folding the heavy illustration board so it cracked. I dropped the pieces into an ashcan, piling stuff on top of them. Six hundred dollars' worth of pictures for the Department of Sanitation: *Compliments of Mattie Dolan.*

I walked east as far as the River.

It was dusk, warm for March, and you could smell the beginning of spring. I sat on a concrete bench, facing the river, all of the City behind me. I looked at the Island, Welfare Island, with the lights of the cell-blocks and hospital wards coming on, one by one, making a pattern. I thought of the suckers out there in jail, doing time, and the people in the wards, people with the con, coughing up their lives, old cokies taking the cure, old whores getting rid of the clap, women whose husbands had beaten them up, crippled kids, living on the City, people in the Emergency, smashed up in accidents, cut up in knife fights, played out, dropping on the streets, picked up by a cop, tired of living. And the drunks out there, seeing snakes, wrapped in sheets dipped in ice-water, beaten by the ward boys if they yelled, dying, dying, dying for a drink, just one drink to take the shakes and the snakes away. Out there, on that Island, I was watching a whole town, bigger than most American towns—a great big garbage can for the City, a garbage can for the City people—and everyone there a sure loser, even the guards and the doctors and nurses trying to live on what the City paid them. Further on, up the River, was

Ward's Island and the Potter's Field, where they bury them in open graves, graves the size of the excavation made for the cellar of a good-sized building. Thirty of them in a row, wrapped in canvas, under a prayer that probably doesn't belong to their religion if they have any, because they are given religions by lot, unless they are wearing something Catholic. It makes a triangle, from the neighborhood, to the Island, to the Potter's Field, with not very many stops on the way for the poor suckers who don't figure things out and get themselves an angle.

I got up and walked west, through the alley of rich houses, then turned uptown and walked toward home, in the dark, thinking of Carla Adams and of how much she reminded me of Fred.

CHAPTER FIVE

Rusty was in the bedroom, throwing clothes into his footlocker. His glasses fogged and he pulled them off, looked at them and threw them at the wall. They didn't break. I picked them up and handed them to him.

"What's the matter?"

"I'm getting out of this rat-race for good."

"What's up? What happened?"

"That drunken slob in the kitchen."

"Oh, *oh!*"

I walked through the front room to the kitchen. The old lady sat with her head on the table, her face on the wet oilcloth cover, keening away to herself: "*I'm going to take a dose of something. Get out of it all. Once and for all, get out of it all.*"

"Come on, quit it!"

"I'll be glad when I'm dead and buried. I'll be glad when I'm out of it all."

Everyone who lived in the house had heard this before.

"Nobody's better off dead," I said. "When you're dead you don't know anything."

She lifted her head from the oilcloth.

"Honest, Mattie—"

"What the hell happened?"

"Oh, his Jew girl friend was up here, telling me how I shouldn't drink, tryin' to get me to go to a doctor, take the cure. Is it any of her business?"

"No."

"So I told her to shut her kike mouth. And he had to get mad about it."

"Where is she?"

"She's gone. She started bawling and went. He's goin' now, too."

I took two dollars out of my wallet and gave them to her; it was a mistake. When she had the money in her hand she had courage.

"Dirty kike," she said.

"Lay off it, Ma."

"Dirty little sheeny," she said.

"Cut it out, Ma."

"I'll show him he can't insult me in my own house."

She got up, catching the edge of the table, staggered, and teetered toward the bedroom. Rusty turned around.

"Keep away from me, Ma," he said. "Keep your hands off me. I don't want to hit you, but if you don't keep away from me I will."

"A fine son you are! I may take a drink once in a while but at least I'm not a dirty Jew like that sheeny you're going to marry."

Rusty's body became as stiff as a steel beam and the ends of his fingers trembled. Like a fool, she kept it up.

"You might have been marrying a Christian girl, at least, instead of disgracing the whole family, marrying a no-good kike whore."

After a second, cold-blooded, he slapped her face with his open hand. She went down. He fell on the bed and started to cry: *You dirty old slob. You dirty drunken old slob.* His head and shoulders shook and with them the old bed shook, making a noise of creaking springs. I helped her up and led her to the door.

"Go down to the corner and get yourself a drink."

"Yeah, Mattie. Yeah."

She was stunned, for Rusty had hit her hard, and there was a scarlet mark on her cheek. She put a hand up to her face, touching the red place with her fingers.

"Rusty was a good boy," she said. "He was always a good boy."

She went through the door and I heard her clumping down the stairs. She had been getting worse, these last few weeks. Sooner or later Bellevue would get her and not let her go.

I went back into the bedroom. Rusty was closing the lid of his footlocker. The white stenciled lettering still showed on the lid:

1st. Lieutenant John Francis Dolan
0-1997826
709 Bombardment Squadron
447 Bombardment Group
U. S. A. A. F.

"I'll give you a hand with that, Rusty."

"Thanks, Matt."

He stood, looking at his name on the footlocker, with his red hair disarranged, his long, earnest face in a frown. He was beginning to look more like a schoolteacher than a boy from the neighborhood.

"Come on, Rusty. Let's go."

He put on his hat and coat and looked at the place for the last time. It looked the way it always did, dark, damp, and a rancid smell came from the kitchen, mixed with the smell of stale coffee grounds. The old lady's *Daily Mirror* was on the kitchen table, soaking up slop like a blotting paper.

"I shouldn't have come back here at all," he said. "When I left the Army I should have gone to live in the dormitories at Columbia. I shouldn't even have come back here for a visit."

"Take it easy, Rusty. Take it easy."

We carried the footlocker down the stairs. In the street I looked for a cab, but there wasn't one in sight.

"I'll take the bus."

"With this?"

It was heavy.

"That's all right."

We carried it to the corner.

"How about a beer?"

"Why not?"

We left the footlocker where we could watch it and went into the bar. Rusty paid for the beer with two dimes.

"I shouldn't have hit the old lady," he said.

"It's not the first time she was hit. Or the last."

I drank my beer and ordered another, reaching into my pocket for money.

"No, Mattie," he said. "I'll pay."

"Jesus, are you a plunger," I said. "You shoot forty cents as if money was water."

He smiled. He didn't feel comfortable with me.

"What are you so worked up about, Rusty? What are you all the time fighting with?"

He looked at me, across his beer.

"You, I guess."

"Me?"

He put the beer glass on the bar.

"Oh, not just you. You and people like you."

"What are you blaming me for now? What did I do?"

"You're the heart of the problem, Mattie. In the old days, in medieval times, they would have had a simple answer for you, a simple way to explain you."

"How?" I said. "Tell me about me."

Rusty smiled.

"They would have said you'd made a deal with the Devil. Sold your soul to Old Nick, just for the right to have your own way. It's a nice, simple explanation."

"How about now? How would Mr. Charles Austin Beard explain me?"

He shook his head. "I don't know about Beard. But there are a lot of bright people who would call you a victim of your environment." He took a pull at his beer. "But I don't agree with them," he said.

"No?"

"No."

There was tension between us; I didn't want a fight.

"Aw, Rusty," I said, "just because I see things different from the way you do—"

He interrupted. "What do you believe in, Mattie? For sure?"

I finished my beer and put down the glass, making a final, definite noise. I looked right into his pale blue eyes.

"What do I *believe* in?"

"Yes."

"Me," I said. "Mattie Dolan. One guy I can depend on."

He nodded. "That's right."

"What do you believe in, Rusty? God? The Devil? Or just the fact that a law degree will make you rich?"

He thought for a moment.

"People," he said. "Human beings."

I looked around the saloon at the lumps of men standing at the bar, staring at their beer; I looked through the dusty window into the grey wasteland of the street, grey as glass in an old dry cellar, too blank, too meaningless even to be dreary, the landscape of the end of the world.

"You believe in that?" I asked, waving a hand to include East Yorkville. "You believe in those slobs, slobs that live like that and like it?"

"I believe in people," he said. "And I guess I believe in God."

"You believe in the old man?"

No answer.

"You believe in the old lady?"

No answer.

He stood in his cheap overcoat, thinking about what he believed in.

I ordered another beer. One of the day-drunks sitting at the bar lifted his head and I knew that he wanted to join the discussion.

"*Nobody asked you,*" I said, just as he opened his mouth. He went sulkily back to his drink, tracing a pattern in the wet. I touched Rusty's arm.

"People are suckers, Rusty," I explained. "Just suckers. Sure losers. Otherwise, why are they so bitch-awful miserable? Why do they spend their time grumbling about what the smart guys have—money, clothes, cars, women? I know what I want and I'm going to get it. If I can take it from some sucker, so much the better for me. That's why the suckers were put on the earth. To be taken by the smart guys, bled till they're dead."

Rusty studied my face, then looked at all of me, up and down, looking at me the way you'd look at a new animal in a cage at the zoo. I grinned; he made me uncomfortable.

"You're a monster, Mattie," he said. "There was a part of you left out. Or maybe something extra put in. Something we recognize, but don't understand."

"Guts, maybe," I said.

"No." He shook his head. "No, Mattie. Evil."

"I don't get it," I said.

"Forget it, Mattie. Let's not have an argument."

"No. Sure. Why should we?" I said.

I waited for him to go on, to tell me about his girl friend and how it was going to be in the future, after he graduated from school. I was prepared to listen to him, just to make him feel better. But he didn't say anything. He just looked through the barroom window, long and hard at York Avenue, at the women pushing baby carriages, at the old guys who wavered on canes, at the dust-grey street and the mattresses piled high in the bedding shop across the street. Then he finished the dregs of his beer and put out his freckled, knuckly hand.

"So long, Mattie," he said.

We shook hands.

"Good-by, Mattie," he said.

"So long, Rusty."

The red bus stopped at the corner for him and one of the passengers helped with his footlocker. Inside the bus he bent down, so that his face showed at the window, and waved good-by to me. The bus rolled off, reluctant to start, fat and swaying as it climbed the hill.

"Your brother, ain't it?" the bartender asked.

"That's right," I said. "My brother Rusty."

"He goin' somewhere with that trunk?"

"He thinks so," I said. "He's sure of it."

PART VI

CHAPTER ONE

RENTZAU PUT THE tips of his fingers together and pressed so that the knuckles of his hands went white. He wore one of those officer's rings, designed so that at a distance people mistake them for West Point rings.

"I'm very much disappointed, Dolan. Very much disappointed. Not about the drawings so much as the fact that you haven't been happy here."

"I'm happy. I'm happy as a lark. But that doesn't mean I'm fat *dumb* and happy. Thirty-five-a week, less income tax, social security, your phony health plan and what it costs me to work, in cabfares and lunches—it comes to less than the twenty a week the government gives me. And on the Fifty-two Twenty Club my time belongs to me. I'm my own boss. I can watch for the breaks."

He nodded, deciding not to argue with me.

"Tell me, Dolan, as a personal favor, why did you throw the drawings away?"

"Because they stank."

He laughed.

"An art critic, too."

"I know what I like."

"And what you like is not Bramwell's, eh?"

"I've got nothing against the store. I learned something here."

"What?"

"I learned how much money is rolling loose, waiting to be picked up by anyone smart enough to smell it."

Rentzau laughed.

"You're a character, Dolan. You know I could write to the government people. It might make it harder for you to get back into the Fifty-two Twenty Club."

"What would that get you?"

"Nothing," he said. "So I won't do it."

He stood up.

"Good-by, Dolan. Good luck with your saloon."

"What?"

"Good luck with your saloon."

We shook hands.

Outside, I understood that Carla Adams must have told him that I was going to open a place. For a moment I was mad. Then I laughed. I had a certain clown value with these people and I was beginning to understand how to make that work for me. I went to the cashier's window and drew my money, then took the elevator to the salon floor and walked to Carla's office. She sat behind a french-grey desk, wearing a black dress worth a hundred and fifty dollars and a string of pearls worth, maybe, a thousand. Her hair was piled on top of her head and it looked as if it had been varnished. She looked expensive and efficient, almost too perfect.

"Hello."

She looked up and recognized me, then smiled.

"The future Mister Dolan. Did it work?"

"Like a charm."

"Good for you. Are you looking for a job?"

"Jobs are for suckers."

She laughed.

"What are you doing on Friday night?"

This was Wednesday.

"Nothing. Why?"

"I'm throwing a party at my place. Why don't you come?"

I looked at her, trying to figure out what went on behind that enamel.

"What are you looking for? Laughs?"

"No. I want you to come. Really."

"Okay."

Suppose she did want me for laughs? I might meet people there who would be able to do me some good.

"Bring your girl friend," she said.

"What girl friend?"

"Haven't you got one?"

"Why, sure. Sure I have."

"Well, bring her. Eight-thirty."

"Okay."

"See you Friday."

I went out and took a look at Fifth Avenue ... all the storefronts made out of brass and glass and stone, with millions and millions of dollars worth of merchandise behind them; all the people, hurrying along with their heads down, holding their hats on a windy March day; all the doubledecker buses with steam on the windows, weaving in and out of traffic, looking dangerous, as if they were going to tip over; all the angry cabbies trying to make their turns into sidestreets choked with trucks; all the private limousines, black and shiny and a block long, with thin chauffeurs sitting in front, looking as if they owned the world and didn't give a damn. There was a cold-looking cop on the corner, handling traffic, his breath making steam, looking fat in his overcoat; underneath it you knew he wore no blouse but a million sweaters and a pistol belt, and you knew that in his stomach there was probably a taste of rye to keep out the cold that sifted through all the clothing he was wearing. Up in one of the big windows of the University Club sat a fat rich bastard with a dollar cigar, reading a magazine he probably had privately printed, for him to look at only. He looked away from the magazine and down at me in the street for a second. I stuck out my tongue and gave him the bird: a long Bronx cheer that he couldn't hear but could see plain enough. He had made his pile and now he sat, reading and smoking and looking through the window at the rest of the world as if it didn't have the right to be there, the way a cop on horseback looks, up there above the crowd, with his polished putties and his knees against the silky brown hide of the horse, acting as if he could spit on the crowd, acting as if his god-damned polished and curry-combed horse was better than the people down on the street.

I looked up and down the avenue and decided I didn't like it. It was sucker bait, Fifth Avenue, except for the people sitting on top of it, like the fat bastard in the window, smoking his dollar cigar. A guy like me, with brains and nerve and savvy, was better off sticking to what he understood, what he knew he could lick.

What I understood was the neighborhood, so I caught a cab and rode home. There, at Eighty-sixth and York, was Murph standing in the gutter of the street, holding a rubber ball in his hand, playing ledge-ball with a crowd of kids about sixteen years old. I sat in the cab, watching Murph throw a home run. Then I paid and got out.

"Murph!"

He dropped the ball and it rolled away; one of the kids picked it up.

"My old pal, Mattie!"

We shook hands.

"When did you get out?" I asked.

"This morning."

"How?"

"Bail. We got bail. Vincie Rhattigen fixed it up."

"Good deal."

"Yeah. Good guy Vince. Good guy."

The Wop pushed his body away from the wall, walked over and said hello.

"I thought you were working, sucker," he said.

"I just got fired."

"Have you got any scratch? To spring for a beer?"

"Sure."

"So let's go."

We went into Greene's and drank beer.

"What do you think you'll get?"

"Suspendeds," said the Wop. "Vincie says we're a cinch for suspendeds, being veterans. Even if they don't find the dough."

"Yeah," said Murph. "Vincie says suspendeds is all we'll get. He got a lawyer for us."

"It's funny where that dough went," said the Wop.

"Some fat boy in blue got it," said Murph. "Some cop."

"Do you think so?" I said.

"Sure," said Murph.

"Yeah," I said. "It could be, at that. I wouldn't put it past a cop."

"Yeah," said Murph. "It was a cop all right. Don't you think so, Guinea?"

The Wop nodded.

"I guess so."

"Have another beer, fellows," I said.

"Thanks."

"Thanks, Mattie."

Greene brought the beer.

"How's your girl friend Gina?" asked Murph.

"All right."

"I sure would like to get into *her* drawers," he said.

"Why not?" I said. "It's a free country."

CHAPTER TWO

Gina waited at the corner, her short street coat wrapped tightly over the thin long dress. It was Friday night.

"What did you wear that for? Do you think you are going to some Hunky wedding?"

"It's the only thing I got dressed up."

It was the formal her mother made for the Christmas dance at John Jay, made of something that looked like cheesecloth, held in back by a pink bow.

"Go home and change it. It's all wrong."

"Aw, Mattie, I hadda sneak out. If I go back now I'll never get out again. I had to get out before she got home."

"I'll go with you," I said.

"Gee, no, Mattie. She doesn't know I go with you."

"So I'm not good enough, huh?"

"It's just, you know, when you weren't working—"

"Frig her."

At Carla's house, Ada the maid opened the door to let us in. She wore a black sateen uniform with a white apron and a starched cap.

"Come in, honey."

She took Gina's coat, bugging her eyes at the dress.

"Big dog, tonight, white trash. Big dog."

She took my hat and coat.

"Go on downstairs and join the quality."

The cellar of Carla's house was fixed up as a barroom, with pine paneled walls, a pine bar, a juke box and a row of quarter slot machines. There were forty or fifty people, holding drinks, milling around, under the reticent amber side-lights. The women were wearing street clothes.

"See, bitch," I whispered to Gina. "What did I tell you?"

"I'm sorry, Mattie."

"Sorry! You make me feel cheap."

Carla sat on the bar, trailing a pair of sleek silk legs, talking down to a dozen people. When she saw me she yelled: "DOLAN! *Come here, you bastard!*"

I left Gina standing in the doorway. A thin yellow boy passed with a tray and I took a drink without breaking my stride.

"Listen, folks!" Carla said, loud enough for everyone to hear, even above the juke box, "Listen. Meet my deadend kid. In person: the future Mister Dolan."

She was high in the way you can get if you drink good liquor in the right frame of mind.

"Lay off it, will you?" I said. "Wait till I have a drink, at least."

"Have all you want, Mattie. Where's your girl?"

"Over there."

"Jesus Christ!"

I don't know what she had expected but the sight of Gina certainly shook her. She vaulted down from the bar and went to Gina, leading her into the room. When I turned around Gina was sitting at one of the tables with a group of people. An old man with a boiled face and white hair was holding a glass of champagne while she drank from it. He looked like a rich grandfather, of the kind you see in the movies. The good-natured, benevolent kind. I watched her sip the wine and giggle, then dab her lips with a napkin. *Let the bitch get slopped,* I thought. *Let her get paralyzed drunk and be raped by that old goat,* I thought. *Who cares?* Wearing that god-damned homemade dress, she made me feel cheap as a nickel.

There was an instant of dead silence and I heard her voice come across the room, a high, tinny, kid's voice: "Oh, no. I go to school, John Jay, where Mattie used to go."

I turned back to the bar, hoping no one would know I was Mattie. A pop-eyed woman in a flame-colored dress touched my arm and said, "What are you? You look like a wrestler, but what *are* you?"

"I'm just what she said I was: the future Mister Dolan."

She took her hand from my arm.

"Well, gee, fellow, don't get mad about it."

I stood at the bar, watching the party. Gina, trying to make me notice her, finally waved. The old man looked up and smiled.

"Mattie! Come here."

The champagne sounded a little in her voice.

I nodded.

"I'll be over later," I called.

The room was filled with cigarette smoke and the smell of expensive perfume. It was a big, expensive party, with everything on the bar and a buffet table against the wall, being attended to all the time by the yellow boy in the white coat. People were playing the slot machines, feeding them quarters and laughing when they turned up lemon after lemon. Someone hit the jackpot and everyone laughed when the quarters rolled with a money noise on the floor.

"Hello, Mattie," said someone beside me. "You look bored."

It was Ambrose, leaning on the bar, his face half-lighted by the overhead lamp.

"Hello, Ambrose."

"Call me Howard."

I looked at him; he smiled.

"No hard feelings?"

"Of course not."

"I'd give you back the money if I had it."

"The money doesn't matter. Forget about it."

He moved a little closer; he had a confidential manner.

"Do you know Carla Adams?"

"Sure," I said.

"Astonishing girl."

We both looked at Carla, who was entertaining a group of people, apparently telling a dirty story, because when she stopped talking everybody roared.

"Are you with someone?" Ambrose asked.

I shook my head.

"Just a tramp from the neighborhood. I brought her for laughs." I nodded toward Gina. "She was on her way to a racket on Third Avenue. That's how come the get-up.

"She looks young," he said. "And just a wee bit tiddly."

"Just a tramp from the neighborhood."

He put his hand on my forearm.

"I know a more amusing place than this, Mattie. Why don't we go there?"

All I could think of was the Wop, Guido, who had cleared five thousand cash, and when I thought of the money, in my mind I could see the fourteen thousand resting in the dark, in my tin box in the bank vault.

"Why not?" I said.

When she saw us at the door Gina broke away from the table, running so that her long dress flowed behind her.

"Where you goin', Mattie?"

I took her wrist in my hand and twisted.

"To the men's room. To make wee-wee."

"Oh."

I let go of her wrist.

"Go on back and sit down. That way you don't look so stupid wearing that lousy dress."

I turned around; Ambrose waited at the foot of the stairs. He had heard everything, but he was too crafty to smile.

"Eddie Riley's, driver," he said in the taxi. "Down in the Village, south of Waverly Place."

"Yeah, sweetheart. I know where it is."

"Do you?" Ambrose laughed. It is funny, the way they like to be recognized and kidded. "They know me well."

They knew him all right, Riley's is one of those Village places: a basement with whitewashed walls, a seven-foot ceiling and dozens of round hard-topped tables the size of a derby hat. There is a dance floor: twelve square feet of parquet—and beyond that a stage raised a foot from the floor, just large enough for two upright pianos, back to back.

"Scotch, Mattie?"

"Okay."

The whiskey came.

"How did you know my right name?" I asked.

He smiled.

"Carla told me about the future Mister Dolan."

"That dame, Carla."

"Unbelievable woman. She likes you."

"She thinks I'm good for laughs."

"She likes you. What was it she said about you?"

"What?"

"Oh, yes. She said that your instinct for evil hadn't been corrupted."

He laughed, thinking that over.

"Perfectly astonishing woman. You know she was born in a barroom?"

"Lay off me, will you?"

"Sorry. I was talking about Carla."

"I know. Astonishing woman."

I tried to imitate his speech.

"Don't be rude, Mattie. Please?"

He was hurt.

We watched the floor show. Riley must have paid off to every cop on the vice squad. Half the jokes were double-talk to me, because they have their own language, like thieves or sailors or theatrical people. They would call me a piece of rough trade.

A guy who liked it, but didn't admit it, was just trade. To one another they are Queans. There were three hundred people in Riley's cellar, though the occupancy sign limited it to one hundred. A uniformed fireman looked in for a minute, tipped his hat, grinned, and went out. He was taken care of.

When I got up to go to the john, Ambrose caught my hand and held it.

"Don't vanish, Mattie, please don't. You won't regret it, I promise you that."

"I told you I was sorry about the other time."

"That doesn't matter."

"I'll be right back."

In the toilet, a kid my age looked me over and said: "West Side?"

I shook my head. The odor of the pink crystal puck in the urinal trough blended badly with the whiskey fumes in my head. I was mulled; my lips were rubbery.

"East," I said. "East Yorkville."

"Jesus," he said, "the old tank I'm with is so hot he's steaming. I'm going to take him for a C at least."

He had a mean, lipless mouth.

"You mean these suckers will *give* you a C? You don't have to rob it off them?"

He produced a thin, mean smile.

"They're suckers. Sure losers."

"How much do you take out of the racket?" I asked.

"Hundred, hundred and a half a week, with what you can steal. Some of them are cheap. Five bucks, ten bucks. One little runt tried to give me three."

"What did you do? Clout him?"

"What's the use to clout him? I took all his clothes—suits and ties. I made him tell me the ones he liked best, then I took 'em. He was a stingy punk, like a poet."

"He ought to be willing to pay," I said.

The kid looked at me.

"Are you from Rausch?"

"Who's Rausch?"

"Who's *Rausch?* The pimp, you dope. I thought you were in the racket."

He buttoned himself and went out. I stood leaning on the porcelain trough, half drunk, needing air. *Jesus,* I thought, *a pimp for guys.*

I walked back to the table, along the edge of the dance floor. Men were dancing with other men, women were dancing with other women. Ambrose got up and pulled back my chair.

"You're just in time for the best thing in the show," he said. He pointed to the stage. Two buck niggers were at the pianos, beginning to beat it out, sweat shining on their black faces, reflected light on their white teeth. The pianos were stripped and fitted with mirrors screwed in place to reflect the keyboards. I watched the big black fingers, strong as iron, thick and short, not piano-player's hands at all, way down, all the time, down on the bass so the beat of the rhythm got into my brain, mixed up there with the whiskey... the tom-tom rhythm startled occasionally when one of them tickled a high note, clear and sharp as an electric shock.

They played and people kept quiet, leaning forward and listening, all three hundred of them soaking up the beat of the black fingers on the bass, bouncing back from the low ceiling, becoming part of the dense air in the jam-packed room.

"Mattie! It's time to go."

Ambrose shook my arm. I was too groggy to argue, and I went back to sleep in the cab. When I woke up the cab was parked, with the motor running, on a downtown sidestreet in front of a building that looked like a Protestant church in a poor neighborhood. It was brick, square and ugly, with a pair of low blue lights showing at the stone doorway.

"Where is this?"

"Turkish bath," Ambrose said. "It will help you to sober off."

"Oh, no." I sat up in the taxi, drunk. "Not for Mattie Dolan."

"Please, Mattie. It's just to get you sobered up. I feel responsible."

The driver snarled with his horn.

"Make up your mind."

"Don't be nasty," said Ambrose. "The meter's running and you will be paid."

"I want to go home," the hackie said.

"Come on, Mattie. It *will* do you good."

What could I lose?

I stumbled, getting out of the cab, and Ambrose caught my arm. He held me until I was steady, then paid off the cab, tipping the driver a dollar. He turned back to me as the cab gears were shifted into first.

"How are you, Mattie? Four Oh?"

"All right, I guess."

It was a cool, clear night and the street stretched straight toward the River like a canal, with a belt of bright stars overhead. I guessed it was somewhere east, in the Thirties.

"Let's go in."

"Okay."

There was a marble counter with a wire cashier's cage, and behind the counter were a couple of hundred boxes, numbered drawers with polished brass knobs. Even in the lobby you smelled the steam and the dampness of the baths inside and there was a vagrant liniment smell. Ambrose unbuckled his watch and handed it to the clerk. Then he handed the man his wallet.

"Leave your money here, Mattie. It will be safe."

Ambrose registered with phony names: George Murphy, Howard Murphy, and smiled at me when he wrote them. The clerk gave each of us a key that hung by a ring from an elastic wrist band. We went upstairs to a double room with plywood walls that reached only halfway to the ceiling—a cubicle with two army cots made up neatly with hospital spreads.

An old attendant wearing blue swimming trunks handed us bathrobes that smelt of lye. We undressed, then descended the cast-iron stairway to the baths. It was dark, with just a blue light at each turning on the stairs. Although you couldn't see anyone, you sensed that people were inspecting you from some recess in the darkness.

We went into the hot room and sat on wooden deckchairs with towels spread over them so that you wouldn't scorch your skin. The wood was hot as iron that has been left in the sun. The room was big—about thirty chairs—and the bright light blinded you after the dark of the stairway. There were old-fashioned naked electric bulbs hanging from the ceiling in wire cages, so that the light was metallic and hard. An old guy of sixty, with muscles like knots in heavy rope, gave Ambrose and me tin cups, big ones that held a pint, filled with iced water. The cold tin-and-water taste was good after all the whiskey. It cut the fur on my tongue and teeth. I started to take a gulp, but the old guy with the muscles said: "Seep it, sawney. Seep it."

So I sipped.

After a while I began to sweat, sitting in the chair without moving, sometimes permitting the icy cup to touch my stomach and enjoying the shock. There were a dozen men in the room, naked, with sweat rising on their bodies so that they looked as if oil had been rubbed on their skin, and the curves and shadows of the muscles were defined, as they are on a colored fighter. I felt good, not wanting to move, half asleep, half awake. But when Ambrose said, "Shall we go?" I got up and followed him out.

We passed through a narrow tiled hall, cold as a cellar, into the steam room. It was like being wrapped in hot fog. You could hardly see through the bank of steam that rose through gratings set into the walls, and for a moment I thought that Ambrose and I were alone in the room. Then, when my eyes were used to the steam, I saw others, just bodies in the fog and steam, pink blobs that moved around, moving as if they were floating on air, gliding, because you couldn't see their feet. Then Ambrose came through the fog, whispering: "Come on, Mattie. Come on, I'll make it right with you."

I moved away; he whispered faster:

"Fifty dollars, Mattie. A hundred. Anything you want."

In the street it was almost morning, with grey-pink streaks in the sky toward the East River, and some low clouds. The street was empty, with a lonesome look as though no one had walked along it for years, the way streets downtown look on Sunday when all the offices are closed. It might have been any street in the Thirties—loft buildings with dusty windows, and a narrow sidewalk so that trucks could back right up to the loading platforms. Across the street in the doorway of a closed-up sandwich shop that had a sign in the window: MALTEDS—Any Flavor—21¢, an old drunk with long grey hair slept under a blanket he'd made out of newspapers. Nothing showed but his head, with a red face swollen up and the grey-mop hair, and his feet, in a brand-new pair of GI shoes. The rest of him was under the newspaper. I knew that the cop on the beat hadn't been through this street yet, because he would have warmed the bum's feet with his club, and I wondered if the place, the Turkish bath, paid off to the police, because a raid in there, at three in the morning, would turn up some business for the Magistrate's Court. We were standing on the steps, looking for a cab, and I turned to look at the place. It was red brick, with a pair of stone columns in front, and granite steps that led to the door, steps of the kind you see leading into an old-fashioned school. Like the rest of the street, it looked dead, like a boarded-up building no one ever went into.

"Shall we go to my place and have breakfast, Mattie?"

I had almost forgotten he was with me, while I stood on the steps, looking at the street, and the sound of his everyday voice startled me a little.

"Why not?"

In his bathroom, I shaved with his razor and used his after-shaving lotion, Russian perfume that smelled like leather and came in a cut-glass bottle. He had a pair of military brushes with polished cherrywood backs. I used them too and scrubbed my teeth with a new toothbrush I found in the medicine cabinet. I felt as though time had stopped, or shifted, and as though I were someone else, moving in a different layer of existence, and the gap in time since I'd been in the neighborhood might have been weeks, months, instead of just a few hours.

After breakfast we listened to records.

"Do you like music, Mattie?"

"Sure."

"I have three thousand records."

They were in specially bound books, in cabinets built into the wall, and each record was indexed in a leather book with letter-scalloped sides.

"Why do you want that many? It would take you a year to play them all."

"I have a lot of time," he said. "People like me are alone a lot of the time."

He played some classical music. It meant nothing to me, but as I watched him, sitting in a chair, I knew that he wasn't faking. He really understood it. It was saying something to him.

He got up and switched off the record.

"You'd like something different," he said. "Something a little livelier."

"Whatever you say."

He put on a recording of a lowdown tune, beaten out by two pianos.

"It sounds like the two coons last night."

"It is."

We listened, and as I stared at the sleek front of the expensive machine, I could see the thick black fingers, in the mirror and on the keys, working fast, sure of themselves, letting you know that the man knew how.

"I ought to be going," I said.

"Stay for a bit, Mattie. You can stay as long as you like."

CHAPTER THREE

We sat on the wall, looking down at the River. It was warm enough to go without a coat. Gina had her schoolbooks on her lap.

"Sit still! What are you nervous about?"

"I'm not nervous."

"So sit still."

I picked up one of the books: *Gregg Simplified Shorthand.* I flipped the pages, looking at the pothooks, then tossed the book back to her lap.

"I'm going to flunk," she said.

"What of it? You flunked before."

"I want to quit school."

"Well, quit. Am I stopping you?"

A towboat passed, moving quickly through the water. A three-hundred-pounder in an undershirt, bare arms streaked with engine oil, waved at us from the afterdeck. Gina waved back.

"You told me you loved me, Mattie."

"Sure. I do. So what?"

"How come you left me like that by myself where I didn't know nobody?"

"I told you I was drunk. TWICE I TOLD YOU I WAS DRUNK! What do you want me to do? Shoot myself because I got a little slopped?"

"Only for the old man I might have got in trouble."

"Did he take you home? The old goat?"

She nodded.

"Did he try anything?"

"He was a perfect gentleman. But my mother gave him the devil."

"Did he take you upstairs?"

"I got sick at my stomach. I spoiled my dress."

"So he took you upstairs."

"My old lady started to curse at him. She wouldn't even listen to me."

"Does she know you started with me?"

"She doesn't think I go with you. I told her."

I nodded.

"Don't be sore, huh, kid?"

"Where you been five days? I asked all the fellas, Murphy and that Eye-talian fella. They didn't know."

"What are you? A spy?"

"I only asked."

"Well, don't ask. Don't spy on me."

She looked at me, wrinkling her forehead.

"Where'd'ja get the new suit? And the shoes?"

"In a store, you chump. Where do you think?"

"It looks nice."

"Hundred and ten bucks."

I touched the lapels of my new suit, one I had needed for spring. I lifted my foot and admired the shoe.

"Thirty-five a pair. Peel's. English."

"I got to talk to you, Mattie."

"Talk. I'm sitting here."

"I didn't have no period."

"What?"

"I didn't have my periods. It's too long I didn't have it."

I snatched her wrist.

"Don't hurt me, Mattie!"

"Who's going to hurt you? Did you tell anybody?"

"No. Gee, no, Mattie."

"Well, don't."

"You got to marry me, Mattie."

"Says who?"

"You got to. You promised."

"When?"

"Before. A long time ago."

I wanted to cuff her with the back of my hand, but I didn't. The important thing was to get rid of the kid, then, for all I cared, she could go to hell.

"Look, Gina, I have to think this over. In the meantime, don't say anything."

"All right."

"Not to anybody. Not to the priest, or Webber, or your old lady."

"No."

"Otherwise we're through. I'll leave town. Go to Europe, Alaska, maybe. You won't see me at all any more."

That did it.

"I promise, Mattie. Honest."

"Now go on home, before your old lady gets suspicious."

"She won't be back until late. You want to come up?"

The idea of making love to her, with that vicious little bastard in her stomach, made me sick.

"No," I said. "No. I have to think this thing over."

I walked with her as far as the corner, carrying her schoolbooks under my arm. After I left her I went to Greene's and sat on a stool at the empty bar, staring at my reflection in the mirror, wondering who would know how to help me get out of this one.

CHAPTER FOUR

Carla said: "Why don't you marry the kid, Mattie? It's the right thing to do."

"Are you kidding?"

She laughed.

She was dressed in a black velvet skirt that reached to the floor and a shirt cut like a man's, but made of silk, so heavy that to the touch it seems to be weighted with silver.

"I don't quite see you married."

"Listen, Carla, for seven months I hung around the neighborhood, just like any other slob, looking for an angle. Now I have an angle, and I know where I'm going. If I married that little Hunky tramp I could kiss myself good-by."

"Do you love her?"

"She gives me a pain."

"Are you sure?"

"SURE I'M SURE!"

"Don't get excited, Mattie. You're not the one who's pregnant."

"What if I did have a soft spot for her? She's dumb. She's a moron. Being with her drives me crazy, except when I'm in bed with her. If I married her I'd get to be just like her. Keep going down. I'd turn out to be a slob, just like my old man."

"Have you talked to Gina about it?"

"What do you mean, talked to her?"

"Will she do it?"

"She better do it."

"Girls are funny. You'd better talk to her."

"She'll do it. She'll do what I tell her."

Carla stood up and took her red flannel drawers from the closet. She pulled up her skirt and put them on, making a zipper noise. In chilly weather she wears them right over her skin. When she goes into a restaurant or a night club, she unzips them and lets them fall to the floor, steps out of them, and hands them to the hatcheck girl. She attracts a lot of attention with them, but she says they're just to keep her warm. They are bright red, red as the inside of a fireman's overcoat.

"All right, Mattie," she said, swishing her skirt so the folds were straight, "if Gina wants me to I'll call a man I know."

"If *she* wants you to?"

"That's right. You have her come to see me, if she wants me to help her get an abortion. I don't trust you."

"Have it your way. How much will it cost?"

"Have you got any money?"

"About eighty dollars."

That was what I had in my wallet; I wouldn't have touched the money in the bank to keep Christ from being crucified.

"This fellow comes higher than that. But I'll take care of the money. Call it a wedding present."

"You don't have to do that."

"Forget it. Have a drink before you go?"

"You too?"

"A light one. I'm going out."

I handed her a pale highball. As I bent over, close to her face, it occurred to me that she was probably forty, a year or two older than my mother. She looked like a magazine advertisement, with her hair fixed, and her face groomed, taken care of, given a lot of money and attention.

"How did you like Howard Ambrose?" she asked.

"What do you mean?"

"He says you are a basically fine young man who hasn't had the right opportunities. He says you have a keen, sensitive intelligence."

"Suckers are born to be taken," I said.

"Where did you get your dog-eat-dog philosophy, Mattie? In the Army or the neighborhood, or from your uncle. What was his name?"

"His name was Fred. No. Whatever I know, I learned for myself. And the way I see it, it isn't dog eat dog. It's cat eat mouse. Some people, no matter what you do to them, never have nerve enough to turn and fight. They're mice. Little, nasty, mewing mice. Other people, they know from the beginning that they are at war, with one another and with the world."

I stood up.

"Hell, how long have I got to live? Forty years? Fifty years? Then I'll be dead, under the ground, and it will be too late. How much lousy time do they give you? Damned little. And only a sucker is going to waste it, worrying about somebody else, letting his own life rot away, so somebody else will be satisfied, think he's a fine, honorable fellow, maybe even spend a dollar to have a perpetual prayer mumbled in Latin by a guy who once played substitute guard. Be a hero, in the Army—what does it get you? A gimpy leg. Be honest and work hard. What does it get you? Look at my old man. I can't see it. I want to get a stake. Twenty-five thousand dollars. I'll have it before I'm twenty-one. Then I will run it up, all the way up. How I do it, or why I do it, is nobody's business but my own."

"Mattie you are grotesque. You're a monster."

I laughed.

"That's what my brother said. He called me a monster."

I looked around the beautiful room, the dark walls showing up the pictures in gold, Carla sitting there, at forty, looking better than most women look at any time after twenty. I looked at the crystal glass in my hand; you could buy them at Plummer's for a hundred and twenty dollars a dozen.

"I suppose you got all this, this house and your colored maid, your clothes and the way you look, all by being a member of the Christian Endeavor Society?"

"No, Mattie."

She put down her glass, not looking at me, but staring at the window, where the light was failing.

"No. I stole and lied and cheated and clawed and screwed my way. And it was worth it. I wouldn't change with a living soul. I wouldn't be poor for anything. I'd rather be dead. Because I know what it's like."

"You're a success," I said.

"Yes, Mattie. I'm a success. And I was practically born in a saloon. My name isn't even Adams. It's Adamowski. Sophie Adamowski. I'm a Polack. A Polack from Michigan City, Indiana, one of the toughest towns in the Midwest. When I was seven, my old man had an argument with an open hearth furnace. The furnace won. Both his legs were about gone before they got him out. They brought him home to die because the company quack said there was no use taking him to the company hospital. He died in his own bed, with his hands on a crucifix, out of his mind from the pain in his legs, calling on Christ and the Virgin Mary to let him die so the pain would stop."

She held out her glass; I mixed her a drink, stronger this time. It was getting dark outside but she didn't want the lights, so that, after a little, she talked in dusk, with just her face and her white shirt showing, fuzzy in the shadows of the chair she sat in.

"That was when I stopped being a Catholic. And stopped believing in God Almighty—when I was seven in Michigan City, listening to my poor old man, trying to die, calling on the Saints, hanging onto his life for hours with no morphine because that cost money, and no sleep because of the pain, and no death because God wouldn't give it to him."

She put her empty glass on the table. She was talking to herself, herself and the dark, more than to me.

"My mother was twenty-four—a good-looking, zoftig Polack girl, blonde and pretty. She got a job in one of the bars that catered to steel workers, and her job was to keep the drinkers drinking. She drank along with the men, the kind of job that kills most girls. But my mother was smarter than most. And better looking. By the time prohibition came in she owned the saloon. And the cops were all her buddies. She knew how to pay off. Spend money, make money.

"I went to college. To the State University at Bloomington. I joined the best sorority there: Kappa Kappa Gamma. For two years everything was fine. Then someone told them my mother controlled the whiskey in Michigan City.

"One of the girls had a father who stole half the limestone in southern Indiana, paid off congressmen to keep them quiet. Everyone knew it. Nobody cared. She was the head of the house. One of the girls had a father who went to jail because he made a little too much by being an officer of the Ku Klux Klan. She was all right too. But they threw me out. I quit school and never went home. I went to work in Field's, selling dresses. But I never gave them back their god-damned key."

She walked across the room in the dark and opened the drawer of a desk.

"Look. Look at it."

It was a gold pin shaped like a key. I looked at it and handed it back.

"What would it get you in pawn?" she asked. "A dollar? Two dollars? Five?"

I poured two drinks.

"Why did you show it to me?" I asked.

She sat down with the glass in her hand, the soft grey dying light on her face.

"Because," she said, speaking slowly, "I think you hate human beings almost as much as I do."

"I don't hate anybody," I said. "I just want to be a success."

She stood up and walked to the window, pulling back the drapery so that light came into the room as though she had turned it on with a switch. She let the curtains fall into place and the room was dark, dark as night.

"Yes," she said. "But it's the same thing. For people like you and me, it's the same thing. Just a way of expressing hatred, just a way of making an attitude concrete, just a way of showing them that you are a cat and not a mouse."

"I don't think I get it."

"No," she said. "No. But you will. You will get everything you want. You'll get your saloon—twenty of them."

"Look, Carla," I said, "by the time we fight the Russians I expect to be dealing in major generals."

She laughed. The wisecrack wiped out all that mood.

"Now get out of here, Dolan," she said. "Have your girl friend come and see me."

"Good night, Carla."

"Good night, Mattie."

She kissed me on the cheek, then gave me a push.

"Go on, now. Get out. I'm going to a big, big party and you are not invited."

"Not even for laughs?"

"Not even for laughs."

I walked back to the neighborhood and waited for Gina, so that I could tell her the news, tell her that everything was fixed up.

CHAPTER FIVE

It was a private house near Gramercy Park, brownstone, with a polished brass knocker on the door and a brass nameplate bolted to the stone: DOCTOR HOFFMANN. Underneath the name-plate was the knob of an old-fashioned bell pull. I gave it a tug, then a good pull. Gina was trembling.

"For Christ's sake, don't be scared. The way they do it you won't feel a thing."

"Mattie, I'm scared."

She had been saying that ever since I met her in the Greek soda fountain, a couple of blocks from school.

"What's to be scared of?"

A woman wearing a salmon-colored sweater over a white nurse's uniform answered the door, holding it open just a little, inspecting us through the crack.

"Yes?"

"Johnson," I said. "Mr. and Mrs. Johnson."

"Just a minute."

She closed the door and we stood on the steps, waiting.

"Come on, kid," I said. "Don't lose your nerve."

Gina didn't answer, but looked at the Park, with the wrought-iron pailing around it, the gate for which you needed a key, and the rich kids in shorts and caps, inside the fence, playing with their nannies. There was a nurse in an English uniform, with a long blue veil down her back and a blue topcoat with brass buttons, wheeling a lacquered baby carriage that shone like a Cadillac. She stopped at the gate and unlocked it with a key that she took from her bag, wheeled in the carriage, then locked the gate behind her. It was a nice spring day, bright blue sky, looking higher up than usual, with just a few clouds, very white, high in the sky, catching the sunlight. The air was warm, even now, late in the afternoon.

The nurse in the sweater came back to the door and this time opened it all the way.

"Come in, Mrs. Johnson. Mr. Johnson. Right this way."

We followed her down the old-fashioned hall, past a polished banister. The house smelt doctorish and stuffy, as if the windows hadn't been opened for years. There was a strong smell of furniture polish. The carpet was heavy and springy as turf. There was a dark, carved sideboard in the hall and behind the glass doors were several hundred china figurines, pink and cream and light blue, little statues of men and women and animals.

"Nice stuff," I said to the nurse.

"Yes, it is a good collection. Doctor Hoffmann brought it all from Germany when he came to this country. He was a—different kind of doctor in Germany."

She spoke with an accent that might have been German and her English sounded as though she had learned it in England. She took us into a waiting room off the hall.

"Just wait here, please."

There were three women, sitting with their husbands, close to the men and looking frightened. Across from them, sitting by herself, was a woman of twenty-five, reading a magazine, chewing gum, bobbing one of her crossed legs. She had good-looking legs, long and slim, with a pair of sheer stockings pulled up tightly so that the muscles around her ankles showed. She was wearing a thin silver anklet with a little heart attached to it. I could visualize the guy who had put up the money for this trip.

We sat on a sofa. I took out a cigarette, then decided not to smoke. In there, in the waiting room, you got a strong medical smell, of iodine and ether and what I guessed was blood. After a while a door opened and a fat quack wearing a white coat and a white skull-cap showed in the door frame. There was blood on the coat and it looked fresh. I felt Gina stiffen up.

"Take it easy, kid," I whispered.

The nurse came in and spoke quietly to the woman who sat by herself, the one with the magazine and the nice-looking legs. She smiled, as if the nurse was calling her for a hair appointment, then got up and smoothed her dress. She took the gum out of her mouth and stuck it on the underside of a standing ashtray, following the nurse through the opened door into the operating room. You could see, through the door, the white walls and a cabinet of nickel-plated instruments, and, over in a corner, a big polished nickel boiler, the kind they have in barber shops for hot towels. In the center of the room stood a table on wheels, with chromium stirrups, hanging from bars bolted to the sides of the table. Another nurse was clearing the table of bloody towels and sheets. Beyond the operating table was the door they went through when it was over, so they didn't have to come back to the waiting room. The door was closed, the waiting-room door, and everyone settled back.

After a little the girl inside moaned, then she screamed, low, not loud enough to disturb anyone. But when she screamed, Gina screamed too and suddenly she was on her feet.

"I can't, Mattie. Honest, I can't."

"Sit down," I said. "God damn it, sit down."

One of the women who were waiting reached up and touched Gina's arm.

"It's all right, honey," she said. "It won't hurt you."

Gina pulled away as if the woman had burnt her.

"Don't you touch me, you!"

The man with the woman said, "Mind your own business, bitch." He was a prosperous-looking man of forty, with a good blue suit and a mouth that looked like a line drawn in concrete.

The other people looked away, afraid they would get mixed up in something.

The woman inside groaned again, then whimpered. Gina started to cry.

"Come on, tramp. Cut it out."

Then she started to wail like a baby. I smacked her hard across the face with my open hand and she sat down on the sofa and began to bawl, loud. The nurse with the salmon sweater came out, darting across the room like a cat.

"You'll have to take her away, Mr. Johnson. You'll have to get her out of here."

"Oh, yeh?" I said. "We came here for something, it's paid for, and we're going to get it."

The doctor came out of the operating room, wiping his hands on a towel, blood on the front of his white coat.

"Get her oudt uff here. Right away."

"Says who?"

"I can't do anything for her," he said.

All this time Gina sat, crying and saying over and over again: "I can't do it, Mattie. I can't do it, honest I can't. I can't do it, Mattie."

I slapped her again, hard, and the doctor grabbed my arm. He was one of those fat refugees, but he was stronger than I expected.

"Hier you. Stop that!"

"Yeah? What are you going to do? Call the cops?"

He understood that he was licked.

"Make her stop crying."

"Yeahyeahyeah."

It was no use. When I got her out into the street I was so damned mad at her that I could have done it myself with an ice-pick. I walked her east, on the south side of the Park, to Third Avenue, straight into a saloon. We sat in a booth, in the back.

"Two whiskies."

When they came I drank both of them and ordered two more. I looked at her, sitting there, with her eyes red.

"Jesus. You chump dame."

"I just can't do it, Mattie. I just can't."

"Why? All of a sudden you can't do it? Why?"

"All those people, sitting in the room, that woman, chewing gum, and that doctor with the blood on his coat. Murderers, all of them. Just plain murderers."

"You went to the priest, didn't you? You went to that bastard priest and confessed."

She started to cry again.

"Did you tell him my name?"

"No, Mattie. Honest."

"Honest?"

"Honest to God, Mattie, I didn't." She crossed herself. "Honest I didn't."

"What did you tell him?"

"I told him I was pregnant."

"Didn't he ask you who?"

She nodded.

"So what did you tell him?"

"I told him some man. I wouldn't tell him who. I just told him some man."

"Did you tell your old lady?"

"Oh, God! No, Mattie, no!"

I looked at her, with the tear stains on her fat dumb Hunky face and the red mark on her cheek where I had smacked her, and I hated her. I hated myself for getting mixed up with her.

"So what are you going to do?"

"You got to marry me, Mattie. You got to."

"Is there a law that says so?"

"You got to, Mattie. At least you got to marry me. I'll get a job. Anything you say. You don't have to give no money into the house if you don't want to. But you got to marry me. You got to."

"Why?"

"I was a virgin, you know that."

"Yahhhh!"

"I never was with anybody else. You know that. I love you, Mattie, that's only why I let you do it."

I leaned across the table, trying to smile and be friendly with her.

"Listen, kid. I know I said I'd marry you. But give me a little time. Just a few days."

"You promise?"

"Sure I promise. But don't say anything to anybody. Don't mention it. And be careful with your old lady, in case you get sick in the morning or something."

"What'll I tell Father?"

"Tell him you made a mistake."

"He won't believe it."

"What is he going to do? Call you a liar? Make you show him?"

"Mattie!"

"Oh, for Christ's sake!"

"He's a priest, Mattie."

"So is that God?"

In the cab, going uptown, I had an idea.

"Look, Gina, in a couple of days we'll have a party. Up at your place. Just some of the fellows and girls. I'll tell them, all of them, that we're going to get married."

"Honest?"

"Sure."

I left her at Eighty-fourth and went on to Greene's bar. Murph was standing at the bar, showing his atrophied leg to a fellow, some casual neighborhood canvasser.

"Big piece," he said. "Big piece."

The fellow nodded, paid for Murph's beer, picked up his call book and went out.

"Hello, Mattie."

"Hello, bum. How would you like to go to a party? You and the Wop, and, let's say, Large Will Riordan?"

"Sure, pal. Where?"

"Gina's."

"No kidding!"

"Sure. Why not?"

"Sure," he said. "Why not?"

"Can you get some reefers, Murph? Some marijuana?"

He scratched his head, thinking.

"Yeah. I think so."

"Well get some. I'll buy the booze."

CHAPTER SIX

When we came through the door, Gina asked, "Where are the other girls?"

"They're coming up later," I said. "They work. Do you think everyone is a schoolkid?"

"I don't want to have a party with just you fellas."

I smiled at her.

"Take it easy, kid. The other girls are coming."

I walked into the apartment and the other fellows followed, Murph and the Wop and Large Will Riordan, one of the neighborhood bums, a dark-faced, blue-eyed Irishman. Murph had a grin on his big dumb face. The Wop looked mean, with a mean grin on his Guinea face. Large Will didn't quite get the pitch.

I went into the kitchen with the booze; I had two bottles of whiskey and two of ginger ale. I mixed drinks for all of us, whiskey and water for us, whiskey and ginger ale for Gina. I handed the drinks around and turned on the radio, one of those little things you buy for eighteen dollars. I got some dance music. Gina was standing near the window, scared, understanding that something was wrong. The fellows were sitting in chairs, taking it easy, making themselves at home.

"Come on, Gina. Let's dance."

"Okay, Mattie."

Gina did know how to dance. You know the way those crazy kids are: in a soda fountain, in the corridors at school, in the park, anywhere, they dance with one another, so that they practice all the time.

We danced, and had some more to drink. I mixed Gina's second drink with four ounces of whiskey, enough to get her started on top of what she'd had. After a while she began to get the way she always did when she'd had a drink, careless, forgetting things, and wanting to make love. I danced her over to Murph.

"Hey, Murph? Have you got a cigarette?"

"Sure, Mattie. Sure, pal."

He reached into his pocket and brought out four reefers, marijuana cigarettes, wrapped in brown paper. I took one and gave it to Gina.

"Here, kid. A new taste thrill."

"What is it?"

"Mexican cigarette. Try it."

"No, Mattie. Give me a regular cigarette."

"Come on. Try it."

She put the reefer into her mouth and I lit it for her. I showed her how to draw on it, deep, holding the smoke in her lungs. Murph lit one for himself and he and the Wop were taking turns. I didn't let Gina have too much. It's apt to make you sick, if you take too much when you're not used to it. Then I fed her more whiskey—and danced her around; she started to get the glassy look in her eyes that she'd had on New Year's Eve.

"Where's the other girls, Mattie? Ain't they comin'?"

Her voice was thick, lazy.

"What do you care?" I said. "They're coming."

She giggled.

"I don't care, Mattie. As long as I got you."

"Well, you got me, haven't you?"

She pressed herself close against me, putting her cheek against mine.

"Oh, Mattie...."

I danced with her and so did Murph. The reefer was beginning to work. After she'd had enough to drink I danced with her again and steered her into the hall. I frenchkissed her, holding it, and I could feel her clinging to me, wanting me to love her. Back in the living room, Large Will Riordan and the Wop were dancing with one another, clowning, and Murph was standing near the radio watching them, with a reefed-up look on his face.

The music switched to a slow number, and I had Gina's cheek close to mine. I started socking it to her good and kissing her while we danced, then I steered her into the bedroom and danced her over to the feather bed. I kissed her and pushed her on the bed.

"Don't, Mattie. How about the other fellas?"

"Frig them."

The whiskey and the reefer had worked on her so that her eyes looked as if they were made of glass, and she had a coked-up, crazy look on her face, wild, animal-like, crazy for me, crazy to have me love her. I heard a noise behind me and looked around, holding Gina's shoulders on the bed. There was Murph, with his pants and drawers off, wearing nothing but his shirt and shoes and socks. I had to laugh, because he looked so funny.

By that time I don't think Gina knew the difference, she was so slopped up and so hot. I just moved over on the bed a little and Murph moved in. All of a sudden, after a moment, Gina looked right into Murph's face and screamed. She tried to roll away but Murph held her with his big body and she screamed: "Mattie, Mattie! Don't let him. Don't let him."

I was right on the bed, and I said, "Come on, Gina, give the boy a break. What difference does it make to you?"

She looked up at me and I thought she was going to say something, then she turned away and I watched her grab the pillow and turn her face into it, biting on it, and shaking, and all the while Murph was there, with his dumb red face lit up by the booze and the half reefer he'd smoked.

I got off the bed and went into the front room to call the other guys. They went into the bedroom and after a while I heard Gina scream: "No, no! Don't! Please don't!" and then Gina crying, and then Large Will: "Come on, you bitch, you come across. You let Murph do it, what's the matter with me?"

Then Gina cried some more and I heard the sound as Large Will smacked her, and Large Will's voice: "Why, you tramp!" After that I didn't hear anything except the sound of Gina's crying. Then Large Will came out with Murph. The Wop was in the bedroom and I heard Gina saying again in a weak voice: "Don't. Please don't." But I think that by then she was too far gone to know what was going on. The Wop came out and Murph went in again. I heard him sock her and call her a bitch, then there wasn't any noise for a while. Murph came out, still in his shirt and shoes and socks, staggering a little, pleased with himself.

"I guess I ain't as good as the Wop, here, huh? She dinn wanta let me do it again."

He gave the Wop a shove and the Wop laughed: "Heh, heh, heh!"

I thought that it was time to go.

He started to put on his pants, but he was so drunk that he fell down, laughing, and put them on on the floor, wriggling into them. I went into the bedroom. For a minute I felt sorry for the kid, because Murph and Large Will had slapped her around. Her dress was torn at the top, where Murph had tried to get at her breasts, and he had tom her skirt too so that the dress was held together by a little piece of cloth in the middle. She was lying on the bed crossways, with her dress pulled up around her stomach, and her pants were on the floor where Murph had thrown them. She was crying, with her head in the pillow, hanging onto the feather mattress as if it were a life preserver.

"Listen, Gina," I said, "now I'm not the only guy that had you. Maybe you won't pull that marriage stuff on a guy again, huh?"

She just cried, biting the pillow, and after a while she said, biting into the pillow so that the words were indistinct: "Go away, Mattie. Please go away."

I saw her bag on the bureau top. I took two new tens from my wallet and put them into the bag, then closed it.

"Good-by, kid," I said.

Large Will, the Wop, Murph and myself marched up York in column of squads, turned into Greene's and took a table.

"On me," I said, nodding to Greene.

"Do you think she'll squeal?" asked Large Will.

"Let her squeal," said the Wop.

I leaned across the table.

"Listen," I told them, "you guys stick to the story I give you, because I am in the clear."

"How do you figure that?" asked Murph.

"Did I do anything to her?"

"It was your idea."

"It was my idea to have a party. You brought the marijuana. You guys beat her up. All I did was to kiss her a little."

Murph scratched his dumb head.

"That's right," he said. "Mattie didn't do nothing."

We agreed that if the cops asked questions everyone would swear that Gina took money, and that all of us had been with her before. That way, how could they blame me for the fact that she was going to have a baby? The father might have been anyone's guess out of all the fellows from the neighborhood.

But all that plotting was a waste of time, because everyone was in the clear—

Old lady Tragorna came home from work and found Gina the way I left her, crossways on the bed with her clothes torn, the room smelling of spilt whiskey. The radio was still turned on. People who live in the Tragorna house say you could hear the old lady screaming, all the way to the street, yelling: "*Whore! Dirty little whore!*" They heard Gina scream once, and the sound of the old lady slapping her. Then Gina ran out of the apartment and

stood for a second at the top of the stairwell, swaying, dizzy from the dope and the whiskey. Then she lost her balance and fell, over the railing and down the stairwell, five stories down to the dirty tiles of the ground-floor hall. She didn't move after she landed. The old lady stood at the top of the stairs, crying in Hungarian. Someone called from a front window: *"Police! Police!"* and in a minute the radio car came through the street with its siren going. One of the cops put his coat over Gina and knelt to feel for the pulse at her wrist. The other one put his chain nippers on the old lady to make her keep quiet. Then the City ambulance came and a cop carried Gina down the stoop, wrapped in his blue, brass-buttoned coat.

So, as it turned out, they couldn't have made me marry Gina, because she died that night, out on the Island, and of course the kid wasn't far enough along to amount to anything.

CHAPTER SEVEN

I sat in the bar at Greene's a few days after it happened, on the day that Murph and the Wop were sentenced to two and a half to five years. A plain-clothes detective from the Station House walked into the bar and came straight to me.

"We want to talk to you at the House."

I got off the stool.

"Is it a pinch?"

"So far as I know, they just want to talk to you."

We walked down to the House. In the back room, with the captain there, old lady Webber pointed at me.

"That's him. Mattie Dolan."

I turned to the captain.

"Is she the law? Do I have to listen to her?"

He looked at Webber and said, "You better wait outside, lady. We'll find out what he knows."

They worked on me, five of them.

"Did you know Gina Tragorna?"

"Sure. I used to go to school with her."

"Did you ever have intercourse with her?"

"No."

"Did you ever give her liquor?"

"No."

"Did you ever give her marijuana?"

"No."

One of the cops put his hands on his hips and leaned over so that his face was close to mine. He spoke in a gentle, fake voice.

"Did you ever kiss her?"

"Yes."

"Did you ever fool around with her? Love her up?"

"Sure. Everybody did."

"Was she a virgin?"

"No."

"How do you know?"

"Everybody knows she was a tramp. She took money for it, even."

"Listen, you," said one of the cops, "the kid's dead. Watch out what you say."

"I didn't mean anything," I said. "But everybody knows she was going around with a rich old guy, and taking dough from him."

"What old guy?"

"I don't know. I only saw him a couple of times."

After a while they gave up.

Outside, the captain said to old lady Webber: "What do you want me to do?"

"Arrest him," she said, pointing at me.

"For what, lady? The way it looks, the kid was a tramp." He took a copy of the *Daily News* from the desk. The front page carried a picture of old lady Tragorna, holding the mop handle. The paper was two days old. The captain glanced at the story, then folded the paper and put it back on the desk.

"The way it looks, lady," he said, "she wasn't much better than a prostitute. Her mother said as much, downtown. She said the kid had been running around with a rich old man, fifty years of age, out drunk, and that she took money from him. We talked to the girl's parish priest. He says she was carrying on with a man.

Both of them told us that the kid hadn't even been seeing Dolan for months."

The captain stood with his blouse unbuttoned, shaking his grey head.

"I don't see what you want us to do."

"You mean there isn't any charge?"

The captain was irritated.

"Oh, lady, if you could prove that this boy had intercourse with her, he would be technically guilty of second-degree rape. She was under eighteen. But you can't prove it. If we beat it out of him he'll go back on it later. And if you could prove it, I don't think you'd get an indictment. The boy is a war veteran. The kid was a tramp."

"She was a child!"

"So is this boy. He's nineteen. And you should see the kids we pick up for soliciting. Fourteen, some of them. Thirteen, even."

It was all over, and Webber knew it. She walked across the room and slapped me hard, across the face.

"Here, lady, you can't do that."

She turned and walked out of the Station House. The captain watched her, then turned to me.

"Dolan," he said, "there is nothing I would like better than to take you back in the cell-blocks and work you over with a rubber hose." He stopped and touched the badge on his chest. "But I like this shield too much. Now get out of here."

"What are you mad at me for?"

"Get out of here."

In the house that night the old man sat in his chair, staring at the wall, with the *Daily News* folded in his lap. He didn't look up, but he spoke to me.

"You can pack your stuff, Mattie, and go."

"What?"

"You can pack and go, Mattie," he said. "We don't want you here any more."

"What's the matter with you all of a sudden?"

He shook his head, looking at the wall.

"You're just no good, Mattie. Just no good."

I went into the bedroom and packed my bag, then walked through the front room to the kitchen. The place looked just the same. The old lady sat at the kitchen table, sober and looking sick.

"You goin', Mattie?"

"Yeah."

I put the bag on the floor.

"What's the matter with him?" I said, nodding toward the front room, where the old man sat. "What's he so mad for, all of a sudden?"

"Some woman, Miss Webber, was up here to see us. She said a lot of stuff. He believed her, I guess."

I stood, with my foot on the bag.

"That old hag," I said. "What does he care about her?"

"He believed her, that's all."

"To hell with him."

I took ten dollars out of my wallet and dropped it on the table.

"Here, Ma. Here's ten dollars."

She looked up and shook her head.

"No, Mattie. I don't want it."

"What?"

"I don't want it. Honest I don't. You keep it."

"Suit yourself."

I picked up the money and went out of the house. Behind me, I could hear her crying.

I carried my bag to the East River and sat on the seawall, looking at the Island, at the big hospital where Gina had died, at the long lighted cell-blocks, where the losers were serving time, thinking of all the people there, the old whores and the old drunks, the cripples and the cokies, the petty thieves and

petty pimps—the City's refuse, human refuse, out there on the
Island, making a town that was bigger than most American
towns, and all the people just as much garbage as the City's garbage, towed past the Island in scows every day. I thought of the
neighborhood, and the people in it, as I sat on the wall with my
face toward the River. I thought of Murph and the Wop going up
to wear out their fingers picking jute, coming out, doing it again,
going back for a longer stay. I thought of the old man, pushing
the hack, watching the weekly take get smaller as people began to
watch their pennies and stopped throwing dollar tips. I thought
of the old lady, getting loaded as often as she could, the old man
hunting for her at night, leading her home as though she were
blind, and of her, finally, ending in Bellevue, dying down there
some night in the midst of delirium and the stink of paraldehyde.
I thought of the fellows with sucker jobs, earning thirty-five a
week, believing the lying boss who told them they were going to
inherit the business. I thought of Rusty and his Jewish wife; and
the old bat Webber at school, going home every night to her four
walls and little kitchen; and the woman whose husband has tin
legs, going out looking for guys so that she won't go crazy, hating
the people she brings home so much that she could kill them; and
all the old girls in the neighborhood movies, tired of their husbands, tired of their houses, leaning forward in the movie seats,
breathing hard, rubbing the legs of some kid from the Fifty-two
Twenty Club who came in looking for a little fun because there
was nothing else to do. I thought of all the boy-crazy kids, with
army patches and naval ratings sewed to their cheap windbreak-
ers, and their dirty knees and dirty shoes and cracked scarlet
fingernail polish—all those kids, wishing the war had gone on
forever so there'd still be soldiers in Times Square, or wishing
they had been old enough to get in on the fun when it was there.
I thought of Ambrose, with all his money, his champagne and
his three thousand records, waiting to be taken, waiting to be
kicked. I thought of Carla, and of Fred.

I thought of all these things and all these people, sitting on the seawall, looking at the Island. I was glad that I had an angle, glad that I knew where I was going. I was nineteen, and around my neck was a chain with the key to fourteen thousand dollars. I had a whole lifetime before me and fifteen months in which to get eleven thousand dollars. By the time I was twenty-one, I would be ready to start living.

I turned around, facing the City, with the buildings climbing toward the mottled, moonstruck sky, and it seemed to me that the City was a jungle, a great American jungle, with the smart guys lurking in the trees like tigers, while the losers scurried in the underbrush, hiding and afraid.

I picked up my heavy bag and started to walk west, out of the neighborhood, into the City.